# Scars and Stars

Dustin Stevens

Scars and Stars
Copyright © 2013, Dustin Stevens

Warning: All rights reserved. The unauthorized reproduction or distribution of this copyrighted work, in whole or part, in any form by any electronic, mechanical, or other means, is illegal and forbidden, without the written permission of the author.

This is a work of fiction. Characters, settings, names, and occurrences are a product of the author's imagination and bear no resemblance to any actual person, living or dead, places or settings, and/or occurrences. Any incidences of resemblance are purely coincidental.

*For Pop...*

*The wrong war, at the wrong place, at the wrong time, and with the wrong enemy.*

-General Omar Bradley

*December 11, 2013*

*Eric,*

*For the past two years your mother and I have made our home in a tiny Upper East Side apartment in New York City. We have been too crazy about each other and too oblivious to the world to think that toiling away for twelve hundred square feet at two grand a month was anything less than the American dream.*

*Not until the news of your impending arrival six months ago did that all change.*

*We have spent every free moment since scouring the real estate market for a new home. Some place with a lawn, with a clear sight line to the sky above, with enough room for you and hopefully many more to grow up. It wasn't easy, but we believe we have found such a place west of here in Pennsylvania.*

*By the time you read this you will already know that full well, but I wanted to point it out again so you know where I'm coming from.*

*How you reading this now came to pass.*

*The move was supposed to have been easy. Your mother went to visit her family for a few days and I called in to work to stay home and pack. First thing Friday morning I took up a post in the living room, starting with movies, music, books. By late afternoon, I moved on to photo albums.*

*I figured I was making good progress, so I decided to stop and flip through a few.*

*One was from my childhood, filled with pictures of my brother and I in matching outfits on Halloween. Holding fish in front of us on family vacations. My eight year-old self in a matching t-shirt and hat from the local little league.*

*Memories I hope you and your siblings get to have.*

*Memories I hope to watch unfold.*

*Putting it aside, I noticed a single photograph stuck to the back of the album. Pressed there by some unknown substance, it stared back at me, both driving the air from my lungs and bringing a smile to my face at the same time.*

*Images from the past can be funny things. It isn't until one levels you that you appreciate how powerful they can be.*

*The photo was taken on the field after the final football game my senior year in college, the last time I ever wore a helmet. The win over State secured the conference title and as the final seconds ticked away, the student body flooded the field, their exuberance too much to be contained.*

*In the middle of it stand myself and my roommate Trent, smiling. We were both muddy, tired, sore. We knew that it is the last time we'd ever play football, but it didn't matter.*

*We were together, we were victorious, we were going to have a good time that night.*

*For a long time I just sat with the photo in my lap, thinking about Trent. The following spring we graduated together, two years later we were groomsmen in each other's weddings. I was there the day his son was born and I know he would have been there the day you arrive.*

*Last winter Trent was taken from us in a car accident. He was on the road for business, rushing home to be with his family for the holidays. A man was driving back from his company Christmas party and had too much to drink, went left of center and hit Trent head on going eighty miles an hour.*

*The collision put Trent into a coma that lasted almost two months. The other driver walked away without more than a few scratches.*

*Trent never woke up.*

*As I sat and thought of my fallen friend and his son, I can't help but wonder about all the things he left undone. Of the life lessons he never got to pass on or the stories that needed to be told.*

*It was such a thought that led me to what I am doing now.*

*I hope this turns out to be nothing more than wasted effort. It is my goal to be there for you through every trial and tribulation you encounter in life, but if for some reason something should happen to me I want to make sure this is taken care of. Of all the stories I ever have heard in my life, this is the most important.*

*Tucked in beneath this letter is an album. To my knowledge I am the only living soul to have ever seen it. If you are reading this, then you are now bestowed with the same honor.*

*Right after staring at the picture of myself and Trent, I made a point to locate this album. It had been years since I'd sent it, but I knew every aspect of it the way someone knows a dear old friend. Even if age has changed them to a mere semblance of their former self, there is an inherent familiarity.*

*I recognized the scent of it, knew every mark on the crusted leather that encased it, even remembered the water stain in the bottom corner.*

*This album, this story, was entrusted to me as a gift. There was no requirement that I pass it on when I go, but I wouldn't feel right unless I did.*

*Some tales are too great to ever let perish. If something were to happen to me the way it did my friend, I must know that it will live on with you.*

*Twenty-seven years have passed since I received this gift and was made guardian of its story.*

*Now I am extending the same honor to you.*

*Your mother will know when the time is right to give this to you. I assure you your eyes are the first to have seen inside this box since I taped it shut a few short hours from now.*

*Enclosed with this letter is an old photo album and a stack of typing paper. You'll need both of these.*

*I apologize if anything becomes jumbled or doesn't make perfect sense, but since finding the album I have been unable to do anything else until it was completed.*

*I haven't ate, I haven't slept, I haven't moved.*

*Sitting here now, I can tell you it has been worth it. Before last weekend I never had any intention of putting this story to paper, but now that it's done I can't help but wonder what took me so long.*

*Contained here is a story of honor and love, of loyalty and casualty, of hope and spirit.*

*Of brotherhood.*

*I have always been proud to call the men in this story my family and I trust you will do the same.*

*Your father,*
*Austin*

# Chapter One

To a six year old boy, few things in life can match the joy of skipping a day of school. So much so that I never noticed the red rimmed eyes of my Mama as she handed me the folded note excusing me from class. I didn't pay attention when Mrs. Hurwood read the note, nodded solemnly, and told me she was sorry for my loss. I didn't even find it odd that my father, the hardest working man I've ever known, stayed home that day.

It should have registered when I came downstairs that morning to find my good khaki shorts, short sleeved white dress shirt, dark blue blazer and matching tie waiting for me, but it didn't then either.

All I knew was I was skipping school for the day.

"My Easter clothes Mama?"

"Yes, sweetie. Go take a bath and then get dressed. Your father will help you with the tie when you're ready."

It wasn't until I heard the voice that I realized something was wrong.

My mother had three distinct tones. One was her usual voice, soft and sweet, melodic to a fault. She used this one almost all the time, especially when talking to my brother or me.

The other two were stronger, forceful, meant what she said was non-negotiable. The first was angry, raised and pitched and full of hurtful venom. I to this day have only seen her use it a handful of times.

Looking back, in each case it was warranted.

The third was every bit as rare, an effort at flat and monotone, a vain attempt to hide a slight cracking. She used it when I was in a car accident in college and almost lost my life. She used it the day she found out about the cancer that would eventually take hers.

And she used it that morning.

I knew better than to argue.

I took a bath, got dressed as ordered, and came down to find my father in his own dark blue suit. He helped me with my tie and together we stood in the living room, tugging at our collars and fighting to ignore the wool that itched against our skin.

The car ride was short, terse and silent, ending at a place I had never been before. It was a stately building with thick white columns stretched around the entire structure and a large carpeted ramp leading up to the front door. Enormous bouquets of flowers were piled everywhere and subdued music hummed over the grounds.

Where it was coming from, I had no idea.

Women in dark blues and blacks huddled and spoke in soft whispers. Many wore short veils down over their faces and clutched handkerchiefs in their gloved hands. Men stood off to the side trying to avoid the awkward displays of emotion, hands thrust deep in their pockets, nodding occasionally to one another.

Some smoked cigarettes, others feigned interest in a dog that had wandered onto the lot.

All looked supremely uncomfortable.

Mixed amongst the crowd were a handful of veterans in full dress uniform. It was my first encounter with military dress and I stood in awe as they milled about. Green trousers and jackets. Tan shirts and ties beneath them. Rows of ribbons and medals displayed on their chests, hats in their hands.

I had no idea who they were, where they came from, or why they were there, but I couldn't shake my gaze from them.

My brother was not yet old enough to join us and I was completely alone in a world of adults. I kept myself pressed to my father's side as we stood against the building and waited while Mama spoke with other women in hushed whispers. Every so often one of them offered a furtive glance towards the door, but for the longest time nobody moved.

We just stood outside, counting minutes in our heads, wondering if it would ever end.

For the briefest of moments, I almost wished I was back in school.

After the better part of an hour, the oak doors swung open and a pastor in black robes stepped forth, hands clasped before him. The crowd fell silent and watched as he walked forward and spread his arms wide.

"Please join me."

Like animals at feed time, the crowd funneled inside. With much jostling, the silent mass made its way into a large room with matching chairs lined into every available inch. The pastor stood by and waited until the room was full before he took his place behind an oversized wooden podium. More flowers were lined three deep behind him and the same low music played throughout the room.

The scents of a thousand fresh flowers hung in the air. Mixed with the perfumes of over a hundred women, making for a concoction that stung in the nose and eyes.

I knew better than to say a word.

It was the first funeral I had ever attended and I still wasn't sure what was going on. I had no idea why over half of the room was crying, why they weren't their usual cheerful selves. I didn't even know that the gleaming wooden box beside him was a coffin.

Despite all that, it was clear that my role was to sit still and be quiet.

"Dear family, friends and loved ones," the pastor began in a deep baritone the moment the music fell away. "It is with mixed emotions that I stand here before you today. I stand with a heavy heart at the loss of a near and dear friend. I am saddened by the loss of a great man from a world that could use more like him.

"At the same time, I am overjoyed to be here. I am happy to celebrate with you the culmination of a truly special person. To honor a life that exemplified what it means to be a man. To be happy in knowing my friend has gone to Heaven and taken his place with the good Lord above."

A soft wail went up from the front row, a stifled moan that swept through the tiny space. From my seat, I craned my neck to see my great-grandmother sitting in a large green chair, a handful of tissues pressed to her face. Her thin and frail body shook with each sniffle as she bit down on her hand and let the tears roll down her cheeks.

The pastor paused and let the moment pass before he began to speak again. As he did, I sat and wondered how I had missed seeing her outside. For the first time I noticed the people on either side of her. Sitting in a line on the front row were my grandmother, my two great aunts, and my great uncle, all in matching green chairs.

Most of them were holding hands as the others wiped away tears.

Mama was soon to follow suit as most of the women in attendance had opened their purses and were digging for more tissues. By the time the pastor called for the Lord's Prayer, there wasn't a bit of mascara left in the room.

The entire time, I pressed the palms of my hands flat on the chair beneath me. I sat on my hands and stared upward, counting the lines in the ceiling, willing myself not to follow suit and let a teardrop fall.

If Pop could stay strong, so could I.

When at last the pastor stopped, I watched as the crowd rose. One by one the rows filed past the large wooden box at the front of the room, my wide-eyed youth still not sure what was occurring around me.

Not even as our row stood and moved forward did realization set in for me.

Not until I put my fingers on the edge of the box and stood on my toes to peer inside did I grasp what was happening.

There, dressed in a military uniform, his white hair parted to the side, lay my great-uncle Jack.

# Chapter Two

To a child weaned on cartoons and Dr. Seuss books, death was not something that came along often or was easily comprehended. My father asked me three times if I was alright and each time I nodded without actually saying anything.

I understood without really understanding.

The ride to the cemetery took just a few minutes and I spent the entire time staring out the front window. Focused on the small purple flag with the white cross affixed to the front of our car, my mind honed in on the cloth fluttering in the wind, shutting out even the voices of my parents.

Just minutes after departing, we climbed from the car and joined the same mass of people moving in the same slow saunter. Much like the moments before the service, women dabbed at their noses and spoke in low voices, men nodded at one another and paced about.

After a few moments the now familiar voice of the Pastor called out, summoning everyone into a loose circle around him. In the center of it sat the same row of aging family members comprised of my great-grandmother, great aunts and uncle.

Just inches away from them, close enough to reach out and touch, was the polished wooden box holding my uncle. An arrangement of flowers rested on the top of it and a large marble headstone stood to the side.

All I could do was stand and stare in wide eyed wonder at it all.

The pastor raised his hands to quiet the crowd and again launched into verse. He held a Bible in his hands and spoke from it, pausing in tune with the loud sniffles and wails from the women around us.

He spoke for a long time. I stood with the late fall sun on my face and could feel sweat forming on my lip and along my forehead. Around us, leaves of brilliant gold and orange rattled in the trees and floated lazily through the air. They stood in large piles and collected as the breeze pushed them back and forth across the ground.

I wish I could remember exactly what he was saying that afternoon. I wish I could say it was beautiful and eloquent and everything a proper eulogy should be.

Truth is, I don't remember.

What I do remember is the look of anguish on the faces of my family as they sat in those chairs. I remember my legs growing tired from standing in one place for so long but thinking that I would never sit again if it meant I had to be as sad as they were. I remember my great-grandmother's body shuddering so hard it lifted her from her chair as she cried.

I remember the pastor saying the words, "Ashes to ashes, dust to dust," holding his arms to his side, then bringing them together and bowing his head.

I remember watching in awe as my great-grandmother willed herself to stand without the aid of her walker. With no regard for where she was or who was watching she pressed her body flat against the box and cried with everything she had.

I wish I could have walked up to her and hugged her, told her I loved her, that everything would be alright.

I wish somebody would have, even if I couldn't.

Nobody did though. Over one hundred people stood and watched as she poured her soul out, their own emotions sliding down their cheeks thick and fast.

She stayed that way until it became apparent she had no intention of leaving, until at long last my two great aunts ambled to their feet and peeled her frail body away. She made no effort to fight them as she went, her fingertips sliding along the smooth veneer, longing obvious in her movements.

Not until she was seated again did the crowd part to reveal the same men I had seen before in full military dress. Arranged in straight lines, each one carried a matching rifle and marched in time, stopping just feet away from the crowd.

Then, without warning, they raised the rifles to their shoulders and fired.

Again.

And again.

# Chapter Three

It was the first gunshot I'd ever heard, the sound nothing short of deafening.

I had no idea who these men were or why they were firing, but I remember the precision with which they did. I remember the gleaming brass of their uniforms and the way the crowd flinched with each shot.

What I remember most though was the silence.

The silence that followed the third round was unlike anything else I'd ever experienced. It boomed louder than a hundred guns could have and hung heavy in the air with an ominous tone that seemed to resonate with sadness.

Several long minutes passed before finally the pastor said, "May God be with you," bowed his head and walked away.

I feel like there was more he wanted to say that day, but didn't. Those three rounds and that heavy silence said everything for him.

Sometimes there just aren't the words.

The crowd paused and watched him depart before following suit, everyone trying to ignore the enormous sadness of the moment. Some people formed into loose clumps and whispered back and forth, others got into their cars and drove away.

Lost in the shuffle, nobody noticed as I slipped off and watched the solitary man alone by the grave. He sat with his gaze aimed forward before reaching into the small green knapsack by his feet. From it he pulled a tattered rag of red, white and blue, twisting the material in his hands.

On wobbly legs he stood and spread it across the top of the casket.

I knew the man was my uncle Cat and that he couldn't walk without his cane. I heard he was injured in the war years before and that his body was never the same. Despite that, I watched as he tossed the implement aside and stood over the casket of his brother. In one swift movement he snapped his heels together, drew himself up arrow straight and saluted.

His body quivered as he held that salute as long he could before collapsing to the ground.

Chills ran the entire length of my body as I watched. Never had I felt so alive, so emotional, so vulnerable, all at once.

I stood rooted to the spot with every fiber of my being on fire until my father came and gently pulled me back to the car. The mere touch of his hand set my skin crawling as goose bumps dotted my body.

On numb legs I walked back to the car, certain that I could never feel that way again.

A few hours later I found out just how wrong I was.

# Chapter Four

Growing up in a small town, there wasn't a lot of variance in the people that lived there. I didn't meet a black person until I was ten years old and didn't befriend one until a family moved in during junior high.

Most folks were white skinned, blue collared, and kind to a fault. They were God fearing, upstanding, and lived their lives the way we're taught to as children.

The only major difference between most people in town and my father was that he was the hardest worker around. Famous for his strength and stamina, he worked far beyond the hours any normal human should be expected to and did it without ever a word of discontent.

Every day he rose before the sun, put on his bib overalls and flannel shirt, and headed to the wood yard that was his second home. Each night he would return home and peel off the same sweat soaked clothes.

To this day I can only remember my father wearing a suit a handful of times. Growing up he referred to it as his "marry-bury suit," which pretty succinctly summed it up. If the suit came out, somebody was getting hitched or had just been read their final rights.

It was much the same way with Roberts family gatherings. It wasn't that we didn't like each other or get along well; it was just that everybody had their own lives to lead. It was very rare that I saw most of my relatives outside of holidays and the only time we ever saw extended family was when a major occasion brought us together.

I guess you could say we were a marry-bury family.

I was still reeling from the scene at the graveside as my father piled us into the car and drove away. The gold buttons on my jacket had a hawk emblazoned on them and I spent the ride studying it as we wound our way through town and out into the country.

The incident scrawled through my mind time after time. With each replaying my uncle held his salute a little longer, fell a little more dramatically. It wasn't until the car stopped that I even realized we weren't going home.

We were going to visit my Aunt Millie.

Aunt Millie was my mother's sister and lived not far from town. Mama used to say she always thought she was better than Birch Grove and everybody always assumed she would leave town and never look back. Instead, she married a doctor and spent her every waking minute touting her newfound affluence for anybody that would listen.

I guess it never dawned on her that she had latched herself to the ugliest man in Ohio in earning this wealth.

That, or in her mind, it was worth the sacrifice.

If not for my aunt's demeanor, visiting her would have been a kid's dream come true. She lived in a big two story farm house that sat fifty yards off of Lake Mendelman. A dock ran from their front yard out over a hundred feet into the water with a motor boat and paddle boat they kept tied to it nine months out of the year. Giant sycamore trees dotted the front yard with plenty of low branches for climbing. One of them even had an old tire swing that swung out over the water.

"What are we doing here?" I asked from the backseat without thinking.

"We're having a visit," my Mama said and together we climbed from the car.

We were one of the first to arrive and within minutes a dozen cars pulled in behind us. I recognized a few of my aunts, uncles and older cousins streaming from the cars, but for the most part I was again a child among strangers.

"What's going on?" I asked my father as we climbed the steps to the enormous front porch and walked towards the door.

"It's been awhile since we've seen each other," he replied. "We're going to have a nice lunch and talk for awhile."

Reading between the lines, this meant I was in for an afternoon of boredom.

Still, I knew better than to say anything.

The house smelled of honey and fresh baked bread as we entered and Aunt Millie swung out from the kitchen with an apron wrapped around her neck. She was drying her hands on a dishtowel as she grabbed my mother in a hug. "Oh, how was it?" she asked, feigned concern in her voice.

"It was…it was bad," my mother answered, the hurt in her voice very much real.

"I wish I could have been there, I just had to stay and get everything ready," Aunt Millie replied, her eyes already moving to the next people streaming through the door. "Food's in the kitchen, go ahead and help yourself."

I looked uncertainly up at my father, who said, "Come on, you must be hungry."

I wasn't, but went along for his benefit as much mine.

Neither one of us much cared for Aunt Millie.

Following my father, we made our way to the kitchen and grabbed matching plates. We filled them high with mashed potatoes, noodles, turkey, and green bean casserole. Together we found a small table in the corner and settled down to eat alone.

My father wasn't from Ohio and sometimes I got the impression that he felt even more out of place at family gatherings than I did. It was easy for a kid to disappear in a crowd, but a man his size stood out no matter how hard he tried not to.

With our heads down we fell to our meals, both taking in heaping spoonfuls. By the time we were done the crowd had swelled, people standing in pairs and trios all over the house, deep in conversation. Many of them held plates of steaming food in front of them, doing their best to talk and eat.

"Come on, let's get up and let somebody else sit down," my father said and we both rose and took our plates to the sink. He placed his in and ran some water over it, then took mine and did the same.

Together we turned and wound our way from the kitchen towards the front of the house where we bumped into my mother talking with an elderly couple in the main hall. "You remember my husband William," she said as my father shook hands with the man and nodded at the woman. "And this is our son Austin."

I gave a half smile as they did the same, both sides dismissing each other within seconds. For several minutes I stood and dutifully tried to listen, followed by several more of watching the people mingling about me. Eventually, I gave up on the situation and made one of the most important decisions of my young life.

    I wandered out onto the front porch.

# Chapter Five

The thin wooden screen door was light and swung free at my touch. Outside, the autumn air was deliciously cool after standing in the artificial heat of the house.

My shoes clicked against the floorboards of the porch as I walked to the edge and peered down at the flowerbeds a few feet below. A handful of red maple leaves were pressed against the lattice encircling the porch. A few more were wrapped around the bases of bright yellow mums spaced every couple of feet.

The screen door swung open behind me and I turned to see my father stick his head out from the house. "Stay on the porch Austin, alright?"

"Yes, daddy."

The door swung back closed and for a few moments I was again alone. I turned and walked in the opposite direction, measuring my steps against the even planks of the floor.

I made it over halfway across the floor before I noticed there was someone else with me.

My great uncle Cat sat stone still in a rocker, staring out over the lake. His left hand gripped the top of his cane and his right was draped across his lap. He was still dressed in his military uniform and his gray eyes stared unblinking across the water.

Pulling up short, I stopped and stared at him. The scene from the graveside played again in my mind and all I could think of was him saluting the casket before tumbling to his knees. A thin chill crept through me as I retreated a few steps and perched myself on the top step, my body angled towards him.

If he saw me, he gave no indication.

Instead, he sat with a steeled façade and stared at a spot on the horizon. For several minutes I followed his gaze in an attempt to figure out what he was staring at.

Nothing jumped out at me.

Eventually the curiosity got to me and I did something that only someone as brash or naïve as a six year old could do.

I asked him what he was looking at.

His features remained fixated, his hand remained on the cane as he watched the water. I waited for him to answer, but no words came. I began to wonder if he'd even heard a word I said.

Several minutes passed before I worked up the courage to try again.

"Uncle Cat, sure is some good food in there. Can I get you something?"

I had hoped the less obtrusive topic might get him talking, but it didn't. He remained motionless, as wooden as the rocking chair he sat on.

Finally I resigned myself to being ignored and said, "I sure am sorry about Uncle Jack."

I pressed my back flat against the post and turned my head to the lake, watching the sun dance patterns across the water.

"He was my brother you know," my great uncle said, his voice deep and graveled.

The response took me by surprise and I jumped several inches up off the porch. My heart pounded in my chest as I turned to look at him, his body frozen in place, his eyes locked towards the distance. "No, I didn't know that."

They were my great uncles. Their being any more than that had never occurred to me.

Something moved behind my uncle's eyes as he shifted his head towards me. The stiff exterior of his face softened and sagged a bit. His right hand released the cane and he leaned forward and rested it against the porch railing. Not once did his eyes leave mine and when he spoke, I knew I was the only person in the world he saw.

"Have you ever heard the story of my brother Jack?"

# Chapter Six

My great uncle was born Richard Roberts, but for the last fifty years, everyone just called him Cat. At the time I didn't think much of the name, and not until long after the fact did I learn it stemmed from a cat fishing accident near their home when he was a boy.

Only twice before had I been in his presence and neither time did he say anything to me. My mother often spoke about him in hushed tones and said that things had happened that made him the way he was.

I had no idea what that meant.

All I knew was the earnest sincerity in his face when he asked me that question. I could sense the gravity in his tone and I bit back my eagerness to hear anything he might tell me.

"No."

The corners of his lips turned up a bit, giving just the slightest indication of a smile. Without comment he lifted a gnarled hand from his thigh and reached for the floor beside him. He pulled the same faded green knapsack I saw at the cemetery up onto his lap and pointed at another rocking chair off to the right. "Drag that chair over here."

I did as he said without pause.

The chair was homemade from thick wood and it took a great deal of effort for me to drag it the ten feet to his side. I left a gap the better part of a foot between us as climbed up and stared across at him.

"What I am about to show you, only one other person has ever seen," Cat said. "The time has now come to pass it on to somebody else."

He lifted his eyes towards the water again.

"I've been sitting here for the last hour trying to think who I should give it to. It was so simple, I should have seen it sooner. Only a child can properly appreciate this story. Someone that hasn't yet been corrupted by society or embittered by the false promises of a government that cares nothing for them.

"Most importantly, only somebody that has a brother themselves will properly appreciate this story."

"A brother themselves?" I asked, furrowing my brow and staring up at him.

His gaze never left the water as he raised a hand for silence. After several moments he lowered his focus and peeled back the flap of the green canvas bag. He reached in with one hand and pulled from it a dark leather album.

Scratches and blemishes crossed the front of it. A few water stains stretched from the corners. He placed it with care, almost reverence, atop the sack and looked down at me.

"You might have photo albums at your house, but I promise you they're nothing like this. Yours might be filled with pictures and papers and awards, but you won't find much of that here.

"This album isn't really an album, but a record. A record of the life your uncle Jack and I lived together. Everything in it has been put there with great care and everything in it has a story to tell. Each item was placed in specific order and even if something doesn't make sense as we come to it, it will by the end.

"Do you understand?"

I stared from my uncle's face to the album and back again.

I did not understand in the slightest, but I nodded my head up and down anyway.

His eyes bore into my own for several moments before he too nodded and turned his attention back to the album on his lap. The cover swung open beneath his aged hand to reveal not a cover page, not even a title.

Just a single object pressed against a solid white background.

The birthday napkin.

# Chapter Seven

Uncle Cat stared at the napkin, his face impassive. I watched for any sign of movement, but for a long time none came.

At last, the crease along the right corner of his mouth played a little deeper into his face and his hand ran its fingers over the page.

I waited until I could resist the urge no longer.

"What is that Uncle Cat?"

He raised his face from the page and turned it to me, then back towards the water. His eyes took on a far away quality and when he spoke it was the rich voice of a man many years the junior of the one before me.

My Uncle Cat wasn't just going to tell me a story.

He was going to relive it.

"My Pappy hung himself in the spring of 1937," he began. No preamble, no back story, just a flat statement that would set the tone for the rest of the day.

"After he did, my Mama had no option but to move us. She didn't want to take us from Birch Grove any more than we wanted to go, but we didn't have a choice.

"She found work in a laundry outside of Burbank, about twenty-five miles north of here. The job was posted in the weekly newspaper that we got whenever somebody left one lying around at church. She wrote to the address to ask if it was still available and a few weeks later a man replied. Said she was welcome to it if she was still interested.

"We packed up everything we could in a couple of peach baskets and the rest we bundled up using our bed sheets as hobo sacks. One bright Saturday afternoon the man drove down in his flatbed pickup and got us, took us up to Burbank."

Uncle Cat paused a moment to collect his thoughts.

"We got us a little apartment above a general store and for three years we went about life the best we could. Mama worked torturous hours at the laundry and many days she would be gone before sunrise and home after sunset. When she did return she was often pale and her dress was soaked in sweat, though she never said a word."

His voice caught a tiny quiver at the last line, but his gaze remained focused on the lake.

Mine remained focused on him.

"Up to that point Jack and I were brothers only insomuch as we were born from the same parents. We weren't enemies mind you; we just didn't cross paths that often.

"See, Jack was a loner by nature. He was two years older than me and he knew Pappy better than I did. He was the one that found him hanging in the mill that day and I think it left a deeper impression on him than he would ever care to admit.

"Not only that, but from that moment on he felt an innate need to assume the leadership role for the family. It ate at him that Mama had to work so hard and it absolutely killed him that he couldn't do more to help her."

He cocked his head a bit to the side and turned his right hand upward. "Of course, this is all hindsight from an old man looking back at the situation. At the time I was just a five year old boy, oblivious to the world around me.

"Every day Mama would go to work, Jack would go to school, and I was free to roam as I pleased. I spent many spring and fall days bouncing through the creeks behind Main Street, looking under rocks for crawdads and salamanders. In the winter I'd sit at the window and watch the people come and go from the general store.

"I'd perch there for hours with a pad and charcoal pencil and draw them the best I could. I'd make up names and stories for them and days would pass without my ever so much as moving.

"Ah, to live the life of a child again."

Uncle Cat turned to me and gave a half smile, then shifted back towards the album. He motioned towards the date written along the edge and said, "In the summer of 1937 my brother and I were invited to our first ever birthday party. The man that owned the laundry had a daughter named Terra that was between Jack and I in age.

"Terra was turning six and her father was throwing a party for all the children in her class at their house outside of town. They were going to have pony rides and food and games, he was even going to dress up like a clown for it.

"I had never met Terra before and from what I gathered she and Jack didn't much like each other. Jack said she was as full of herself as her father and she didn't like the way Jack hardly ever talked.

"One night Mama came home late and announced that Mr. Albon had asked that we come. She said she knew we didn't want to but that she didn't want to risk making her boss angry, so we were all going."

Uncle Cat's face grew into a grin as a low chuckle rolled out.

"My brother and I fought her tooth and nail about it too. Man, we did not want to go to that thing. Didn't matter though.

"The next day we got into our church clothes and the three of us walked two miles out to the Albon farm. Most of the other families in town had buggies and we were by far the last ones to arrive. A few folks pointed and whispered as we walked up, but Mama told us to pay them no heed.

"We joined the party the best we could, though it didn't take long to realize the only thing stronger than our not wanting to be there was the other kids not wanting us there. The minute everybody broke for lunch we took our plates and disappeared to the furthest corner of the yard, content to hide for the rest of the afternoon."

Uncle Cat paused, leaned forward and placed his elbows on his knees. I watched as the corners of his eyes tightened and when he spoke, his voice was a touch lower.

"Just before lunch was served, Mr. Albon asked my mother to help him with some things in the kitchen. She told us she would be right back and we continued playing, never giving it another though. Awhile later we were sitting in the corner eating when Jack said, "Mama's sure been gone a long time." He told me to stay put and disappeared around the side of the house.

"Jack wasn't one to say things he didn't mean, so I listened to him. I stayed right there until I heard the scream."

My eyes grew wide. "Who screamed Uncle Cat?"

He had been so lost in the story that I think he forgot I was there. At the sound of my voice he flinched, followed by several quick breaths.

"I knew the second I heard it, it was my mother.

"As I'm sure you'll discover some day, there are some things a person just knows. The sound of a loved one in trouble is one of them.

"I jumped to my feet and sprinted as hard as I could around the house. I heard her again from somewhere inside and threw myself through the back screen door. The wooden floor pounded loud beneath my feet as I ran through the house checking rooms and finally found them in the kitchen. It was a scene I still remember with as much detail as the day it happened.

"My mother was pressed against the sink, her dress torn and the skin of her shoulder shining bright from the heat. A large red welt crossed her left cheek and her eyes were puffy from crying.

"My brother had his back to the wall, his hair mussed and his face covered in sweat. Standing in front of him with his back to me was old man Albon. His shirt was off and suspenders held his unbuttoned trousers up around his waist. In his hand he held a rolling pin, slashing it back and forth through the air like a sword.

"You just had to go meddling didn't you boy?" he said as he stood holding the pin in front of him.

"You're not hurting my mother anymore," Jack said, his voice low and throaty."

As he told the story, Uncle Cat rubbed the palms of his hands together, his eyes narrowing further with each passing second.

"You're right," Albon said, "I'm hurting you first!" and took two hard steps towards my brother. Without waiting, without even thinking, I grabbed a paring knife from the counter and ran at Albon.

"I crossed the floor faster than I had ever run in my life and just before he got to Jack, I got to him. I plunged that knife into his leg with everything I had. In an instant I heard the rolling pin hit the floor and felt warm blood run over my hand.

"Albon screamed out in pain and backhanded me across the mouth with a vicious swipe. I had never been hit before and the pain was tremendous. I could taste blood in my mouth and before I knew it I was lying on my back in the middle of the kitchen.

"My head hit the floor hard and brilliant colors flashed before my eyes. I lay there helpless, unable to move, and I could hear him say, "You little son of a bitch, you're going to pay for this."

"I raised my head to see Albon coming towards me, but I couldn't do anything to stop it. I was at his mercy, unable to stop anything he might do.

"Two steps before he got there, Jack picked up the rolling pin and hit him across the back of the knee. Albon's leg folded in half and he stumbled forward onto all fours, his body just inches away from mine. Our eyes locked for a moment, both sets flashing with fear, before Jack whacked him hard across the back of the skull."

Uncle Cat wrung his hands for the last time and ran them down the front of his pants.

"Old man Albon was out cold. His eyes rolled up into his head and flopped down on the floor beside me, his entire body limp.

"Mama waited only a second before she helped me off my back. She took a birthday napkin from the counter and wiped my face clean as we all stood and looked at each other.

"After a minute or two, Mama fixed her dress and the three of us walked right out the front door. People were crowded around the front porch to see what happened, but we walked past them without turning our heads or even acknowledging their presence. The minute we got home we packed everything we could and walked two days back to Birch Grove."

Uncle Cat fell silent, though by the end of the tale his voice was just a whisper.

"So that's the napkin Grandma gave you that day?" I asked.

Uncle Cat nodded. "The reason the napkin is in here isn't because of what it is, but what it symbolizes. The day Jack and I really became brothers."

"But weren't you always-" I began to ask, but he raised his hand to stop me.

"That night as we packed our things Jack pulled me out on the balcony of our apartment. He made sure Mama couldn't hear him and told me how he had walked in on Albon..."

My uncle paused for a moment. "Well, a boy your age shouldn't hear such things.

"Jack told me he suspected Albon had been mistreating Mama for some time but he wasn't able to do anything about it. He also told me that I shouldn't be ashamed for what I did. A man has a right to stick up for his family and I should be proud of the stand I made."

My uncle swallowed hard and blinked a few times. "Then he thanked me and told me he was proud of me. Said that if there was ever anything I needed, I only had to look as far as my brother."

# Chapter Eight

After he muttered that last line, my uncle stared at the napkin for a long time. I'm pretty sure there was more he wanted to say, but I don't think he trusted himself to say it. His voice didn't crack, but it had lowered so far I could barely hear it.

No tears filled his eyes, but they were closed tight.

I watched him for just a second, then sat back in my chair and stared out over the lake. The glorious afternoon sun played across the water and I was content to sit and watch it.

If my uncle needed time, I would give him all he needed.

I was so content in doing so, I didn't see him open his eyes or raise his head. The faint sound of thick cotton paper rubbing along metal made me look in time to see him turning the page in the old album. The napkin disappeared from sight and in its place was a piece of paper.

I was only in the beginning of my first grade year and while I was well ahead of the curve for reading, I couldn't yet decipher a word of cursive. Not that it mattered anyway, the writing on the paper was faded so much that in many places it was gone.

I looked from the paper to my uncle and back a couple of times, then focused on my uncle's face as he stared at the note with an expression that resembled a smirk. When he spoke, the sadness and strain from before was gone.

Pointing to the date along the side of the page he said, "1943. America had entered World War II and the country was in a state of patriotic upheaval unlike anything since the Civil War. Of course, we can thank our *allies* the Japanese for that."

I had no idea what World War II, the Civil War or the Japanese even were, but could tell by the venom dripping from the word 'allies' that he didn't at all like them.

"Most of the able bodied men in the country were called to war, and by most I mean any healthy male between the ages of 16 and 40. Many did the right thing and volunteered to go, and after Pearl Harbor who could blame them?

"The rest? Well, they waited for Uncle Sam to tell them they had to go.

"By the fall of 1943 Birch Grove was a ghost town. Most of the men were off to war, many to never return. It made for bad times around here, with folks crying and praying and carrying around the burden of things left unsaid. No way to live, that's for damn sure."

He paused for a second with his gaze locked on the horizon before giving his head a twist to clear it. "Six years had passed since the incident up at Burbank. Not one time in those six years had any of us mentioned it, though my brother had lived true to his word. With each passing day he and I grew closer, forging a bond that would prove invaluable over the years.

"We'd go fishing, hunting, swimming. We'd walk with Mama to church and help her with chores. We'd work at the mill together or chop wood for folks for extra money.

"Now don't get me wrong, it wasn't as if Jack and I suddenly became the best of friends and walked around arm in arm. Jack was still Jack and there would be times we'd go days without as much as ten words being said between us. He was still the same person as before, it was just that he let me tag along with him.

"In the fall of '43, Jack and I were in the sixth and fourth grades. Jack had emerged as one of the smartest people in Birch Grove, not just in the school, but in the town. Me, I hated being cooped up every day and would spend hours staring at the clock trying to make the hands on it move.

"The only thing I watched with more intensity was Mae Rife, but that's a whole other story."

The folds of skin around his eyes and mouth crinkled a bit, but he didn't elaborate further.

He tapped the note with his index finger and said, "One day while at lunch Jack overheard a group of boys complaining that their fathers had been forced off to war. Jack listened for a moment before turning to leave, never saying a word.

"As he walked across the grassy lot behind the school one of the Lewis boys said in overly loud voice, "Yeah, one good thing about not having a father is at least you don't have to see him sent off to war."

He turned his head to me and said, "Mama taught us from a very young age nothing in the world was worth hating. There may be things we don't like or people that make our skin crawl, but nothing was worth the energy of hatred.

"I tell you though, the Lewis boys gave Mama a run for her money.

"The Lewis clan lived up on the north end of town in a small clapboard house. By all accounts the father was a pretty good guy, worked at the post office for years.

"His boys on the other hand, were the spawn of Satan himself. It took everything my brother had not to turn around and go after him right then, but to his credit he didn't. Lord knows I would have flown at him the second a word was uttered in my direction.

"Stronger than I ever was, Jack set his jaw and continued across the open lot. As he walked though, the Lewis boys began to follow. With each step, they lobbed a torrent of insults at him, each one a little more vile than the one before.

"One of them said, "Hey we didn't mean you Roberts, we meant the other guy whose old man hung himself."

"Another fired, "It's probably better anyway, we've got no use for pussies over there."

The old wrinkled hand holding the album clenched itself into a fist. It was obvious the story was having an effect on my uncle, even all those years later.

"On the first day of school every year I made it a point to arrive early. It was the only day of the year I arrived early or even on time. Do you know why?"

The direct question caught me off guard and it took a moment for me to stammer, "N-no. Why?"

"Because seating was always done on a first come, first served basis. The earlier you showed up, the better seat you got for the year. Every year I would go extra early on the first day to claim my seat next to the window.

"Most days I'd stare with longing out at the late autumn and early spring sun and watch for any signs of wildlife that might indicate the fish were biting.

"That day it gave me the perfect vantage to see everything out in the yard as it unfolded."

He opened his mouth to speak twice, each time closing it without saying anything. On the third attempt, he found the words.

"Jack held his gaze and continued on his trek until finally Scot Lewis, the oldest, crossed the line. Jack was just about to the front door when Scot said, "Hell, ain't no way of knowing if that old bird was his father anyway, his mother being a whore like she is."

"The comment stopped Jack cold. He pulled up just short of the door and placed his book and lunch sack on the ground against the building. In slow, deliberate movements, he turned to face the crowd.

"Sitting against the window, I could tell something huge was brewing and started waving my hand like crazy. I asked Miss Tilton if I could go to the bathroom twice, only to be told both times that I could wait until recess like everybody else.

"Outside Jack turned and stared at the three Lewis boys in turn, pointed at Scot and said, "You just messed up."

"Oh yeah, what are you going to do about it?" Scot sneered.

"I'm going to kick your ass and there ain't a damn thing you can do about it."

"And what about them?" Scot asked, gesturing to his brothers on either side of him.

"Unless they want their ass kicked too, I suggest they stand down," Jack said. "Nobody calls my mother a whore."

"I sat and watched as Scot laughed nervously and turned to say something to his brother on the right. The words never got out though, Jack was too fast for him.

"He tackled Scot before he had a chance to move, burying a shoulder into his ribs and driving him to the ground.

"The crowd around them stood frozen in shock as Jack sprung to a knee and snapped a hard right to the nose of Scot Lewis. Scot was already coughing from the tackle and when Jack hit him he coughed harder and covered his face as blood oozed between his fingers.

"Jack cocked to fire a second punch at him but before he could Burt and Terry Lewis grabbed him from behind. The second I saw them enter the fray I jumped from my seat and sprinted from the classroom. Miss Tilton hollered and yelled at me as I passed but I ran right by her, down the hallway, and out the front doors.

"Burt had Jack by the waist from behind, trying to control him as Jack flailed about. Terry stood in front of them trying to land punches when I slammed headlong into him from behind. The force sent him sprawling forward onto his stomach and as he attempted to rise from the grass, I stepped forward and swung a kick clean across the bridge of his nose."

Uncle Cat turned his head and looked at me. "That kick hurt my foot like hell. I can only imagine what it must have felt like for him. A plume of blood exploded down onto the grass and Terry fell flat and didn't move.

"Scot regained his feet and tried to come after me, but his eyes were teary and puffy from the punch Jack had landed. He stumbled forward and tried to throw a roundhouse, but I sidestepped him and tripped him to the ground.

"I fell to a knee beside him to finish the job but before I could, Burt flew into me and we both toppled over. We rolled twice on the grass and he came up on top before Jack hit him with a vicious knee to the side of the head.

"Grabbing me by the back of my shirt, Jack hauled me to my feet and the two of us stood back to back with our fists raised, facing off against the crowd.

"Anybody else?" Jack demanded, one of the few times I've ever heard him looking for a fight. The wild look in his eyes was one I usually wore, not him.

"Nobody said a word as we lowered our fists and our breathing slowed to normal. The world was silent except for the sound of slow clapping from inside the school. It grew louder until eventually the principal, Harold Marcus, sauntered out the front door and onto the lawn."

Uncle Cat turned an eye towards me, then looked back at the book and continued, "Harold Marcus was a real sanctimonious bastard. As a child he lost a bout with polio and walked with a cane and a limp. It left him ineligible for the draft and made him about the only man left in Birch Grove older than us. Guy had a real problem with it too, kind of like he was less of a man because he couldn't go to war. Spent every free second he had trying to prove otherwise.

"The clapping continued as he walked up and without a word handed us a piece of paper, *this* piece of paper. He looked at the Lewis boys lying on the ground, handed a second piece of paper to a boy nearby and said, "Give this to them when they wake up."

"He gave each of us one last look, turned and walked back into the building. Inside, I heard Miss Tilton call the class back from the window and watched as faces disappeared from behind the glass.

"What's it say?" I asked after a few minutes.

"Jack looked at me, then walked over and collected his book and lunch sack. "Let's go."

"Where we going?"

"He held the note up and read,

*Dear Parent,*

*You are receiving this note for the same reason you are receiving your boys home in the middle of the afternoon. They were involved in an altercation on the lawn of the school today. Not only is fighting not allowed at Birch Grove School, neither is the disruption of classes in progress. For their actions, they have been expelled indefinitely.*

"He flipped the note over to the opposite side and continued,

*Mrs. Roberts,*

*Because your sons gave the Lewis boys the thrashing we at the school have been wanting to for quite some time, Jack and Richard may return starting on Monday. Must be nice to know you have somebody looking out for you like that.*"

The upturned corners gave way to a full smile as Uncle Cat stared out. "Not only were we not in trouble, well not too bad anyway, we were *envied* by the Principal of the school."

He turned his eyes to me and said, "Oh, Mama was plenty mad when we got home and had us doing the most God-awful chores every minute until we went back on Monday. The entire time she wanted to know what had caused us to do something like that and the entire time I told her I didn't know, which at the time was the truth.

"Jack, well, he was Jack. He didn't say anything. Far as I know, he never did tell what that damn Scot Lewis said about her."

Uncle Cat ran his tongue over his bottom lip, then relaxed his hand and rested it back on the album. He traced his finger along the faded pencil script and said, "This right here is the reason that note made it into the album. That one line...*Must be nice to know you have somebody looking out for you like that.*"

He looked at me again and saw the confusion on my face. "Like I said before, it'll all make sense in the end."

# Chapter Nine

The sound of the screen door swinging open jolted us both from the album. In unison we turned to see my mother through the heavy insect screen. "Austin, you're not bothering your uncle are you?"

"No Mama."

"Would you tell me if you were?"

Before I could answer Cat said, "Oh now, he's fine. We're just out here talking, aren't we?"

"Yes sir," I said.

My mother frowned a bit, but let it pass. "You boys need anything? Glass of lemonade? Sweet tea?"

We each murmured a no and my mother's frown grew a little deeper as she retreated back into the house. We watched the door for a few seconds to make sure she wasn't returning, then turned our attention back to the album.

Carefully he peeled back the note and flipped it to the next page.

I admit I flinched when I first saw the misshapen object. It was long and jagged, colored black and gray. It kind of resembled some sort of overgrown bug, but it was obvious that whatever it was had never been alive.

"What is that?" I asked.

"That is a sliver of wood."

I studied the object, the answer not quite satisfying my curiosity. "Where'd it come from?"

My uncle tapped the page with his index finger and let his gaze wander to nowhere in particular. His eyes clouded over, and I could tell he was retreating back to a time long ago.

"The winter of 1947 was one of the harshest these parts have ever seen. The river froze up about mid-November and didn't even begin to thaw until mid-April.

"School was cancelled for over a month and a half. The businesses in town were only open on Mondays and Thursdays so folks could stay home and the owners didn't have to heat the buildings.

"The first cold snap came down from Canada and it just kind of settled here. The world took on a gray tint and the wind blew for days on end. Around mid-December, the snows hit.

"Nobody ever mentions the Blizzard of '47 because technically it wasn't a blizzard. It was more than like one long storm that lasted over three months. Every single night we'd clear as much away as we could and each morning we'd wake up to find several more inches of fresh powder."

My uncle shook his head as he recounted the memory, no doubt recalling the hours spent with a shovel. "At that time Mama was working at the sundry store in town. With the store being closed, she worried herself sick wondering how we were going to make it through the winter.         "Our family had one old pair of wool coveralls somebody brought back from the First World War. They were a little short and snug, but they sure were warm.

"Each day Jack and I would get up early. One of us would chop wood and tend the chicken coop while the other pulled on the coveralls and set off for the day, shovel in hand. Day after day we'd walk the town, clearing sidewalks for five or ten cents apiece.

"Most folks refused to believe the snow could go on for months the way it was and were happy to give us their money, always insisting it was for the last time. Neither one of us ever said word, we just kept right on taking their money.

He paused again, mirth lines present at the corners of his eyes.

"Each year at Christmas, Mama selected the largest from our chicken coop. She'd then present it to a less fortunate family in the area and wish them a Merry Christmas from all of us. Hard to believe there were many people around less fortunate than we were, but somehow she always managed to find them.

"Not once did Mama ever make any fuss over who she gave the chicken to. Fact is, I don't think she ever told a soul beyond our family and the family she picked. She never did anything just for the attention.

"At some point, an appreciative family let it slip that we gave them a chicken. Most people that it was a nice gesture and never gave it a second thought.

"Most, but not all."

The way he muttered that last line made the hairs on my neck stand up and I could tell he harbored deep resentment for the story he was about to tell.

"If the Lewis boys were vermin, the Carpenter clan barely qualified as fleas on vermin. I don't remember a single one of them ever having a job and the word around town was they owned a moonshine still that fed their own habit and little else.

"Every one of them was rail thin and wiry, heads full of stringy hair and rotting teeth. And I do mean every one of them, mother included."

Any other time I would have thought something like that was a joke, but I could tell he was completely serious.

"Christmas Eve we woke up to find six inches of fresh fallen snow on the ground. Jack and I had agreed we'd take Christmas day off from shoveling, but we weren't about to miss two days worth of income.

"It was my turn to shovel and I remember waking up in complete darkness. When it got that cold we closed off most of the house and drug our mattresses into the kitchen. We'd hang blankets over the windows and pile the stove high at night and no matter how often we put wood in overnight, it would be dark and cold the next morning.

"We used to keep the coveralls between as at night so we could pull them on without having to crawl out from under our goose down blankets. Beside me, Jack tugged on a pair of jeans and a couple of heavy shirts. When we were both dressed we'd tiptoe out so we didn't wake Mama sleeping beside the stove.

"Looks like another half foot or so," I said as we stood outside the door and pulled on our gloves.

"Yep," Jack agreed and tugged a knit cap down over his ears.

"Where all did you hit yesterday?" I asked.

"The usual spots. Be sure to go down the main drag, then head east down Sycamore Street and work your way back up this way. The Lee's, Johnston's, Hardy's."

"You got the Hardy's yesterday? I thought he wasn't going to bother until it was all done?"

Jack blew a plume of hot breath into the air and said, "Poor guy couldn't get out his front door. Guess he decided it was time."

"Bet that was some fun digging."

"Over three foot," Jack deadpanned.

"The two of us stood there like that for a couple more seconds before I said, "Well, I better be off."

"Without a word I grabbed the shovel leaning against the house and headed out. Even using it as a walking stick, it was slow going. The powdery snow was too thin to pack tight and every step I sunk halfway to my knees. It wasn't long before my boots were completely filled.

"I was just about out of the bottoms, cussing and spitting, when I saw them."

I waited for him to continue but when he said nothing I asked, "Saw what?"

"Tracks."

My eyes grew large. "What kind of tracks?"

"Human tracks."

"Humans? Walking around in the snow at night?"

My uncle didn't answer the question. Instead, he said, "There were three sets in the snow and as I stood and surveyed them I could tell they swung a loose semi-circle towards the back of our place. I was almost a quarter mile away and had no idea how old the tracks were, but I knew I had to get back in a hurry.

"I took off through the snow with everything I had, plowing along in my own fresh trail. Snow continued spilling down into my boots and after about a hundred yards or so I kicked them off and ran in my stocking feet.

"Normally my feet would have been numb in seconds, but I couldn't feel a thing as I stumbled and flailed down the path. Adrenaline surged through me and I could feel sweat rolling down my back under the heavy wool coveralls.

"I used the shovel as best I could to keep me upright, cutting a path straight for the front door. When I got there, I found only the two sets of tracks Jack and I made just a few minutes earlier.

"This told me two things. First, Mama was still inside and safe. Second, Jack was outside with whoever made those tracks."

Uncle Cat paused for another second and leaned forward onto his elbows. He looked down at the ground in front of him, then raised his head.

"I shrugged off the heavy wool suit and stood in my long underwear, cold air enveloping the wet flannel. I looked down at my feet to see I had a thin trail of blood behind me, though I wasn't sure where it had come from.

"Shovel in hand, I followed Jack's footsteps around the corner of the house and inched along until I heard voices coming from the barn. I peered around the corner to see Jack was on his knees on the dirt floor, staring wild eyed up at old man Carpenter. One of the boys was on either side of him gripping an arm while the old man stood in front of him, our pitch fork in his hand.

"You people got so damn much you can give it away, then you won't mind us taking what we need," he said as he waved the fork at my brother.

"Jack said something I couldn't hear back at him and one of the boys snapped a quick punch to his mouth. A small line of blood appeared at the corner of his lip as the old man laughed and continued waving the pitchfork.

"That's when I made my move."

My uncle's voice was low and he was staring hard at the ground in front of him.

"Gripping the shovel handle with both hands I sprinted from behind the corner and covered the fifteen yards between us in just seconds. Both the boys looked up in total shock, neither one able to utter a word as I smashed the shovel head against the old man's skull.

"He crumpled on contact. Went down so fast I tripped over him, barely catching myself from falling flat.

"Once he realized what was happening, the older Carpenter boy released Jack and sprinted at me, a crazed look in his eye. I let my momentum spin me around and swung the shovel out as hard as I could. He never stood a chance. The head of it caught him just behind the ear, shattering the wooden handle into a hundred pieces.

"Just like his old man, he went down and didn't move. I turned to face the third one, waving the busted shovel handle in my hand at him. You could tell he was scared to death, just stood there with his hands raised by his side.

"Jack appeared beside me as I lowered the stick and motioned toward the boy with my chin. "What do we do with him?"

"Jack stared at him, then the two bodies lying unconscious beside him. "They won't be any more trouble. We'll leave it up to him to get their asses home."

Uncle Cat exhaled and pushed himself back to a full upright position in the chair.

"We watched from the front step as he woke them up and the three stumbled off our land. By the time they were gone I was trembling with cold and my foot was throbbing. Mama hadn't heard a sound inside the house and was shocked we were still home, let alone almost frozen to death and both bleeding.

"I ended up with a nasty cause of pneumonia and some mild frostbite on my toes, though nothing permanent. Nothing like Jack would have ended up with if I hadn't gotten there in time."

Forgetting, or quite possibly just ignoring, the first rule, I asked, "Did Jack ever tell you what happened before you got there?"

Uncle Cat scrunched his nose. "No, and I didn't even ask. I figured it must have been pretty bad, so I just let it be."

I nodded at his answer, staring down at the shard of wood on the page.

Uncle Cat noticed my gaze and said, "So far you've seen three objects. A birthday napkin, a note from the principal and a piece of wood. Know what each of these things have in common?"

I searched the furthest recesses of my young mind. "Each one has you beating somebody up?"

Uncle Cat threw his head back and laughed, a deep, throaty spasm of sound. "No son, not that. Your uncle and I hardly ever fought. Matter of fact, I think these three were the only fights we ever got in. At least up until we were grown and gone.

"No, what each of these items has in common is they tell a story of me coming to my brother's aid. Each time my brother found himself in a world of trouble and each time I was there to help him."

I nodded again and looked at the thick stack of pages remaining in the album. "So what are all those?"

Uncle Cat picked up the stack and thumbed them with his right hand. "These are Jack returning the favor."

## Chapter Ten

The last line hung in the air as Uncle Cat leaned back in his chair and lowered his chin. Time passed, the only movement the album gently rising and falling with his breathing.

"Just give me a moment," he said at last. "I want to make this as easy as possible."

"Isn't that what the stuff in the album is for?" I asked.

At that Uncle Cat popped open his eyes and chuckled. "Son, these stories are all ones I remember as if they happened yesterday. This album isn't to help me remember, it's so nobody else forgets."

I had no idea what that meant and started to ask him, but I again got the old gnarled hand telling me to stop.

It would all make sense in the end.

With a flick of his wrist, Uncle Cat pushed aside the sliver of wood. I braced myself for what lay ahead, but my trepidation proved unfounded.

Page seven held a small square piece of newspaper, roughly five inches on each side. The top of it was upside down and displayed ground beef on sale at the local grocery. The page was yellowed with time and the words were written by an older typewriter.

Confused, I furrowed my brow and turned my face to my uncle. He paid me no mind as he peeled back the plastic covering the article and unfolded the item upward and then again to the side.

The piece of newspaper doubled in size twice to stand almost twenty inches square.

"*North Korea Crosses 38th Parallel, Invades South Korea!*" Uncle Cat read aloud. "*President Truman Calls to Congress for Action.*"

The article had a picture of a man standing at a podium, his right fist raised above his head.

"June 25th, 1950. If I'd only known…" Uncle Cat said, letting his voice trail off.

"It was a Friday. That summer was almighty hot. Most years we waited until around the 4th of July to start helping farmers take off their wheat, but that summer we were already helping old man Myrtle on the other side of town.

"He was a kind old man who'd lost both his sons to the Second World War and his wife to grief soon thereafter. There was no way he could keep up the place by himself. Winter before that he had hired us to help cut away some felled trees. We'd been working for him ever since.

"That day we were bucking hay, a miserable job any time made that much worse by the heat. Myrtle couldn't afford any of the new equipment available, so we did it the old-fashioned way. One of us would drive the cutter, stripping the straw off at the ground. The others would follow and feed the felled straw through a machine that separated the wheat from the chafe. It was a job that usually used a crew of six or seven men. We did it with three.

"Per usual, we worked until it was too dark to see anything before packing it in and promising to be back by first light. Dog tired and soaking wet, we took off for home, neither one saying much.

"Most nights, town was almost deserted. None of the stores stayed open past nine and this was long before the days of kids hanging around just for fun. We'd walk down Main Street swinging our lunch sacks and canteens, straps slung over our shoulders, a silent sky full of stars overhead.

"Not that night though."

A burst of laughter from inside the house stopped Uncle Cat and again we both turned to see what had happened. We waited for somebody to poke their head out at us, but nobody did.

"That night we heard the commotion long before we saw who was making it. By the time we reached Main Street, the noise was deafening. The church choir was singing *Amazing Grace* from the top of the Tabernacle Church steps and two men were playing bugles as loud as they could. Everywhere people were running and yelling, hugging and praying.

"It ain't the Fourth already is it?" I asked Jack.

"Not for a week or two yet," he replied. "I don't know what all this is about."

"A minute or two later, Ricky O'Malley came running up to fill us in. He was a year between Jack and I in age and both of us had always gotten along well enough with him. "Hey, did you guys hear?" he almost shouted.

"Yeah, we could hear this racket clear out at Myrtle's," Jack said.

"Ricky shook his head and said, "Not that. The war!"

"Jack and I turned our heads and looked at each other, completely unaware of what he was talking about.

"Ricky got so excited at the prospect of being the first to tell us, he almost started jumping and up and down. "You haven't heard yet? North Korea breeched the 38th Parallel today! They're invading South Korea!"

"Jack's face was as solemn as the moment we walked up. "So?"

"So?! So it means we're going to war! President Truman's already sending troops over and is asking for more!"

"Jack and I turned and glanced at each other. "A bunch of us are going to Columbus tomorrow to enlist," Ricky continued. "There's room on the flatbed if you want to come along."

"I'll be honest, the idea of enlisting had never crossed my mind before. I tried to say something, but before I could Jack said, "We promised Myrtle we'd help him get his wheat in. For sure won't be done by tomorrow."

"Ricky's mouth fell open as Jack and I walked on past him. Left him standing right there in the street."

Uncle Cat smiled at the memory and chuckled, rocking back and forth in his chair as he did so.

"We walked on through the middle of town towards home, most of the way in silence. It wasn't until we were almost there that I asked, "What do you make of all this?"

"Jack kept his eyes locked straight ahead and exhaled. "Mama's gonna be a wreck. You watch and see."

"Up to that point, there had been a thousand different things running through my mind. I'll admit, Mama hadn't been one of them.

"Old Jack, he was right though. We walked the last quarter mile in silence and got home to find Mama in tears at the kitchen table. A newspaper – *this newspaper* – was spread out in front of her.

"Her eyes were red and puffy, looked like she'd been crying for days. Her hair was matted and strewn in different directions and you could tell she'd been running her hands through it all evening. I already told you how warm it was, but she had an old sweater wrapped around her anyway."

Uncle Cat's voice dipped off for a second and he regained the faraway look he had earlier. Again I fixed my gaze on the water and waited for it to pass.

"The minute we walked in she jumped up and grabbed us both in a bear hug. For such a small woman, she held us with a strength I didn't think possible.

"After a while she let us go and we all took a seat around the table. She outlined everything she knew for us and we sat and talked until the wee hours of the morning."

Again he paused and stared out over the water.

"Talked about what Uncle Cat?" I asked.

He looked at me and gave a grave smile. "Jack and I had a choice. Either we enlisted right then, or we waited until we got drafted a little while later.

"Neither Jack nor I had ever thought of going into the Army. Our place was there with Mama. Besides, we'd both known our share of veterans walking around with canes and heads full of bad memories. It wasn't our war, we wanted no part of it.

"Word was though, they were offering a signing bonus of five hundred dollars on top of the usual enlisted man pay. Between the two of us, a thousand dollars would pay off the rest of the house. I was twenty, Jack was twenty-two, neither one of us had a wife or kids. It was only a matter of time before they came for us anyway.

"So, we both decided to do the only thing we could do. We'd fulfill our responsibility to help Myrtle bring his crop in, then we'd head north and enlist."

# Chapter Eleven

My uncle placed the album on the ground and rose to his feet. I could hear his knees strain as he stood, culminating in a short of burst of loud popping sounds. An inch at a time he walked to the closest porch support post and leaned against it.

"Hurts my knees to stay seated like that for too long. Need to get up and move around a little."

Without thinking, I hopped down from my chair and walked to the opposite side of the post. I matched his pose and waited, hoping he would continue.

He did.

"My brother and I finished gathering the crop two weeks later on a Thursday. We worked six days a week like always, every one from dawn until after sunset. It was a pretty light crop from the heat and we got it off in record time.

"Looking back, I'm not sure if that was a good thing or bad.

"The next day, Mama took off the only day I ever remember her missing and the three of us spent it together.

We went fishing, we had a picnic, we sat on the front step and watched the breeze blow through the willows.

"None of us spoke of where we were going or of what might happen when we got there. A few times I saw Mama's eyes well up or heard her voice crack, but to her credit she never once broke down."

Uncle Cat adjusted his weight against the pole, using his cane to prop himself up as he went. Once he was comfortable again, he continued.

"That night Mama made the finest meal I have ever had in my life. Fried chicken, homemade dumplings, baked beans. Cornbread, fried okra, sweet corn. It was a meal fit for kings.

"The three of us sat around the table and ate and talked and laughed for hours. We all acted like if we didn't acknowledge what was coming, maybe it wouldn't really happen.

"Just before midnight, my Mama took a small white envelope out of her apron and drew a single silver chain with a cross from it.

"I wanted to get you both one to wear around your neck, but the store in town only had one," she explained, her voice thick with guilt.

"Jack and I both knew what the necklace must have cost, and we both knew she'd never spent anywhere near that much on herself in her life.

"I'm sorry you don't each have one," she said, "but maybe you can share somehow."

"I opened and closed my mouth a few times hoping to find the right words. Across from me Jack stared down at the table, his only movement a muscle twitching on the side of his neck.

"I just wanted you both to know that Jesus and your Mama love you and will always be with you," she whispered before running from the table in tears."

My uncle pushed himself from the post and returned his weight to the cane. "I jumped up and started to go after her, but Jack grabbed my arm. I tried to pull away, but his grip was firm, his eyes set on the necklace. After a few minutes he said, "Take your shirt off."

"I wasn't sure what was going on, but Jack seemed pretty serious. Without a word I took my shirt off and watched him pick the necklace up from the table and remove the cross from the chain.

"He motioned for me to follow him with a jerk of his head and together we walked to the stove. The cook top was still hot from dinner and Jack laid the cross right on top of it . We both watched as the metal began to glow in the dim light.

"Jack grabbed an oven mitt from the nail beside the stove and said, "You might want to find something to bite down on. This is going to hurt a little bit."

"I still wasn't sure what he was thinking, but I found a wooden stirring spoon and clamped it between my teeth anyway. In one swift movement Jack grabbed the cross from the burner and pressed it to my bare chest, dead center of the left pectoral," he said, tapping his chest with a finger.

My eyes grew large and my jaw dropped a bit. "Didn't that hurt?"

He looked at me and gave a half twist of the head. "Man alive did it ever. I bit clear through that spoon, snapped it off clean in two different places.

"Jack held that cross to my chest for just a few seconds, but it felt like a lifetime. As soon as he was done, he put it back on the fire and pulled his own shirt off, me still standing there gasping in pain.

"At that point I was about half mad at him for doing it. I snatched up the glove and the cross and pressed that thing against him quite a bit harder than I needed to. Didn't matter though, he never said a word."

Uncle Cat poked at a nail sticking up from the floorboards, first with his cane, then with the toe of his shoe. "A few minutes later, Mama returned. She'd been crying pretty hard, but had it all bottled up for the time being. "What in the world is that smell?" she asked, her nose crinkled. "Nothing I cooked smells like that."

"She saw us sitting with our shirts off and it only took a second for her to put it together. "Oh, boys," she whispered.

"In the silence, Jack rose and picked the cross up from the table between us. He threaded the chain back through its eyelet and handed it to Mama. "You said you wanted us to have something that reminded us that Jesus and Mama would always love us. Well, now we do."

"Jack held the necklace out for her to take. "And now you have something to keep with you too. A piece of us that is always close to your heart."

"Mama's hands trembled as she took the necklace from Jack and put it around her neck. Tears poured down her face as she grabbed us both and held us tight.

"This time, we both hugged back. We hugged Mama and each other. We hugged our home and the river bottoms and Birch Grove. We hugged and hugged and stayed that way clear until morning."

Uncle Cat kicked at the nail once more. "Looking back, we were also hugging goodbye to our innocence and life as we knew it."

## Chapter Twelve

"Uncle Cat, if you gave the cross to great-grandma, how did it get here?"

The question surprised him and he flinched at the sound of my voice. I think it reminded him that he was on a porch with me and not back in 1950.

"Oh," he said, clearing his throat, "this isn't the actual cross that Mama got for us. She still wears that one around her neck.

"On the plane home we decided to put this album together and wanted to include a cross. Between us we had forty-six cents and sweet talked a lady in Los Angeles into giving us one for that."

"Hmm," I said, nodding at the answer. "On the way home from where?"

A smile cracked out from the left side of his mouth. "Not just yet, son. So, where were we?"

I cast a quick glance at the album lying by the rocking chairs. I considered going and getting it, but instead just shrugged my shoulders.

"That's alright, I know what's coming anyway," he responded. "The next page is a piece of paper about three inches by five inches. It's got two holes punched through it and the letters F-C-K-Y scribbled across it in faded pencil."

"A piece of paper with holes punched through and letters written across it?" I asked.

Uncle Cat smiled out at the water and again held his hand palm up towards me. "The next morning we got a ride to the recruitment center in Columbus from Bruce Rife. He heard Jack and I were going to enlist and said we could ride up with him on his weekly trip.

"We met him in town early so he didn't have to see us say goodbye to Mama. The entire ride Bruce tried to make light conversation but neither of us felt much like talking. He dropped us off in front of the recruiting depot around noon, leaving us standing alongside the curb with our half empty duffels.

"Some people would call it packing light; but that would denote we actually stuff to take with us."

The screen door swung open behind us and my second cousin Ginnifer walked out into the afternoon sun. "Mama wanted me to ask if y'all want anything to drink."

Her tone did an excellent job of relaying the disdain she felt for the task. Not that her face needed any help in the matter.

I looked at Uncle Cat, who replied without turning around. "No Ginny, tell your Mama we're just fine out here honey."

That was the answer she was hoping for, the door swinging closed before he was even done responding.

"The recruiting center was an old butcher's shop from back around the turn of the century. It was converted during the First World War into a draft office, shut down after the war, and re-opened during the Second World War. In a perfect cycle they closed it after V-J Day, only to re-open it again when North Korea invaded South.

"Lord only knows how many times it's been closed and re-opened since.

"Walking into the recruiting center was like stepping into an alternate universe. The walls were lined with glossy pictures of men in uniform and maps of faraway places I'd never heard of. Weapons and munitions stood lined up in display cases around the room and a man in a sharp dress uniform sat behind a large desk.

"As we entered the room a small bell tinkled on the door behind us. When he heard it the man stood up and saluted us. He stood rail straight for several seconds before dropping his arm and smiling, shaking both our hands.

"So I take it you boys are here to do your duty in bringing those Communists to justice over there?" was the first thing he said to us. Not hello, not his name, "So I take it you boys are here to do your duty in bringing those Communists to justice over there?"

"Looking back it should have been a gigantic warning flag, but it wasn't. I had only a vague idea what Communism even was. I just knew I wanted to wear a uniform like his, know the right thing to say like he did, be important like him.

"The man knew what he was doing too. Within minutes he had us both bent over the desk, signing away the next year of our life to the United States Army.

"In the movies they always make it look so big and grand. You go into a fancy office, you receive royal treatment, they present you with an official request from the President himself asking you to be part of the military.

"Turns out all it really takes is twenty minutes and an old butcher's shop."

My uncle turned and plodded back to his rocker. He picked the album up off the floor and placed it in his lap, then turned the page to reveal exactly what he said it would.

"Most of the volunteers came in together the week before. Army policy was to try and keep everyone that signed on together in the same platoon. Said it helped with morale and survival rates to have friends serving together.

"Everyone that came in the week before was sent to Fort Benning, Georgia. They even got their own private bus and all forty-seven of them rode down to training together.

"By the time we signed up, their platoon was already full. They paired them with some group from Cincinnati and between the two that was that.

"Instead of a bus full of boys we'd known our whole life, Jack and I got Greyhound tickets."

He looked at the ticket on the page before him and pointed at the writing scribbled across the bottom of it. "F-C-K-Y. Fort Campbell, Kentucky."

## Chapter Thirteen

"The next bus south to Kentucky didn't leave for several hours. We had the entire afternoon to sit and rethink what we were doing, but it didn't matter. They could have spent the time showing us bloody, gory war movies and it wouldn't have changed a thing.

"We were both so excited to be in that room, with all those pictures and trophies and weapons that we both felt like we were going to burst. We stayed in that office for as long as we could and when the recruiter left for lunch we stood outside and peered in the windows."

Uncle Cat pulled up short and focused hard on the horizon again. He snorted and muttered, "If we'd only known.

"The bus we were on was a newer Greyhound, polished silver with bright red and blue paint. It came down from Rochester, swung through Cleveland and picked us up in Columbus. By the time it got to us most of the seats were taken and we were forced to split up.

"Jack pulled up short and splashed himself into the first available seat he found. It was in the front row and was already half-taken by a large woman in the seat beside it, but he didn't seem to mind. He always liked it up front, being able to see out without anything blocking his view.

"Me, I went on back to the final empty seat on the bus. It was in the next to last row and on the aisle next to a nice lady named Dorothy Bixby."

My uncle smiled and bobbed his head as he spoke. "Dorothy Bixby was in her mid-thirties from a small town not much bigger than Birch Grove between Cleveland and Columbus. Several years earlier her sister had moved to Nashville, Tennessee and she was on her way down to visit.

"She and I took to each other right off and within five minutes we were jabbering along like two old women at a church social. She told me all about her kids and her husband and their little house with a picket fence. In return I told her all about Mama and Jack and going off to war.

"She had a big basket of food with her for the trip and the whole way down she gave me fruit and fresh muffins. Fastest four hours I have ever spent."

Uncle Cat leaned forward and returned his elbows to his knees. He smiled and shook his head from side to side, looking at nothing in particular.

"The bus dropped us off alongside the road just before sundown. Dorothy gave me a hug and more muffins, told me to be careful and that she would be praying for us. I hugged her back, thanked her, and laughed as Jack's eyes bulged at all the food she gave me.

"The two of us stood beside the road and watched the bus disappear around the bend before tossing our bags on our shoulders and setting off down the dirt road. It was almost two miles from the highway to the fort and we took off our shoes and slung them over our shoulders too.

"We walked barefoot along the dirt road munching on muffins and for a few minutes it was like we never left home.

"It was the last time Jack and I were ever together without a worry in the world."

A few long moments passed as we watched a boat move into view. A pair of people, too far away to make out, could be seen fishing from either side of it.

"When we were in sight of the front gate we stopped and put our shoes on, then walked the rest of the way in. We got within about thirty feet when the sound of a bolt action rifle stopped us dead in our tracks.

"Stop, put your bags on the ground, raise your hands in the air and identify yourselves," a deep voice boomed from the darkening evening.

"We both about jumped out of our skin. I dropped my bag and threw my hands in the air so fast I almost came up off the ground. Jack was a little more prudent, dropping his pack with one hand and producing our enlistment papers with the other. "Privates Jack and Richard Roberts reporting for duty, sir."

"A light flashed on above us and a short, squat guy stepped from the guard house. A second man stood behind him, remaining in the shadows and keeping his gun trained on us. Who he was expecting to walk right up to the front gate of a fort in Kentucky and start trouble, I don't know.

"The first guy took the papers from Jack and read them over. He looked back and forth from the papers to each of us a couple of times.

"They're clean," he said over his shoulder. He handed the papers back to Jack and said, "You boys got here a little late. About the only thing you can do now is go down to HQ and let them know you're here. We'll radio ahead and tell them to be expecting you. I'd take you down in the jeep, but we're pretty shorthanded out here tonight."

"What do we do when we get to HQ?" Jack asked.

"Guy in there name of Helton, he'll set you up."

"We both nodded at him and passed through the guard house to the other side of the gate. We walked along in the darkness and within minutes we were standing in HQ in front of Helton.

"Captain Helton was about as out of place in the Army as tits on a bull. He was a tiny guy that smiled when he talked and seemed like he'd have a hard time using a flyswatter, let alone shooting at someone.

"Where you boys from?" he asked as he entered us into the fort log.

"Birch Grove, Ohio," Jack answered, standing tall and staring straight ahead.

"Helton chuckled and asked, "That as small as it sounds?"

"I responded, "Even smaller," and that got him laughing again.

"Well, you boys got in too late for chow, so I'll send you straight on over to the barracks. You might be able to snag something from the guys there."

"He motioned to a fort map hanging on the wall, pointing to a black square in the middle with his finger. "This is the HQ, where we now stand. You boys are going to take a left out of here and head west, then make a right just past the OC. Head down a little further to barracks R and that's you. Can't miss it, has a big R painted in red on the side of it. Ask for a guy named Marks, he'll take care of you."

"Together we made our way past the Officer's Club and over to our barracks, which was easy enough to find. Most of the barracks stood silent, largely dark at that time of night.

"Barracks R looked like New York City on New Year's Eve. Music poured from it and men were sprawled around the entrance, smoking cigarettes and talking.

Bursts of laughter and light spilled from every open door and window.

"Both of us stood there for a good long while, staring at the party going on in front of us before Jack finally nudged my arm and said, "Come on, looks like it's time to face the music."

"To this day I don't know if he meant that as a joke or not."

## Chapter Fourteen

Uncle Cat broke off in the middle of his story and returned his attention to the album. He looked down at the bus ticket staring up at us and in one deft flick of the wrist dismissed it to the side.

In its place sat the Jack of Spades.

"Do you know what this is?" Uncle Cat asked me, tapping the page with his fingertip.

"No sir."

"That's good. This is a playing card, one of the worst inventions on the planet."

I didn't know a whole lot about the planet, but I didn't see how that little thing could be all bad. "Playing cards are an evil creation because they are never found alone. Whenever you see these, you see gambling, you see drinking, you see women.

"One time though, in just one particular instance, a playing card saved our butts."

My face registered complete confusion as I tried to comprehend what my uncle said.

"Jack and I resigned ourselves to the fact that barracks R was ours and walked to the front door, trying our best to act like we belonged. Some of the guys outside looked at us funny as we passed, but they moved aside and let us pass just the same.

"A barracks is a place where people in the Army sleep, more or less just one long room. There are a couple of small areas with toilets and showers on the far end, but otherwise everything is out in the open.

"In the case of Barracks R, everything being out in the open wasn't a good thing. A cloud of smoke hung heavy over the room. Loud music played. People were all over the place, most grouped in a big cluster in the center of the room, but none of them so much as looked at us.

"We ambled forward to the edge of the circle and took in the scene. Dozens of sweaty and shirtless men were circled up, smoking cigarettes and throwing cards down. With each card that was thrown a new cheer went up from the crowd, most of them at least a couple years older than us, if not more.

"The two of us stayed that way for awhile as people came and went and money changed hands. After awhile a black man peeled himself off from the group and turned to head for the door. I grabbed his arm as he passed and asked where I could find Marks.

"Without warning he whirled and slammed his fist into the side of my head. Pain shot down my skull and a dull pinging noise settled in my left ear. I stumbled a bit and heard him say, "Don't ever put your hands on me, punk."

"I didn't even wait for my eyes to uncross. I planted on my foot and threw myself at him. My right shoulder slammed into his chest and both of us toppled to the ground. I came out on top in the pile, but before I could even cock my arm back several sets of hands jerked me off him and pinned me to the ground."

Uncle Cat watched the fishermen move further along the shore line, reeling and casting their lines as they went. He shook his head twice and said, "I didn't realized until I hit the ground that the music was off and the room was silent. Jack was pinned to the ground beside me and a group of men held back the black man I'd just been tangled up with.

"A big man with a thick chest and veins running down his arms emerged from the middle of the group. He walked between the three of us and looked hard at the black man. "Dwayne, calm your ass down."

"That's all it took to make him stop struggling, but you could tell he was still plenty mad.

"The big man walked over and looked down at us. He didn't look angry, but he sure wasn't happy either.

"Who the hell are you and what the hell was that all about?"

"Dwayne started to shout out, but the man raised his hand and said, "I'm asking them." He turned his attention back to us. "So?"

"Jack glanced over at me and said, "We were just trying to find a guy named Marks."

"The guy looked back and forth between us. "I'm Marks. What's it to you?"

"We just got here. Captain Helton sent us over."

"Marks smirked and turned his attention to the men gathered around. A mischievous grin spread across his face and he bobbed his head up and down. "Since these two seem to be in a sporting mood, let's have ourselves a little fun."

"He turned his head towards us and said, "We found out a little bit ago that we leave for Korea tomorrow. Now, some of us have been here doing this shit for several months now. I know I for one ain't too happy about being told at the last second that I have to babysit a couple of greenies."

"He turned his attention back to the room and said, "So what we're going to do is have Dwayne and the scrapper here cut cards. Kid wins, we welcome them to the unit, we all get rip roaring drunk, we head off to kick some ass in the morning.

"Dwayne wins, we all get rip roaring drunk and let the ass kicking begin with these two tonight. That sound fair to everybody?"

"A loud cheer went up from the room as I was jerked to my feet. Somebody produced a small wooden box and a deck of cards and within seconds, Dwayne and I were positioned on either side of it.

"Marks held his hand in the air to quiet the room and said, "Since you are our guest, for the next few seconds at least, you can go first."

"I looked at the stack of cards in front of me, breathed deep and reached down towards them. Part of me wanted to bolt for the door, but one glance at Jack still pinned to the floor made that impossible. I closed my eyes, grabbed a thick wedge of cards, and held it up for the room to see.

"A slight groan went up around me and I heard someone mutter, "Kid drew a damn King." To this day I don't know what suit it was. I never even looked."

I looked over at my uncle and could see his hands shaking in the afternoon sunshine as he spoke.

"Dwayne looked right at me, tried to stare me down, and reached for the pile. Without moving his gaze one inch he grabbed a stack of cards, picked it up and looked at it. A grin spread across his face and for a moment I thought we were done for. The crowd seemed to inch in closer as he said, "Looks like we tied."

"For every groan that was heard when I drew a king, there were at least ten cheers when he matched it. Not a good sign from our new teammates.

"Marks stepped back to the side of the table and raised his hand in the air. "Alright, alright. This is an easy enough problem to solve. This time, Dwayne, you go first."

"Dwayne licked the tips of his fingers and rubbed them together. A few members of the crowd shouted encouragement. Again he kept his eyes locked on me as he picked up a stack and showed it to the room. A mixture of groans and cheers greeted the ten of hearts.

"I glanced over at Jack, who was now sitting up. In the tension of the moment, he had been forgotten. Everybody was crowded tight around the table and for just a second I thought again about running, but to where? We were at a fort in the middle of nowhere.

"The second time I reached down, I drew with my left hand. My right I coiled into the tightest fist I could. If I didn't beat the ten of hearts, my first swing was going at Dwayne's head.

"I cut the deck once more and prayed I would pick the same card as last time. I didn't, but I didn't have to."

A tight-lipped smile spread across his face and he tapped the page with a heavy finger. "Good old Jack of

Spades. I think everyone last person in the room except Jack and I groaned when I pulled it, but we didn't care.

"Marks took over on the spot. He stepped in between Dwayne and I and said, "Alright, that settles that. The rest of you get back to the game while I get our new guys set up."

"Just like that the radio kicked back on, followed by the crowd regrouping around the table. Marks led us to two bunks in the back of the room.

"Jeremiah Marks, but everyone just calls me Marks. I'm the NCO around here, rank of Sergeant. I'm just one of the guys though, so you can me Jerry or Marks but never Sarge you got that?"

"Both of us nodded our heads.

"He looked at me and said, "So where you boys from there Jack?"

"Actually, he's Jack," I said. "And we're from Birch Grove, Ohio."

"Marks looked at Jack for a second and nodded. "And what's your name?"

"Name's Richard, everybody calls me Cat."

"Marks snorted loudly. "Cat, huh? That cause you're a pussy?"

"I said nothing, just pulled back the sleeve on my left arm. Marks' eyes went wide as he stared at the scars stretched tight over it. "Jesus, I was just messing with you.

Anybody that flies back at Dwayne like that can't be a pussy. What the hell happened there? You in a fire or something?"

"Cat fishing accident," I said and left it at that.

"Marks looked at my arm again and shook his head. "These here will be your bunks, for the next eight hours or so anyway. All your clothes and most of your equipment are in the trunk at the foot of the bed. You'll get your rifle first thing in the morning before we take off."

"He turned and moved back towards the center of the room. "I wasn't really going to turn the boys loose on you, but it sure was a hell of a show. You boys want a beer or something to eat, help yourself."

"With that, he disappeared into the crowd and we collapsed back onto our bunks. We didn't know it, but we'd just gotten orientation and basic training both in about five minutes flat."

## Chapter Fifteen

My cousin's husband Paul passed through the front door, nodded at us, and walked to the far end of the porch. He lit a cigarette and blew out a long plume of smoke, pacing a tight circle.

Uncle Cat slid his eyes to him and closed the album. He picked up the knapsack from the floor and draped it across his lap, engulfing the album beneath it. "Yeah, I tell you, this lake has some of the nicest bass in Ohio in it. When I was a boy we'd sit down here for days on end, pulling them out by the truckload."

Paul took two more drags on the cigarette before he tossed it into the yard. He cast a disgusted look at my uncle and let the door slam behind him as he walked back inside.

My uncle waited a few seconds before dropping the knapsack to the floor. "You ever been to the dump with your Pa?" he asked.

The question surprised me and I could feel my eyebrows rise. "Yes sir, to drop off a load of shrubs we pulled from the side of the house."

"When you went, did the odor of the place hit you like a wave? Did you wish you could close the door and never have to smell or be near such a mess again as long as you lived?"

"It almost made me vomit," I said, a touch ashamed. "Papa had to let me get back in the truck before I got sick."

Uncle Cat chuckled. "Now imagine it ten times worse and you have what that barracks smelled like the next morning. Men were strewn everywhere, their bodies thrown across bunks and mattresses pulled to the floor. The smell of alcohol, sweat, and vomit hung in the air. The entire room looked like a natural disaster just blew through.

"With all the commotion, I'm not sure that I ever actually fell asleep. I just know that at some point I kind of drifted away and a few minutes later it was light outside. Jack and I were about the only ones in any shape to move, so we got up and out of there as early as we could. We put on our new summer fatigues uniform, packed up the few remaining items from our foot lockers and crept outside.

"We left barracks R and wandered back into the main building we'd been in the night before. Captain Helton was nowhere to be found but a young brunette girl gave us directions for how to draw our weapons and where to ship off.

"It took almost an hour for us to be issued our rifles, each one recorded by make, caliber, and serial number. We then had to sign a document stating that we would only use our weapon against our enemy and in the face of danger.

"Looking back on it, I'm almost ashamed at how exhilarating the whole thing was."

My uncle stared out into the distance and shook his head. It seemed like there were a hundred things he would like to go back and tell that younger version of himself, but couldn't.

Instead, he could tell only me.

"We walked out into the morning sun with our new rifles gripped in front of us and felt like we were on top of the world. We had an old Wingmaster at home for shooting birds and an ancient single shot for deer, but nothing anywhere near an Army issue rifle. Both of us were dying to hit the firing range and try them out, but we never got the chance.

"We were halfway across the parade grounds headed straight for the range when Marks found us. "Hey, you Birch Grove boys going with us or not?"

"In all our haste, time had gotten away from us. Together we spun around to see our unit filing towards the front gate. Dread flooded through us as we slung the rifles over our shoulder and sprinted back across the grounds to join our unit. Marks jawed at us the whole way there, but between my own ragged breathing and the gun clattering against my back, I couldn't hear a word he said.

"Probably better that I didn't. Marks could be a mean cuss when he was mad.

"We weren't the last people to make it onboard, but not by much. They were loading everybody into two transport trucks and the first one was already full. The second one was getting there fast as we climbed in.

"Two rows of grim faces that looked like they'd been awake less than five minutes lined either side of the truck. I didn't recognize a single one except for Jack, so I just sat and stared at my rifle the entire time."

My uncle placed the palms of his hands across his thighs and looked down at them. After a few seconds he gave me a sheepish look and rubbed them along the front of his pants several times.

"Where were you guys going?" I asked.

"Louisville International Airport," my uncle replied. "The trip took over an hour with the sun beating down us, bouncing along the road towards Louisville. By the time we got there over half the men in our truck were vomiting over the side. Man did it ever stink. I don't even want to think about the poor folks riding behind us."

My stomach turned just thinking about it, but I didn't say a word.

"Airports were a lot different back then than they are now. Not that many people flew anywhere, so we more or less had the place to ourselves. Our trucks bypassed the main terminal and drove us right out to the tarmac. An oversized Army plane sat there waiting for us and we unloaded straight from the truck to the plane. We dropped our gear into oversized storage lockers as we boarded and that was that. Nice and easy.

"Jack and I grabbed seats in the front row, as far away from the restrooms as we could get. The plan for trying to avoid vomiting soldiers worked well for awhile, but before too long there wasn't a seat onboard that couldn't smell the stench.

"Five hours later we stopped for a few minutes in San Francisco to refuel and six hours after that we touched down in Hawaii. Far and away the longest day of my young life."

My uncle again leaned himself forward onto his elbows. I thought I caught an upward flicker in the corner of his mouth, but I can't be certain.

"There really isn't an easy way to get an Army to Korea, especially in 1950. Most aircraft just don't have the capability to carry an entire unit that far. Even if they did, taking them one at a time would be foolish. Instead, they crammed as many of us as they could on a boat and shipped us over.

"The western most port of departure for the United States military was in Pearl Harbor, Hawaii. If any of us needed a harrowing reminder of exactly what we'd just gotten ourselves into, right there it was."

I didn't even know what the word harrowing meant, but I waited in patience just the same. Uncle Cat tapped the next page in the album with his finger, a page that had a date scrawled across it in black felt marker.

"On December 7, 1941, the Japanese were fearful of America entering World War II. They thought if they hit us with a pre-emptive strike they could cripple us in the Pacific to the point we would have to leave them alone.

"All they really managed to do was piss us off.

"Once our unit got there, ten years had passed. The place was more or less rebuilt, though the scars still remained.

"In total we spent three days on Oahu while we waited for others to join us. By the time we were ready to ship out, four more units had swelled our ranks to several thousand troops, the basis of what would become our battalion.

"The last night there we were sitting around playing cards, passing the time as best we could. Out of nowhere Marks showed up and told everybody to get dressed and meet him outside in ten minutes, we didn't need our weapons or our gear.

"None of us knew what to make of it, but we did what he said. We all met him outside and followed as he led us down towards the water. Up to that point, none of us had actually ventured down to the harbor's edge.

"When we got there, Marks lined us up single file along the bank and called out, "Hit it boys." A bank of floodlights pierced the darkness, shining past us and out over the water.

"There, tucked away in the clear waters of the harbor, sat the *Arizona*. A few low whistles went up from the group, but for the most part the men were silent.

"Enough of the ship remained that it was obvious what it was, but it was also clear that it could never be salvaged. The remains of two different smoke stacks still poked above the water, sitting atop the shattered hull of a once magnificent battleship.

"We all stood and gaped at it for a long time, the world silent in the moonlight. After a while Marks said, "I brought you down here tonight because I wanted you to see what serving your country really means."

"I think he had a big speech all planned out for us, but he let it go at that. Without another sound he parted the crowd and walked back towards the barracks.

"Over the next few minutes, the rest of the men drifted back as well. Some went to pray, some went to sleep, some even went back to playing cards.

"Jack and I were the last to leave. By the time we made it in most everyone else was asleep.

"Six hours later we boarded the *U.S.S. Lincoln*, bound for Korea."

## Chapter Sixteen

Uncle Cat flipped the page with the date written across it, replacing it with a page that looked even less descript. I stared a long time at it and tried to find whatever it was, but in the end it looked to me like a plain white page. "Did somebody take something out of here without telling you?"

My uncle gave a soft laugh and shook his head. "Oh, no. You are now the only other living person to have seen this album, so I assure you nothing has been stolen."

He reached over with his calloused hand and took mine, then rubbed it over the page. I could feel the ridges of small circles under my fingertips, over a half dozen in total. "What is it?"

Uncle Cat released my hand and said, "Those are known as Dramamine patches. You put them on your neck to keep from getting sea sick."

I had never heard of sea sickness before, much less Dramamine, but I nodded just the same.

"The next morning we were up before dawn. Each of the units grouped themselves together and we all made our way down to the shipyard.

"A fine mist rose up from the water's edge and added to an already ominous feeling in the air. We couldn't see more than a few hundred yards in any direction. We didn't even know where we were until we almost walked smack into the side of the ship.

"They knew we were coming and had four wide wooden ramps stretched out waiting on us. With our packs strung across our shoulders, we boarded the *Lincoln*. Once we were all on deck, Admiral Dominic Myles welcomed us and explained how things would work.

"The morning sun was just above the horizon when he motioned to the Captain of the ship, who sounded the horn and pushed off from the dock. The moment the heavy sound of the horn filled the air, scads of sailors appeared from everywhere. They scattered into a hundred different directions and within ten minutes we were steaming westward towards nothing but open water."

Uncle Cat stopped for a moment and traced the horizon in a complete semi-circle. The lake before us was nowhere near that wide, though from the look on his face the lake wasn't what he was looking at.

"They separated each of us into our individual units and pointed us in the direction of our quarters. We were to be known as the 63rd regiment, housed on the C deck, three floors below.

"Before then I had never been on anything larger than a fishing boat. I had no idea ships could be so large and so small at the same time. I stood on the deck and marveled at how it seemed to stretch on and on in both directions.

"That awe disappeared as soon as I went below deck and saw my bunk mounted to the side of a wall. It folded down just between the ones above and below, affording a total of about five inches to move around.

"Needless to say I spent as little time as possible there."

Uncle Cat held his hand up and waggled his pinkie and thumb showing me the prescribed distance.

"Not that that was too hard to do. Our schedule was surprisingly light, giving everyone plenty of time to become nervous.

"Each morning we woke up with the sun and did calisthenics on the deck. After that, we were pretty much free until the evening when we would do them again.

"In between, men found all sorts of things to keep themselves occupied. Of course there was card playing. Some guys wrote letters home. Marks walked us through some of the stuff we missed in training, like simple marching cadences and how to stay in formation.

"Everybody seemed to pass the time a little bit different, but the one thing we had in common was we all got sick."

Uncle Cat tapped the page with the tip of his finger without looking down. "In total it took four days to make the trip to Korea on some of the roughest seas the Admiral said he'd ever seen.

"All day long waves crashed against the hull of the ship, sloshing water on to the deck and sending ocean spray high into the air. Before long you got used to always being wet and having the taste of salt on your lips.

"At night, the ship would sway and creak non-stop. The chains on our bunks would rattle with every movement, sleeping was darn near impossible."

My uncle paused again, staring forward. He wrung his hands a few times like they were wet and licked his lips as if tasting the sea before continuing.

"On the night before we got there, the Admiral called all four regiments together on deck.

"Gentlemen, I have called you all together here tonight to let you know a few things," he said. "First, the North Koreans have continued their steady progression down into South Korea. So far they've overwhelmed the South Koreans and have driven them back into the southern tip, known as Pusan.

"Second, we are headed straight for Pusan."

"The Admiral paused and waited for the murmurs around him to die down. Jack and I stole sideways glances at each other, but said nothing.

"The four regiments here are going to form the Fifth Division. Your orders are to land at Pusan and make your way to the Eighth Division. There you will be joined by two more divisions where General MacArthur intends to drive the North Koreans back far enough to bring in a major allied force."

"The Admiral stood and surveyed the crowd for several seconds in silence, contemplating his words. "Men, I have been here and watched you for several days now. I can say without reservation that it has been my absolute privilege to be associated with you. You have conducted yourselves to the highest of military code and I can feel a confidence emanating from you that tells me those damn Commies are in for a world of hurt. Give 'em hell for us boys."

"The second he was done, the place erupted with applause and cheers."

My uncle dropped his head again and shook it hard, muttering in what sounded like disgust.

At the admiral, at the situation, or even at himself, I wasn't sure.

## Chapter Seventeen

"The next morning Admiral Myles assembled us again and introduced us to our new Commanding Officer, Captain Harold Williams. We'd heard a few days before he was expected to take over, though most of us were hoping it was just a rumor.

"Everything about Captain Williams was plain and ordinary. He was a little guy and everyone kept saying he had a touch of Napoleon Complex. More alarming to me was the reputation he had as a shoddy leader. Word was he was fresh out of West Point, the kind of guy that relied more on textbooks than instincts.

"Admiral Myles introduced him to us, saluted and promptly left the deck. You could just tell he didn't like him, a fact he didn't much try to hide from us.

"Captain Williams ignored the Admiral. He marched out and stood with his hands behind his back.

"My name is Captain Williams. You may call me Captain or Captain Williams and that is all. I have been appointed commander of the 5$^{th}$ Division and as such serve as an extension of General MacArthur himself. Any problems you have with me, you have with him and with the United States Army reaching clear to the President. Is that understood?"

"He stood and stared out at us for several seconds as if he was expecting a response. There was none.

"As I'm sure you have heard, the 8th Division has been driven back to Pusan by the invading North Koreans. It is the belief of General MacArthur that an amphibious assault is the best way we can be of aid. I have been there for the last several days mapping out the best way to do that."

"He paused for a moment to make sure we grasped how vital he was to the operation. "Our troops are bunched on a small landmass south of Pusan measuring five square miles. We are to put in one mile due east of them. At the same time, the 3rd and 4th Divisions will match our position to the west.

"Upon arrival, we will sit tight and wait for the 4th Division to maneuver around the North Koreans to the north. Once all our forces are in position, we will converge on them from every direction."

"Again he paused as if waiting for some sign of approval of his plan. There was none.

"The way this will work," he went on, "is the *U.S.S. Lincoln* will transport us within a mile of the South Korean coast and we will rendezvous with our amphibious assault vehicles. They will take us to shore, where you will secure the beach and begin working your way inland.

"From this very instant, you have one hour to collect your gear and be back on deck. If you are late, you will be swimming to shore."

"Without another word he turned on his heel and stomped away."

My uncle stood and shuffled over to the pole in front of him. He leaned his left shoulder into it and said, "As soon as he was gone we all went straight back to our bunks to collect our gear. The second we were down there and safely out of earshot, the place went crazy."

"Everybody just went crazy?" I asked, eyes bulging.

My uncle shook his head. "No, I mean, the men were livid.

"We had just received the most self-indulgent and utterly worthless briefing anybody had ever seen. Not once did he mention what kind of enemy numbers we were looking at. He didn't tell us where they were located or if we would land while facing enemy fire.

"Beyond that, the plan itself was flawed. A choke method only works when an enemy is pinned down. All we were doing was creating a cross fire amongst ourselves."

My uncle kicked at the floor with his foot and shook his head.

"One hour later we reassembled on the deck. There was already tension, and that was before we met our second rate Captain and heard his third rate plan. Nobody said much of anything, but you could feel unease in the air.

"Right at an hour after Captain Williams dismissed us, the amphibious assault vehicles pulled up alongside the *Lincoln*. Using the same wooden ramps we used to board, we all loaded onto the transport and headed towards the beach.

"The entire time Captain Williams stood on the deck of the ship in his dress uniform and watched.

"It only took about ten minutes for us to cover the last mile to shore, but that was enough for almost a dozen men to fall prey to sea sickness. The smell of their vomit mixed with the brine of the water and by the time we arrived, almost every one of us was green with nausea.

"Jack and I were two of the last ones to board, making us some of the first to hit the beach. Side by side we jumped into the knee deep surf and scrambled up onto the shore as fast we could.

"We high stepped our way free of the water and flung ourselves down onto the sand. Men filed in on either side of us as we peered down the barrel of our rifles for any sign of movement.

"Several tense minutes passed, but nothing showed itself. Once our entire unit was on land, we pushed our way across the beach and into the forest."

My uncle looked down at me for a long second and motioned back towards the chair with his head. "Go ahead and turn the page. My knee hurts too much to keep walking back and forth."

I matched his gaze for a few seconds before turning and running to the album. Bending at the waist I reached down with one hand and flipped the page. A strange serpentine pattern of tiny particles stared back at me, the entirety of it forming a loose S on the page. "What is that?"

"Sand," my uncle answered. "Jack and I decided sand was the best thing to put here because it was our absolute first and most lingering impression of Korea. It was in our boots the second we touched down and it stayed there every single day we were in country. It ground into our clothing, it grated our skin, it got stuck in the corners of our eyes.

"Sand."

# Chapter Eighteen

My uncle closed his eyes and leaned his weight against the post. I watched as he rubbed the tips of his fingers together and could almost see him feeling the grit of sand between them.

"We were in Korea less than five minutes before we made our first mistake," he said, his gaze far away from the front porch. "We landed outside of Pusan without a single shot being fired. We all came in expecting to be met by heavy machine gun fire and a hail of mortars, but when nothing happened we got lazy.

"Lieutenant Rollins was the senior officer among us and took control, ordering us to move forward. Just like that we fanned out and went crashing into the forest. The foliage was thick and many men took to swinging knives or bayonets to clear a path. They paid so much attention to the dense brush in front of them, they never once bothered to glance down at the ground.

"We were fifteen feet in when we hit the land mines. Lots of them.

"The first wave went off to our right. On pure instinct, we threw ourselves to the ground, which set off another half dozen or so just seconds later."

My uncle closed his eyes and inhaled deep. "We lost five men right there. I didn't know any of them beyond facial recognition, but it didn't matter. We had been in Korea for ten minutes and already men around us, men we knew, were dead.

"Just as important, our air of invincibility was dead with them.

"Rollins called for an instant retreat and as fast as possible we scrambled back to the beach. Everyone was confused and scared, some were outright pissed off. Chatter spread through the lines as Rollins called Marks and the other sergeants together to devise a plan.

"Ain't this some shit? Been here five minutes and we're light ten percent of our regiment," a voice spat. I turned to see a man kneeling beside me with dark tan skin and blonde hair in a deep widow's peak. There was a small scar in the shape of a V over his right eyebrow and the muscles in his neck twitched as he moved his head from side to side.

"Walked right into that one didn't we?" I replied.

"Hell yeah, we did. Buddy Turner," he said and stuck out his hand.

"Richard Roberts, everybody calls me Cat," I said and shook his hand.

"Yeah, I know who you are. Everybody does after that little scrap you had with Dwayne the other night."

"I cast a look down the line to see Dwayne calmly smoking a cigarette and asked, "Is that guy as crazy as he seems?"

"Buddy looked at me, then down the line to Dwayne as well. "Some of the guys are asking the same thing about you. Seems a man would have to be crazy to pick a fight with Dwayne on their first night."

"So I'm in deep shit already?" I asked him.

"I didn't say that. Truth is, most are kind of glad a greenie came right in and stood up to him. Showed his ass he ain't as scary as he thinks."

"Jack joined us as we squatted in the sand, taking up a post beside us without saying a word. A minute or two later Marks broke free from the meeting with Rollins and signaled us all to gather around. He dropped to a knee and spread a map out as everybody crowded in tight.

"So here's the deal," he said, pointing his index finger towards the map. "We're on Tenos Beach here, just east of Pusan. We're going to move a quarter mile east up the coast to the Paching River and follow it inland. The river's the only place we know we can travel and be safe from land mines.

"Recon tells us there aren't any North Koreans in the area, so we'll sit tight until dark and then get to it. Any questions?"

"A man with a heavy southern accent asked, "It's not even ten hundred hours. What the hell we supposed to do until dark? Sit here in the open and hope nobody comes looking for us?"

"Marks removed his helmet and scratched at the close cropped hair on his neck. "That's what I just asked Rollins. Williams told him something like this might happen and if it did, this was how we were supposed to proceed."

"A series of groans went up around the circle. One guy even muttered, "Should have known some half baked shit like that came from him."

"So we're just sitting here?" the southern accent asked again.

"Marks looked up at him and said, "No. We've got half a dozen soldiers to bury," then stood and walked away."

My uncle shifted his weight from the pole and stepped to the edge of the porch. He sat with his legs hanging over the edge and placed the cane down beside him.

"The next page in the album is a dog tag. Soldiers wear them around their neck as identification. If something happens to them in battle, it states their name, rank, social security number, and blood type.

"Jack, Buddy, myself, and a guy named Baker were all assigned to one of the fallen. Since we were the new guys, Jack and I were sent in after the body. That meant we had to crawl on our bellies back into the forest and drag the man out behind us.

"When we got back, we all just sort of stood and stared at him for several minutes. Somehow he looked even younger than we did, easily could have been another kid in the halls of our school.

"Baker was the first to move, walking up to the body and pulling the dog tags from around his neck. "Private Justin Briggs," he read aloud, then handed one of the tags to Jack and the other to me. "Standard rule of soldiering, hang on to a tag from any man you bury. Helps make sure every one of our boys are accounted for after the fact."

"We each stowed the tag in our packs, then helped Buddy and Baker bury Brigg's remains."

"Is that Brigg's dog tag on the page over there?" I asked.

Uncle Cat shook his head. "No, not the original anyway. A few months later we lost our packs and all the tags we had in them. I never forgot his name though and when I got back I had the tag made.

"Truth be known, I never forgot the names of any of the soldiers I laid to rest. I thought about having tags made for them too, but in the end I didn't."

My uncle fell silent.

"Why not?"

"Because there were twenty-eight of them," he said. "But he was the first.

"Like most things, after awhile a person can develop a tolerance for pain. There are some details to the story that have gotten fuzzy over the years, but the way I felt as I dug that first grave...that's something I'll never forget."

## Chapter Nineteen

My uncle gestured over his shoulder with his chin and said, "The next page is a shell casing for an M-1 round."

The only word in that whole sentence I understood was shell. In my mind I envisioned him walking the beach, waiting for dark, picking up seashells.

"An M-1 was the standard issue weapon of the United States Army during Korea. Today it would be a peashooter next to an M-16, but back then they were heavy duty. Amazing degree of accuracy up to several hundred yards away and a lighter muzzle flash for firing under darkness."

My uncle motioned back towards the book and said, "Over time, it was easy to scavenge weapons. I picked up a sidearm from a fallen Korean guard and a K-Bar knife from a Marine headed home.

"Starting out though, it was just me and the M-1."

The front door swung open behind us. My great-grandmother, aided by her always squeaking walker, took several small steps out on to the front porch and asked, "How you getting along out here Cat?"

My uncle turned and said, "Just fine Mama."

"Are you sure? I don't like you being out here all by your lonesome. You should come inside and get some food."

"I'm not alone," he countered. "Austin and are having a talk."

My great-grandmother smiled and maneuvered herself back around towards the door. As she did, her eyes focused on the book lying open on the floor and she drew in a sharp breath.

I could tell she knew what it was, even if she'd never looked through it.

The door slammed shut behind her without another word from anybody.

"Tenos Beach was our camp until almost nine o'clock that night. Burying the men only took a few hours, leaving the rest of the day as an extensive exercise in patience. Some of the men built small fires and cooked food; some curled up on palm fronds and attempted to sleep. Most of us were wired so tight we just sat and waited, counting the seconds until nightfall.

"When night came we headed out towards the Paching, moving in a double file along the beach. We walked at a slow but steady pace, hoping to keep our noise down as we went. I would have preferred double time if only to burn off some excess energy, but the packs were too noisy to allow it.

"When we got to the river, we dropped back to a single file line and began to wade upstream. We cut a path in water up to our knees, thick cloud cover above blocking out any moonlight. A lot of the boys had a time trying to walk along over the rocks, but it didn't bother me any. I was pretty used to it.

"We moved inland after well over a mile. Our boots were waterlogged and every bit of gear we had was soaked by the time Rollins turned us back into the forest.

"The second our feet touched shore, we went to an even higher state of alert. Every sound got at least five men's attention, every step was taken under the greatest of care. It was slow and painful going, took us almost two hours to cover the few miles to our assigned position.

"Along the way, word had filtered back that we were to attack at dawn. Turns out, that was wrong twice.

"We didn't have to wait that long, and we didn't do the attacking."

My uncle ran a weathered hand back through his mane of thick gray hair. "Rollins set up camp in a clearing with thick timber flanking us a quarter mile in both directions. Jack and I both knew there was no way we could sleep with battle just hours away. Instead, we both paced the length of the line, walking from one end to the other.

"We were several hundred yards away from the clearing when the first cracks of rifle fire snapped through the night. Our nerves were already on end and we both jumped the second the shooting started.

"Rifles clutched in front of us, we tore through the forest to join the line. As we did, more than a few of our men sprinted past us in the opposite direction. No weapons, no composure, no nothing. Just running like their hair was on fire.

"To be honest, I don't know that I ever saw a one of them again.

"Side by side we made a beeline for Rollins screaming into a radio at the rear of the clearing.

"Where you want us?" Jack yelled.

"Rollins jerked the phone away from his face and screamed, "South! Swing south! We're getting shredded down there!"

"I think he might have said something else, but I couldn't hear him. We were already on our way to the south, the forest a blur as it filed past us. Smoke hung heavy in the air and the screams of soldiers filled our ears.

"I have no idea how far we went, though it felt like a long way. Gripped by apprehension and adrenaline, we pounded along until Marks called out for us to join him. In unison we dove behind a felled tree just seconds before a mortar exploded right where we'd been standing.

"Keeping my head as low as I could, I worked my rifle up onto the tree and snapped shots out into the night. Jack did the same beside me, firing at anything that moved.

"For a long time, that's how things went. It was so loud, with pockets of bright light followed by intense darkness, people stumbling back and forth. We lay behind that tree and continued firing long after their last return volley before we stopped to listen.

"You boys alright?" Marks asked in a loud whisper.

"Yes sir," I said. "How's everybody over there?"

"We lost Abbott and Musey. Unger's pretty bad off but alive."

"I turned my head to Jack and whispered, "We know any of those boys?"

"He shook his head, but said nothing.

"What's the plan Marks?" I asked.

"Far as I can tell, you two are the end of the line," he said. "Sit tight. It's almost five now, morning can't be far off. If they're going to try anything, it'll be right before daybreak."

"I grunted in response and turned my attention back to the woods. "I only brought three clips with me. I thought we were taking a walk, not going into battle."

"Jack rolled over onto his side and fished two clips from his pants. "This is everything I have left. After that, I guess we use bayonets."

"I grunted again and kept my eyes on the woods. The night sky had lightened to a shade of dark gray and I breathed a silent prayer that morning was almost on us."

My uncle paused and for a moment studied the palm of his hand.

"I had barely finished that prayer when they came at us. The first thing we saw was silhouettes, bouncing through the woods like ghosts. We both fired as fast as we could, which set them to screaming as they ran forward. The entire woods seemed like it shook with the sound. Seemed like there must have been a thousand of them coming at us.

"It was light enough to see them falling each time I fired, but there always seemed to be another to take its place. We both stayed right where we were and fought down to our last clip of ammunition when Marks called over and told us to get the hell out of there.

"He didn't have to tell us twice.

"Together we rose to our haunches and slipped back deeper into the woods, firing the entire way as we went. To our right I could see muzzle flashes and hear men cursing in English, to our left there was nothing but empty forest.

"We stepped backwards as fast as we could, picking our way through trees and fallen soldiers. More than once we stopped to pull ammunition from someone that wouldn't be needing it any longer.

"Overhead, the sky continued to lighten. I had no idea how far back we had retreated, but it must have been far enough for the North Koreans to stop and regroup again. An eerie stillness gripped the world as silence fell, accentuated by a thick fog of smoke floating through the trees.

"Everybody sit tight!" Marks yelled. "Remember last time. They're grouping up to make another push!"

"We stayed that way for a full ten minutes. Jack and I did another ammunition check and I gave him an extra clip I'd picked up. Hunkered down and motionless, we were just about to pull on back to the clearing when the Koreans made their move.

"During the retreat I didn't realize they'd gotten so close. Out of nowhere they sprang from the ground and charged for us, no more than fifty yards separating the two sides. Guttural screams accompanied them as they charged forward, our gunfire doing nothing to slow their approach.

"Little by little they closed the space between us until there wasn't a gap left at all. The first to reach us was a small Korean no older than me that leapt over a downed tree with a pistol in hand. I put two bullets into his chest and rolled to the side as he crashed to the ground, already sighting in on my next target.

"The sound of metal scraping beside me jerked my attention to the side to see Jack engaged in bayonet fighting with a Korean, another rushing him fast. I slid to a knee beside the man I'd just shot, snatched up his pistol and fired a round into one man while Jack thrust his bayonet into the other.

"Without pause, Jack wheeled and aimed his gun right at me, firing at a spot a foot above my head. On instinct I dropped myself towards the ground as a pained cry rang out and an inert body toppled over me.

"You two get the hell out of there!" Marks called through the woods and we retreated towards his voice.

"I'm not sure if the Koreans thought he was talking to them, but they started to fall back as well. We found Marks lying behind a makeshift cover of bodies, blood covering his left leg. Grabbing either side of him, we hoisted him onto his feet and helped him along, moving as fast as we could.

"Where the hell is everybody else?" I muttered.

"Half didn't make it," Marks said. "Other half got the hell out while they could."

"You alright?" Jack asked.

"Aw hell, it's just a scratch," Marks said. "I was retreating and tripped over Abbott. His damn bayonet got me in the thigh."

"Carrying him, it took us about twenty minutes to get back to the main camp. When we arrived Rollins looked like he might shoot himself as he directed people around and continued barking into his radio. There must have been twenty or thirty wounded and dead soldiers strewn about the clearing.

"We found an empty spot along the outer edge and propped Marks up against a tree. Jack fetched him a bandage and we helped him tie it around his leg the best we could.

"As we started to walk away, he looked at us and said, "Hey, you boys ever been in combat before?"

"We both shook our heads.

"I'll tell you this much, I take back that crack I made about not wanting to go into battle with two greenies. I'll take you watching my ass anytime."

My uncle raised his head and stared out over the water. "Just like the dog tag, that's not the real M-1 shell I fired that day. The real one is still somewhere in Korea right now, buried beneath decades of soil.

"The reason we included it was to mark our first ever experience in battle.

"A man can train himself for the sights of war, but it's impossible to prepare the other senses. There's no way to condition for hearing the screams of men and there is no way to recreate the smell of lead and blood in the air.

"We had now seen it all first hand, and we would never forget it again."

# Chapter Twenty

"Let's take a walk," my uncle said. The gathering inside was still going strong and I could hear pockets of laughter escaping through the windows and out into the afternoon air.

The tale of the fire fight had taken its toll on him. Beads of sweat dotted his forehead and his breathing was a bit faster.

We walked side by side through the front yard and followed a foot path down to the water's edge. The trail cut through tall grasses that came to my waist and swayed with the breeze.

As we grew closer, the sun danced bright off the water.

Ten feet from the water's edge the path expanded into a gravel bar that ran twenty yards in both directions. My uncle motioned for me to follow him and together we walked past it to a stretch of soft brown sand where we both took a seat.

"We lost almost two-thirds of our men that first night," he opened without preamble. "Dwayne, Marks,

Buddy, they all made it. Baker and many others weren't so lucky.

"By the time the fighting ended and we were certain the Koreans were done for the morning, the sun was well on its way into the sky. We didn't have time to give proper burials to all the fallen, so instead Rollins sent us out in pairs to collect dog tags. It was hasty and it was crude, but it was the best we could do given the circumstances.

"Jack and I were among those that went out to collect and by the time we got back, Rollins had received our new assignment. We weren't the only ones to face an attack and many of the other units were just as bad, if not worse off, than we were.

"Instead of our original orders, we were going to push northwest and align ourselves with the 73$^{rd}$ and 85$^{th}$ regiments. From there, two units of South Korean soldiers would join us and we would sweep from west to east across the island. The idea was to free up Pusan and all the forces bottle-necked in the south.

"It sounded like the kind of plan Captain Williams would devise. Everybody tossed each other uneasy glances as Rollins spoke.

"I remember somebody asking, "So how far we talking?"

"We're looking at twelve to fourteen miles," Rollins replied.

"By when?" Buddy asked from off to the left.

"Nightfall," Rollins responded.

"More murmurs went up from the men.

"Rollins sighed and looked around the circle. "I don't like it any more than you do, but these are our orders. We'll be leaving in ten minutes and humping hard, so leave everything you don't need."

"As it turned out, that was one of the worst pieces of advice I ever received."

My uncle picked up a small stick from the ground beside him and traced a few lines in the sand. Using it as a pointer, he narrated, "South Korea is shaped kind of like a sock, dropping down in an elongated loop to the south. We were down here by the toe, just outside of Pusan. We had to go north a little ways up the foot and loop around to meet up with the rest of our forces."

Still using the stick, he outlined their path for me.

"It took us most of the day to make that hike. Many of us had been awake for two days and many had injuries ranging in severity. The mid-summer sun beat down on us as we walked and we stopped at every spring we found to drink and fill our canteens.

"We walked in a single file line through the forest with scouts posted a quarter mile out in every direction to watch for encroaching enemies. Twice during the hike Jack and I had to take our turn keeping watch, but the trip as a whole passed without incident.

"The sun was sinking low on the horizon when we made our way into camp that night. Many of the men we found there were dirty and had the look of recent battle, though none wore near the exhaustion we did.

"Rollins ordered us all straight to rest and for the first time since leaving home, I slept soundly through the night.

"The next morning Jack and I rose early and made a lap around the camp. In all there were close to four hundred Americans, a few hundred more South Koreans set up just beyond. By the time we made it back to our regiment, most of the men were awake and moving about. Many were heating dehydrated food over fires and making coffee in the morning sun.

"Jack and I found Marks shaving over a pot of hot water and sat down beside his fire. Buddy dropped in a few minutes later, followed by two more men I recognized from the night in R Barracks.

"Marks watched us all sitting there in silence as he finished shaving and said, "I won't pretend you boys are all sitting here for my company, so I'll get right to it."

"He drew a map in the sand just like this one and said, "The plan is for us to stretch the six hundred men you see around us over a half mile wide and swing from west to east across the breadth of Pusan. As we proceed, we should free up reinforcements from the city."

"When's this?" Buddy asked.

"Move out at first light tomorrow," Marks said. "I know yesterday was rough going, but at least we've got a full day now to recover. Take advantage, get plenty to eat and as much rest as you can."

"How's your leg?" one of the boys across the fire asked.

"Marks gave a reflexive tap at his left thigh, the limb swollen much larger than his right. "I'll live."

"Our goal accomplished, we all set off in different directions. Jack and I spent most of the day alternating between sleeping and eating. Once in the afternoon we had to fetch water, but that was all.

"Around dinner time, Buddy took us from fire to fire and introduced us to the guys he came in with. They were from just outside of Louisville and almost all of them shared a thick southern drawl. Most had the look of farm boys turned soldiers, with deep weathered tans, close cropped hair, and unfailing manners."

My uncle motioned back up towards the house and said, "That night we were sitting by the fire about to turn in when Marks found us and motioned to follow him. Neither one of us had any idea what it was about, but we jumped up and ran after him quick as we could.

"He didn't say anything as he led us through camp and into a tent. Rollins was seated inside at a small folding table serving as a makeshift desk. Papers were strewn across it and he was examining one with a magnifying glass as we stood and wondered what was going on.

"Everything stayed that way for several minutes until Marks cleared his throat, forcing Rollins to look up. It seemed he had aged several years overnight as deep wrinkles creased his brow and his hair was matted to his forehead.

"Sergeant Marks tells me you boys handled yourself pretty well under fire," he opened.

"There was nothing in that statement resembling a question, so we both kept our mouth shut.

"Also tells me you boys helped carry him out of there," he said and again paused for a response that never came. "Last night, I lost five officers in this regiment alone. Sergeant Marks here has suggested that I promote you both to Corporal."

"I couldn't help but let my gaze shift towards Jack, who continued to stare straight ahead. Rollins noticed and smiled, that being all the sign he was looking for. "Congratulations gentlemen. Sergeant Marks will present you with your proper insignia."

"We each murmured 'thank-you' and saluted before following Marks out into the evening air.

"Is that true?" I asked as soon as we cleared earshot, astonishment plain on my face.

"Right as rain gentlemen," Marks replied. "You covered my ass, now I'm covering yours."

"He handed each of us ours bars and shook our hands. "I'll see you boys at dawn."

"The next page in the album is the insignia given to a Corporal. Both of us would rise to ranks higher than that, but that one made the album because it meant the most.

"It was given to us under the recommendation of our superior officer for excellence in battle at a time when we were just a week into the Army. The other ranks we received were for excellence as soldiers, but that first one was for excellence of character.

"Neither one of us had been around long enough to really know much soldiering. Everything we had done the night before was pure instinct. We had been shoved into the craziest of situations and made it out the other side.

"It might sound a little corny or outdated, but to us it meant a great deal."

## Chapter Twenty-One

I expected my uncle to take a short pause before continuing with the story. Each time before, he would finish a particular page and retreat back into himself for several minutes. His eyes would glaze over and his breathing would slow as he stared off at some distant point.

Whether he was collecting himself for the next item, reliving the previous one, or trying to compose himself before going on, I'll never know.

For the first time though, he pushed on without delay.

"That night the sleeplessness returned," he began. "The day of rest managed to relieve the exhaustion and the impending march set our nerves on edge again. Adding to it was our new rank, though Buddy and some of the others encouraged us to wear them with pride. They told us we'd earned them, and that was all anybody really cared about.

"At dawn our division assembled itself on the periphery of the gathering. The makeshift camp was thrown together in a thin spot of the forest without a clearing of any size we could use as a drill ground. Instead, we arranged ourselves the best we could amongst the trees.

"There was an uneasiness in the air as we stood and waited, punctuated by Rollins pacing back and forth in front of us. After almost an hour of inertia, the South Koreans joined us, falling in place at the rear. Their commander ambled by us and strolled to the front, where he was promptly given a good tongue lashing by Rollins.

"I was too far back to hear what was said, but it looked like he gave him hell.

"It was not a good sign that the men who were going to be fighting with us were almost an hour late for our first day together. Very few of them had anything resembling uniforms, most were bare footed and carrying antique weapons.

"One man even came along carrying a club with barbed wire wrapped around it. It was the only time I ever noticed it though, so I'm not sure if he found a rifle or if a rifle found him.

"Once we had everybody assembled, we set out. Rollins fanned us out and took the lead, picking our way through the countryside. To the rear was the South Korean leader, Major Pak.

"The regiment was broken into rows of four across with gaps of ten yards or so between each group. The idea was to allow immediate support in the event of enemy fire and to keep casualties at a minimum if ambushed.

"I walked in the middle right position of a group. On my right was a barrel-chested soldier from our regiment named Benny Butler. He had the thick arms and legs of a man that could bale hay for days and had the scratches on both arms to prove he had. On my left was Jack and to his left was Buddy.

"The going was slow, trekking our way through the thick forest. After the scene on the beach, everybody was paranoid of land mines and was careful to choose each step they took. We were also sure to be as quiet as possible and by noon we'd covered a total of about six miles.

"Sometime around midday, with the sun high over our head, we came across a stream and the line was ordered to stop. As soon as they saw the water, many men fell to their knees and removed their helmets, lapping it up in handfuls or sticking their entire head in.

"We should have known it was the most obvious place for an ambush. It was the only water we had come across all morning. Any leader worth their salt would recognize that was the easiest place to hit an oncoming enemy."

My uncle fell silent for a moment before tossing the stick in his hand into the lake. He scoffed aloud and shook his head.

"The *tat-tat-tat* of machine gun fire took every one of us by surprise. One guy was bent over scooping up water when a bullet struck him from behind and tossed him face first into the stream. For a moment everyone stood and watched as blood fanned from his head in great looping arcs, floating ribbons of red encasing his body.

"A moment later, the reality of it registered with us and we dropped to the ground.

"As a group, the four of us crawled our way to a tree stump and began returning fire. The opposite bank of the stream was a solid wall of vegetation, punctuated every few yards by the muzzle flash of enemy fire.

"The leaves were too thick to make out any particular targets and at first we just shot blind, spraying everything in sight with bullets. Before long, the leaves were cut to ribbons and dark shapes began to emerge.

"The initial outburst lasted about fifteen minutes, dying out as fast as it had started. Taking their dead and wounded with them, the North Koreans retreated backwards and disappeared without a trace.

"We lay entrenched where we were for several minutes before emerging and moving forward across the stream. Marks came down the line and made sure each of us were alright. He told us we were going to cautiously pursue and that scouts had been sent on ahead.

"For the rest of the afternoon, things went back to the way they'd been all morning. The sun blazed down on us and our fatigues clung to our skin with sweat. A couple of times we thought we heard enemy fire, but it was our own guys getting antsy. Just one long nerve wracking march.

"At dusk that all changed."

With his finger, he drew another diagram in the sand. "About fourteen miles northeast of Pusan, the forest gave way to a valley. We were still pushing west to east when we stumbled on it, the forest receding and giving way to a sharp decline. What had been soil and trees all day long was now nothing but flinty ridge and rock.

"The marching procession ground to a stop as everyone tried to figure out what to do. A few of the men stepped from the trees and made their way to the edge of the ravine. They took off their helmets and let the light breeze rush up the rock face and wash over them."

My uncle paused again, his tone shifting.

"Instead of leading with machine gun fire this time, they started by lobbing shells at us. Big phosphorescent shells that bathed us in blinding light and gave their machine gunners targets to aim at.

"The first shells landed a few yards down from us, shaking the ground we stood on. Right after them came the repetitive tatter of machine gun fire and the whizzing of bullets flying through the trees.

"On first impact we flattened ourselves to the ground. We stayed that way until there was a break in the volley and I had just about wrestled my gun out from under me when the second round of shells hit.

"One found its way to where we were lying and smashed into the ground between Buddy and Jack, sending neon light, dirt and gravel spewing into the air. It hit right at the edge of the ridge, causing the ground beneath Buddy to give way and sending him sliding down the front of the rock face.

"Without thinking I dove forward onto my stomach and thrust the barrel of my gun down at him. My arms dangled out over the rocks as he grabbed hold with both hands.

"Jesus Christ Cat, don't you let go! Don't you drop my ass!" he kept yelling. "And don't you dare touch that trigger!"

"Fragments of rock kicked up around us as I tried to wrestle Buddy back over the edge. One of them caught me on the forehead, sending a trickle of blood down the bridge of my nose.

"Hey! Can I get some help here?!" I screamed over my shoulder and felt hands grab hold of my ankles. They drug me backwards with Buddy still clinging to my rifle as scattered fire continued to chip at the rocks around us."

My eyes grew wide. "None of those bullets hit you guys?"

My uncle shook his head. "No, they sure didn't. It was like a scene from a movie or something, one of those things that you'd never believe unless you were there to see it.

"That's not to say nobody was hit though. When Buddy and I were in the cover of the woods, I turned to see who'd pulled me out. It was Jack alright, though I barely recognized him.

"Shrapnel from the incoming shell that first sent Buddy over the edge had torn into the side of his face. Small pieces of twisted metal jutted out from his left cheek. Blood flowed from the wounds and dripped off his chin.

"Jack, you need a doctor!" I yelled. He ignored me and began firing rounds at the opposing hillside.

"For the moment I gave up on getting help and joined him. Beside us, Buddy and Benny did the same.

"Once the firing died away, I took a clean t-shirt from my pack and tore it into long strips. I doused all of them in water and wrapped them around Jack's head.

"He gave token resistance to it, but didn't fight near as hard as I expected.

"The entire unit spent the night on the edge of that ridge, alternating in groups between keeping watch and trying to rest. Every hour or so a few random rounds would come in, just enough to keep us awake and thinking about an attack that never came.

"The next morning Rollins made his way down the line and told us the North Koreans had moved on. They'd left behind enough gunners to keep us agitated, but nothing close to a serious fighting force. He was mid-sentence explaining all this when he noticed the makeshift bandage Jack was wearing.

"What the hell happened to you?" he spat.

"I took some shrapnel," Jack replied.

"Rollins ordered him to remove the dressing and grimaced when he saw Jack's face. It was already swollen twice it's normal size and was deep purple and blue. Flies were buzzing around him and it needed to be cleaned immediately.

"Damn, damn, damn," Rollins muttered aloud.

"Sir, I can go on," Jack said.

"I know you can, but I can't let you. We're going to need you Corporal, stay here and have the medics tend to that wound. Take advantage, get some rest and get healed up. You can catch back up with us when we start moving north."

"Old Jack didn't take well to being left behind, but Rollins insisted. He informed the rest of us we were moving out immediately and moved on down the line to see to the rest of the men.

"I watched Rollins walk away and gave an awkward shrug. "Thanks for pulling my ass out of there last night."

"Don't do that," Jack snapped. "This isn't good-bye, I'll be back by nightfall. I'm only staying now because he gave me a direct order."

"I nodded and said, "Get that damn thing cleaned up anyway, huh? Girls back in Birch Grove won't think you're so pretty with metal sticking out of your face."

"Jack nodded back and assured me it wasn't his face the girls back home were interested in.

"I left Jack on the ridge that morning, certain I would see him again that night. I had never known Jack to lie about anything and there was no need to think he'd start then."

He fell silent and looked out over the water again.

"The next page in the album is a twisted piece of metal about a half inch long. It isn't one that they pulled out that morning, but rather one that worked its way to the surface many years later and had to be removed. Just the same though, it is an actual piece of that shell."

My eyes grew wide with astonishment. "You mean he walked around with metal in his face for *years*?"

My uncle turned sad eyes towards me and said, "Son, we could go over to that grave right now and I promise you we'd still find pieces of that shell in your uncle."

## Chapter Twenty-Two

The fishing boat we'd watched all afternoon came closer, the sound of their trolling motor making a gentle hum. As they approached the man in front flipped it off and the boat coasted through the water towards us.

"Any luck?" my uncle called.

The man in back reached into a reservoir and produced a nice stringer of fish, smiling wide. "Enough crappie to feed us for a week."

"Crappie, huh?" my uncle said. "That's some damn good eating right there."

"Yeah it is," said the man in front. He too smiled when he talked and wore a black and red plaid flannel unbuttoned over a stained white tank top. A floppy fisherman's cap was tugged down onto his head and small lures were hooked to the side of it.

"You from around here?" the man in back asked. He had a bald head that was dark brown from the sun and speckled with liver spots. He had a thick white moustache and wore a plain t-shirt under bib overalls.

"This is my niece's place," my uncle replied, casting a thumb up towards the house. They both paused like they were waiting for him to continue, but that was all he said.

A few awkward moments passed before the man in front said, "Well, we got another couple of hours of daylight, better get to it."

"Alright then," my uncle said, "good luck."

He raised his hand and waved at them and I did the same. The men waved back and turned their motor back on, within minutes well down the shoreline.

My uncle paused a moment to collect his thoughts and said, "Just like Rollins said, we moved out right then. Jack wore the sourest expression I had ever seen while he watched us go, but he stayed behind as ordered. Buddy and I fell in step beside each other and as we made our way around the ravine I could feel Jack's eyes watching us.

"We spent the rest of that day the same way we spent the one before. Once we were around the valley, we were right back into forest. Moving was slow and tough and three different times we were rotated out to sentry positions.

"After only a day of marching, our numbers were already a bit concerning. Word had worked down the line that many of the South Koreans froze under fire. They just stood there and watched as North gunners mowed them down. A fair numbers of those who were smart enough to move threw down their weapons and ran all the way back to Pusan.

"What started as over six hundred men the day before was already down to four-fifty.

"We heard a couple random shots fired throughout the afternoon, but for the most part the day was calm. Sentries on our east flank managed to flush out a pair of gunners before the main detachment was within range, but otherwise there was no sign of the enemy."

My uncle paused for a second and coughed a deep throaty cough. He raised his hand to me as if to say excuse me and rose to his feet. The coughing continued for several seconds as he turned his back to me, culminating with a hack and a spit.

I stared straight out over the water, careful not to let him think I was watching. I heard him take several deep breaths and after a moment he retook his place beside me.

"Darkness crept towards us and with it came the realization that we hadn't slept in over two days. As we pressed on my eyes grew hazy from the sweat and grime that filled them.

"Twice throughout the day Marks made his way down the line, asking us how we were doing and telling us it was only going to be a short while longer. His own leg had swollen again and he was limping. I could see a heavy bandage wrapped tight around his thigh and he winced often as he walked. Benny made the mistake of asking him about it once, something that earned him a severe tongue lashing in response.

"Nobody asked again.

"By nightfall on the second day, we had made it just past the Zanti River. Marks had told us earlier that's where we were going to bed down for the night, and I spent most of the afternoon sniffing the air for the scent of river water. So intent was my search that I didn't notice the rest of my group stopped until I was a good ways past them.

"Roberts! Where the hell you going?" Marks hollered out. "You going to take them slant eyes on all by yourself?"

"It took a moment for the comment to register and I could hear men chuckling. I stood rigid at first before softening up and laughing along with them.

"I was on my third chuckle when the branch beside me exploded."

My uncle again paused for a second, cleared his throat and began anew.

"There were almost fifty yards between me and the rest of the unit, but from where I was it looked more like five hundred. I melted straight down into the ground and worked my gun into a firing position as the trees seemed to spit bark around me."

My eyes grew wide. "How many of them were there this time?"

My uncle cast a sideways glance at me and shook his head. "Only one.

"From where he was perched, the shooter couldn't see the rest of the unit. To him it looked like I was out scouting alone and he could score an easy kill before dark.

"Many of the men saw me fall to the ground and burst out laughing. They must have thought I tripped because they hollered and called me all sorts of names. It wasn't until a few more bullets ripped into the trees that they gathered what was happening and grabbed their rifles to come help.

"As soon as they did, Rollins was there to call them back. Kept telling them it could be a trap, a single gunner firing to lure more out into the open. He was of course right, but that didn't help me much. I was under the cover of trees, but if I moved so much as a foot in either direction I would have been exposed."

I furrowed my brow and looked up at him. "So what did you do?"

My uncle held up his hand and smiled with the corner of his mouth. "Have you ever seen homemade camouflage?"

I wasn't even sure what camouflage was, but I was pretty sure I'd never seen my parents make it before.

"Camouflage is the stuff you see on soldiers on TV. You see it when your daddy goes hunting; sometime you even see it on the side of cars and trucks out on the road."

He paused again and looked at me. I now knew what he was referring to, but I must have still been wearing the look of confusion on my face.

"Well, never mind that just yet," he said. "I lay there on my stomach for over ten minutes, each round coming a little closer to my head. I wanted to curse and yell for my men to do something, but I didn't want to give away my position. The sniper already knew where I was, no use in helping him pin me down any further. Instead, I stayed quiet and prayed that the bullets would stop.

"And then they did.

"Lieutenant, what's going on?" I asked, certain it was some sort of trap.

"I don't know," Rollins called back. "I was just about to send Peters and Bloom out to find the bastard when it stopped."

"Well if you didn't get him and I didn't get him, why'd he stop firing?" I asked. I was certain this must be another trap, but I didn't want to say the words.

"Because I got him," said a familiar voice from the gathering darkness behind me. "And I'm coming in, so everybody hold your fire."

"I knew the voice in an instant and rolled to face it, though I hardly recognized Jack as he emerged through the trees. His face was wrapped in some sort of black cloak and he had stripped off his jacket. Greasy soot covered his arms and I couldn't see him until he was just a few feet from me.

"Where the hell did you come from?" I asked.

"Call me your guardian angel," Jack said with a half smile and stuck out his arm to help me up. The whites of his teeth showed bright against the soot on his face as I accepted the help to my feet.

"No seriously, where the hell did you come from?" Rollins asked, approaching from the opposite side.

"Jack looked at the ground, then raised his head and exhaled. "Lieutenant, I did as you said and got my head cleaned up. Soon as they were done, I kind of faded into the background and lit out after you all."

"Rollins nodded his head upward. "So you went AWOL?"

"Jack grimaced. "Yes sir."

"Rollins spat and turned away for a moment. "By all rights I should write you up and turn you over to military police. At the same time, you just took out a sniper and saved an officer's life. What say we just call it even and agree to never disappear like that again?"

"Jack nodded. "Yes sir. Thank you sir."

"Rollins nodded at him and passed his eyes over Jack. "Now again, where the hell did you come from?"

"Sir?"

"Rollins motioned at Jack and said, "You look like shit and smell worse. You're covered from head to toe in mud and you managed to somehow outshoot an enemy sniper. Anything you care to share?"

"Most of the men had gathered in tight to listen, nudging me a little closer into the circle. Jack glanced my way and said, "Following your orders, I stayed behind to get my face looked at. I was in better shape than most, so I spent the first half of the day helping as much as I could. That's what most of the smell is from.

"Some time mid-afternoon, one of the medics pulled me aside and took a look. By then my face had swollen even further, so digging out the metal took a little more effort than either one of us liked.

"All told he pulled out seven pieces of shrapnel, said there was probably more in there but we'd have to wait until the swelling was gone."

"A murmur went up from the crowd, but Jack continued on in his matter-of-fact style. "When he was done, he handed me some ointment and gauze, went on to other soldiers in need. I put them both on my head and as soon as I thought nobody was watching, I lit off through the woods."

"Damn, didn't they drug the hell out of you?" Buddy asked from the crowd.

"Jack's eyes shifted to him. "Nope. I told you boys I'd be back by nightfall and I knew I wouldn't make it if I was doped up."

"Jack turned his attention back to Rollins and said, "You guys leave a hell of a wake behind you, so it wasn't hard picking it up. I stayed a few dozen yards off of it the whole time just as precaution, wasn't long before I came across that sniper's trail. Picked you guys up just past the ravine and tailed you here. I could tell by his patterns and movement that he was alone and traveling light.

"As far as this," Jack continued, motioning to his head, "I dumped my canteen on the ground and smeared the mud on my face and arms. Took the bandage off, soaked it in the mud, then put it back on."

"Good way to get infection," Rollins said.

"Better than having a bright white target bobbing through the woods," Jack said. "After that, following the guy was easy. He was sloppy, no doubt thought he was alone. I got to within a hundred yards of him when he started firing, unaware I was behind him. He didn't even know I was there until he felt my knife."

"Rollins snorted and said, "So you're saying you didn't outshoot an enemy sniper? That instead you snuck up and gutted him without him hearing a sound?"

My uncle chuckled. "Jack stood there and looked at him for a few seconds, trying to figure out why Rollins sounded surprised. "Uh, yea?"

"A few whistles went up from around the group and a couple of the men coughed and muttered 'bullshit' under their breath.

"Jack never stood for being called a liar and a small flash of light passed behind his eyes.

"The body is still laying over there if you want to check it out," he challenged.

"Everybody stood quiet after that, not real sure what to do next.

"Alright men," Rollins said, "let's get back to what we were doing before all this commotion started. I want sentry outposts every hundred yards. Two men per post in four hour shifts."

"The group stood for a few more seconds before drifting away. When we were clear, I turned to Jack and said, "You saved my ass for certain. He was zeroing in on me in a big way."

"Jack snorted. "If I had known it was you he was firing at, I'd have taken my time putting him down. As was, it was quick and painless."

"As we talked, a man with a medic's insignia made his way over to us. He stuck out his hand as he approached and said, "John Persyn, company medic. I understand you're the Roberts boys?"

"We each shook his hand in turn and he added, "Couple of modern day heroes from what I hear."

"Jack and I shot a quick glance at each other and I said, "More like repeat customers for you I'm sure."

"Persyn laughed and pointed to Jack's head. "Heard your story. How about we get that bandage off your head and get that wound cleaned out."

"Both of us dropped down on a felled tree as Persyn unwrapped and cleaned Jack's head. The swelling was still pretty significant and the bruising heavy, but Persyn said he was lucky to avoid infection. When he was done, he held up the filthy bandage and asked, "You want to keep this as a souvenir?"

"Jack just shook his head and pointed to his face. "I think I'll have plenty of souvenirs right here."

My uncle turned his shoulders and glanced back up at the house. "Turns out they were both right. Jack still has his souvenirs from that day etched across face, but we couldn't very well stick those in the album. Instead, Jack went out into the woods and made some more homemade camouflage, just the same way he did all those years ago."

## Chapter Twenty-Three

The sun was just starting to slide down in the sky when my uncle finished telling me about the sniper. The world was at peace around us, the only sounds being water lapping up onto the sandbar and tall grass rustling in the breeze. Several long minutes passed and I could see the fishing boat make its way to the far corner of the lake and start working back towards us.

The air was shattered by the sound of my father's shrill whistle and on instinct I jumped to my feet to see what was wrong. I must have been hidden by the tall grass because as soon as I took my feet, my father waved and returned into the house.

I took my seat again in the sand as my uncle looked at me and laughed.

"That night we slept little, if at all. Every time I closed my eyes, I saw those bullets getting closer and closer to me. Poor Jack had even less of a chance than I did, his head throbbing beneath the new dressing.

"We figured somebody might as well get some rest, so just after midnight we took over a sentry spot. We spent the rest of the night leaning against either side of tree, silent and staring out into the darkness.

"When the first streaks of dawn appeared we headed back to camp and found the place already busy. Men were running back and forth, fires stamped out, packs hitched into place.

"What's going on?" I asked a man running by. "We got a bead on their position?"

"Visitors coming, just found out," he said over his shoulder and kept on going.

"Jack let out a low whistle and said, "All this commotion, you'd think Truman himself must be stopping by."

"Hell, I'd almost prefer to see him out here," Rollins said from behind us. He walked up between us and we stood three across watching the camp scramble things together.

"So who is it?" I asked.

"Who you think?" Rollins said. "Our fearless leader has decided to grace us with his presence."

"We each turned and looked at him.

"Please tell me you don't mean Williams?" I muttered.

"Rollins made a face. "Yep, sent a runner out here this morning. Said he'd heard we were running into fire and wanted to come give us a hand. Show us how this was supposed to be done."

"Aw hell," Jack muttered. Rollins and I both nodded our heads in agreement.

"A few seconds passed and Rollins spat at the ground. "You boys better get your gear packed up, we head out as soon as he gets here. Should be any minute now."

My uncle snorted and shook his head. "Rollins was right. Williams showed up ten minutes later and we rolled out less than two minutes after that."

Contempt rolled from my uncle's tongue as he said, "That cocksure bastard strolled into camp like he was G.I. Joe himself. Every so often he'd point out a pack that wasn't done to regulation or a fire that needed a little more dousing. Like he'd ever spent a single day in the field and had any idea how things were done.

"What made it even worse was the South Koreans stood in awe of him. Once he knew he had an audience, you'd have thought he was Bob Hope."

I had no idea who Bob Hope was, but I remained silent and let him continue.

"The Americans were a different story though. We paid him his due by saluting or doing as he said, but there was a terse silence to our movements. Faces were hard and jaw lines were set tight as we listened to what he said.

"Once camp was broken in a way that satisfied him, Williams called for us to move out. Wasn't five minutes after that we started running into problems.

"Given the terrain of the land, we had been marching in a formation that was two long lines, staggered rows with sentries posted on our flanks anywhere from fifty to one hundred yards out. We used this formation because it kept us spread out a little bit and best prepared us in case of ambush. Our flanks were always covered and we could still move with some reasonable degree of speed.

"Williams didn't like it though, especially as the trail pinched inward a bit. We weren't a half mile down the path when he called for a halt to the entire thing. Pushed everyone into a single file and removed over half the sentries. The remaining sentries he brought in so they flanked us by about twenty yards."

My uncle dropped his head and twisted it angrily from side to side. "It didn't take long for Rollins to object and for the other officers to join him. We were near the end of the line and were only hearing piecemeal information, but from the sounds of things it got ugly in a hurry."

"So what did they do?" I asked, for the first time in a while grasping the situation.

"The longer they debated, the madder Williams got. Ended up pulling rank and saying his orders would be followed or everyone would be court martialed for insubordination.

"Everyone was mad about it, but there wasn't anything they could do. Instead, we stayed in a single file and stomped through the woods. Jack was behind me, Buddy in front, Benny in front of him. The sun crawled higher in the sky and sweat trickled down our bodies beneath the weight of our gear.

"You think we're going to stop anytime soon?" Buddy asked over his shoulder as we plodded along.

"Hell if I know," I grunted, sweat dripping from the end of my nose to the ground.

"Naw," Jack said from behind me, "Williams is on a power trip. He's all pissed somebody questioned his orders and hell-bent on proving he was right."

"Damn fool's going to get us killed, you ask me," Buddy said. "Walking through the woods single file like this with a handful of sentries. Koreans could squeeze right in on us and we wouldn't even know it."

"We each shook our heads in frustration and continued forward as the sun passed from overhead on down towards the horizon. Wasn't until late in the afternoon that we stopped.

"To the man, we all dumped our packs and collapsed to the cool dirt floor of the forest. Men drank the last of their canteens or smoked cigarettes, others tried in vain to fan themselves.

"Before long we saw Marks and another Sergeant working their way down the line towards us, stopping every so often to talk to a huddle of men before moving on again. By the time they got to us, they both looked plenty mad.

"First of all, I don't want to hear any bitching. This isn't our plan and we let him know that," Marks said, raising his hand in front of him.

"We all exchanged glances that meant *this can't be good*, but said nothing.

"The trail ahead runs through a ravine. About eighty feet down on this side, at least that much back up the opposite," said the other sergeant, a thin man with a shaved head named Byrnes. "Captain Williams has decided we will follow the trail."

"Several groans went up from around us and a man behind me asked, "How big we talking? Couldn't we just go around it?"

"Marks shook his head. "Looking at maybe a mile down and back. Williams doesn't want to lose the time."

"If the ravine doesn't kill us, exhaustion will huh?" Benny asked.

"Neither sergeant answered. They didn't have to. Instead, they looked at one another and moved on down the line.

"I finished the last of my water and fell flat onto my back. I clamped my thumb and forefinger down over my eyes to keep sweat from running into them, pressing so hard bright lights formed behind my eyelids. Jack dropped himself to the ground beside me and I could hear the metallic clang of his canteen as he took water.

"That's when the call went up that it was time to get moving again.

"With everybody spread out in the woods, somehow we'd ended up pretty close to the front of the line, maybe a quarter of the way back. With an audible groan everybody retook their feet and started forward when shots pierced the air. They sounded like twigs snapping underfoot, the sounds ringing out one right after another.

"Moving from tree to tree, we covered the last few hundred yards to the front of the line. Why we did that I have no idea, but at the time it just seemed natural.

"Our boys were taking fire. We should go help.

"We got there a few minutes later to find Rollins and several others lying on their stomachs, peering out over the edge of the ravine.

"What the hell's going on?" I asked as we slid in alongside them.

"Where in God's name did you boys come from?" Rollins asked.

"Does it matter?" I asked. "We heard shots and came running."

"More than I can say for most," Rollins said and handed Jack a pair of binoculars.

"Oh shit," Jack muttered and handed them on to me.

"Oh shit was right. At the bottom of the ravine Williams was huddled with a small group of men. Several other groups were pinned down under cover. More than a few dead bodies littered the trail.

"Where they at?" I asked, checking the opposite hillside for North Koreans.

"Everywhere," Rollins said. "They knew we were coming and drew us in. They've got that side covered and this is the only vantage we have. The way the trail winds down through there, most of our guns are useless from here."

"What about the high ground?" Jack asked, motioning to a rock wall rising behind us.

"Not unless you're a damn mountain goat," Rollins said. "It's too high and too steep."

"I passed the binoculars back to Rollins and said, "So what's the plan?"

"Hell if I know," Rollins said, scouring the opposite side of the ravine. North Korean muzzle flashes continued dotting it and far below we could hear Williams yelling for someone to do something.

"Sergeant Byrnes joined Rollins on his opposite side and said, "Were going to have send someone down in after them."

"How the hell you propose we do that?" Rollins spat. "That's a suicide mission. Captain or not, he's not worth it."

"Send a couple of men down as rabbits, couple more as shooters," Byrnes said. "Rabbits to draw out their fire, shooters to cover them. Work their way from hole to hole until everybody's out."

"Rollins turned his head and glared at Byrnes. "You know I can't give that order. Where the hell you going to find anybody crazy enough to volunteer for that?"

"Byrnes matched Rollins stare, then cocked his neck past Rollins to Jack and I. We both knew what he was thinking, but neither one of us let on. We just kept watching the ravine below.

"Them's your boys there aren't they?" Byrnes asked.

"Rollins cast his eyes towards us and said, "The Roberts? Hell no. I'm not giving up two Corporals because Williams is a fool. Besides, one of them has half his face swollen shut right now. He couldn't hit anything if he tried."

"Byrnes started to persist, but he didn't have to.

"I'll do it," Jack said. "But I don't want him coming with me. There are better shooters in the unit."

"If he was trying to make me mad, it worked. I was on my feet in seconds and checked the chamber on my rifle. Without asking, I snatched up Rollins' from the ground beside him and slung it over my shoulder.

"I just said I didn't want you going," Jack said.

"And I said I didn't want either one of you going!" Rollins said.

"Sergeant Byrnes said we were going," Jack said and in one fluid motion turned on the ball of his foot and bounded down the trail. It took just a split second for me to register what was happening and follow right after him.

"The first cluster of men was holed up maybe twenty-five yards down from us. Jack was far enough ahead of me to draw most of the fire and as I ran I peppered anything moving on the hillside. The ravine was tight and more than once I heard cries of pain as I fired into the brush.

"Jack reached the men a split second before me and slid behind the rocks. When I got there he took one of the rifles from his shoulder and exchanged it for the one in my hand.

"He paused for a second to catch his breath and said, "They'll assume we're going after the Captain, so they'll follow Cat and I down from here. As soon as you guys hear firing, you get on up the trail as fast as you can."

"The men in the group were pale and sweating. Nobody said a word as they nodded their heads. Jack looked at me and said, "How about this time you try hitting a few of them?"

"He was gone again before I had a chance to reply.

"I plunged down after him, snapping off shots as fast as I could. There weren't as many bullets flying at us this time, something I hoped meant I had taken out a few of their shooters and not that they were all firing at the men behind us.

"We reached the second group about fifteen yards further down. Along the way we had to hurdle two fallen soldiers, neither of which were breathing.

"This time we're going to try something a little different," Jack said. He signaled to Williams and the others below, then motioned to us. He pointed back up towards the trail and made a sweeping motion towards them.

"You could tell Williams didn't like being told what to do by a Corporal. He waved Jack off and began motioning in a manner none of us understood. Jack gave him a confused face and made the same set of signals he had before. Williams again tried to change the plan, but we both ignored him and went back up the trail in the direction we'd just came from.

"I fired a couple of times, but for the most part we both just ran as fast as we could. Together we dove in behind the rock pile as bullets ripped into the sod around us.

"When we got there we turned back to see that the bottom group had replaced us at the second rock pile.

"Williams was furious, but he was there and alive just the same.

"Got anymore ideas?" I asked as we sat trying to catch our breath, both tucked behind the rocks. Out of nowhere, the opposite hillside opened up in fire and we turned to see a group of men bounding towards us. We slid to the far side of the cover as a dozen bodies crowded in around us.

"What the hell?" Jack asked the panting men.

"Williams," one of them muttered just as Williams and the last of the group spilled in.

"The rocks weren't really big enough for a group that large. We all knew it was only a matter of seconds before the North Koreans started picking men off the edges.

"Since you two think you're hot shit and like running so much," Williams said, pointing at us, "you're going back down the way you just came. You continue doing your little cat-and-mouse game until I can get us out of here."

"Many of the men around the group gave him a sour glare, but he paid them no heed. Jack matched his stare and said, "We're out of ammunition."

"Without taking his eyes from us Williams said, "Someone give these two a gun." A man handed one out butt first and without looking at it Williams grabbed it and thrust it towards me. "Now get your asses moving."

"This time, we both stared at him. Jack was the first one out, running back down the trail. I was right behind him and made a point of shouldering into Williams as I went. Probably not the smartest thing to do with a blowhard like him, but I didn't care.

"The trail had several more bodies on it than just a few minutes before and it made for much tougher running. When we got to the next rock outcropping Jack muttered, "Ignorant son of a bitch. Look at all those boys he just got killed."

"He might have just gotten us killed," I said.

"Jack looked at me for a second and turned towards the bottom of the ravine. He cupped his hands around his mouth and shouted, "Stay there! We're coming to you!"

"He turned to me and said, "Get ready to run," turned back towards the bottom and yelled, "How bad is he hurt?" When the last syllable left his lips he lunged himself back up the trail, me right on his heels. I didn't even bother to shoulder a gun this time, we both just ran with everything we had.

"We reached the last group of rocks before the ridge to see the trail had claimed a few more lives. "Hey Lieutenant, how about a little cover fire?" Jack called out.

"A few seconds later Rollins replied, "Estrada's halfway up the trail and bleeding. You grab his ass on the way and we'll give you all the support you need."

"We took off up that trail like the hounds of hell were on our heels. Estrada lay in the middle of the trail with blood running from his hip and as we passed he raised his arms towards us. Without breaking stride we each cupped a hand into an armpit and drug him backwards through the dirt.

"The ridge above us ignited with gunfire, matched by North Korean bullets ripping into the ground around us. Estrada cried out as another slammed into his calf, but we didn't stop moving.

"Cheers went up from the unit as we crested the ridge and all three of us dropped to the dirt. Men crowded around, some clapping, others reaching down to slap us on the back. Persyn slid in from nowhere and started working on Estrada while men continued cheering or tossing insults at the North Koreans.

"That all came to a halt though with the arrival of Williams.

"The crowd quieted as that smug prick pushed his way through to us. When he got there he didn't thank us, he didn't congratulate us, he said, "I'm going to have you two court-martialed for that little stunt."

"Rollins turned his head towards him. "Sir?"

"Don't sir me. These two disobeyed a direct order down there and they're going to pay for it."

"They saved your life," Marks said.

"Williams shook his head and said, "That might be, but this is the Army and we have rules. They disobeyed a direct order and they will pay for it." With that he turned and stomped off."

"It didn't even matter that you saved him?" I asked, anger rising in my own young voice.

"No," my uncle said, shaking his head. "Jack and I rose to a seated position and each accepted canteens from some of the men. Rollins waited for Williams to leave and said, "That was the most heroic thing I've ever seen. There won't be any court martial, I guarantee it."

"We each nodded as Rollins moved away to check on Estrada. "You alright?" Jack asked.

"Yeah, you?"

"Yeah. Some fine looking pants we've got on aren't they?"

"I hadn't noticed until he said something, but the legs of our pants were torn to shreds. I ran my hands over my calves a few times to make sure they weren't hit, but aside from a few small scratches they were intact.

"Damn, that was close," I said. My hands began to tremble and for a good while I sat there, staring at the ground, waiting for them to stop. "You want to explain to me what that up there was all about?"

"All what?" Jack asked.

"That whole, 'There are better shooters' thing you pulled up there."

"Jack drew a tight smile. "You do things better when you're mad."

"I started to reply but caught myself mid-sentence. He was right, in a way only an older brother could be."

My uncle paused for several moments again before pointing back towards the house. "We both earned silver stars for the incident. Between extricating the men and pulling Estrada to safety, there wasn't anything a few grumblings of one dead Captain could do to prevent it."

"One dead Captain?" I asked.

"We'll get to that," my uncle said, returning his gaze back out over the water. "Trust me; we'll get to it all before we're done."

## Chapter Twenty-Four

"The incident in the ravine soon became just another day in our life over the next several months. All told, it took us three more nights to finish our swing eastward across Pusan and we earned every inch of it.

"Every tree, every hole, every dip in the landscape allowed for another ambush and the North Koreans took full advantage of them all. The arrogance of Williams seemed to grow every day, so we were always walking into traps. Poor formations, not enough sentries, you name it. I swear he did most of it just to prove he could.

"After the ravine, Jack and I became both heroes and villains overnight. Many of the men admired us for what we did, some even came and thanked us for saving them or their friends. Others thought we were show-offs, glory seekers who needed to be reminded who we were and how long we'd been in the Army.

"That was nothing compared to what we got from Williams though. We took twice as many guard duties and scout positions as others, lugged more water than any five men put together.

"Through it all we never said a word, a fact which only irritated him further."

My uncle again paused for a moment and watched the sun slide a little lower in the sky. For a moment his face was impassive.

"After we liberated Pusan, word came down that MacArthur himself had ordered all available personnel north to the 38th parallel. That was the official boundary between North and South Korea and we were going to try and regain control of all of South Korea.

"Bit by bit we pushed north as the dog days of summer gave way to fall. Around us the torrid heat and humidity receded, shifting to chilly mornings and cold nights.

"Not a single day passed without shots being fired and good men around us falling. On paper, there was no way the North Koreans could match up with us. They were out manned, out trained and out classed in every way possible. Instead, they used guerrilla tactics and a familiarity with the landscape to slowly chip away at us.

"The fact that we had a stubborn ass like Williams at the helm sure didn't help us much either.

"Given our position against the coast, it was impossible for reinforcements to reach us. The shoreline was too treacherous to get aid by sea, the area too hostile for airborne and overland support. Each day our forces grew a little smaller and by the time November rolled around we were at less than half the original force that landed together."

My uncle again paused and I could tell by the slow demeanor and quiet tone that he was preparing himself for what lay ahead. I wanted to move closer to him and tell him it was okay, he could finish the story later, but I knew I couldn't.

He sensed what I was thinking and looked over at me. A half smile crossed his face and he nodded his head once. "You'll have to excuse me. We're coming to a part of the story that still keeps many good soldiers awake at night.

"The Chosin Reservoir is a manmade lake about seventy miles south of the Yalu River, which was important for two big reasons. First, the Yalu was where we believed the strength of the North Korean Army was holed up. If we could get a foothold on the Reservoir, we had a place to launch an attack.

"Second, and maybe even more important, Chosin served as the boundary between North Korea and Red China.

"Like North Korea, Red China was under the control of a communist regime that hated America and everything it stood for. It held no pretenses about its support of the

North Koreans, and offered generous verbal and monetary aid to them.

"On the night of November 27th, that support grew to include their military as well."

My uncle placed a hand on his knee and swung his hips out from under him. He brought one leg up and steadied himself, then climbed to his feet and looked down at me. "Let's walk for a spell."

I sprung up and hurried to his side as we made our way down the sandbar and back through the tall grass dancing in the breeze.

"The night of November 27th was our second at Chosin. We had arrived the day before after fighting our way north for over two months and the entire camp was exhausted beyond belief. Each man there had seen enough death and despair to last them a hundred lifetimes.

"Each day the officers pleaded with Williams for a break to allow the men to recuperate and each day Williams refused and ordered us north. In his mind, he would be recognized as the officer that was the first to reach the North Koreans.

"All it really meant was when we got there, we would have had to face them alone.

"We came upon Chosin late on the 26th, worn out from marching all day. Harsh cold had moved into the country and while we took whatever we could find along the way, it wasn't enough to keep us warm. Every day we trudged forward into a wind that sapped us of our strength and each night we huddled tight around fires in an attempt to get warm.

"When we arrived on the shores of the Chosin, the officers demanded we stop for a few days. There was plenty of water and its beaches offered us the protection we hadn't had in a long time.

"There wasn't any vegetation for several hundred yards down to the water's edge, just rocky shale that became sand. By putting our backs to the water and staying in the trees, we only had to watch one direction. Many of us had lost vast amounts of weight and our feet bled from marching in the unforgiving Army issue boots.

"If Williams didn't stop, he wasn't going to have a unit left. Even still, it took over two hours of heated debate for him to relent and grant a day of rest. That was on the night of the 26$^{th}$.

"The next day we hunkered down in the forest. We built fires, cooked dehydrated meals and slept for hours on end. Late that afternoon Jack and I took our turn as guards to find the forest devoid of activity. I mean *any* activity.

"After growing up on the bottoms, we were pretty attuned to the sounds of woods. Let me tell you, it was unnerving to hear the world so still.

"That evening, neither one of us was able to sleep. Everybody else was well into their third or fourth nap of the night, but we remained awake and alert with our backs to the fire.

"Exhaustion still gripped both of us, but we couldn't let ourselves fall asleep. Years of listening to the forests back home and now months of tromping through the Korean countryside had honed our senses razor sharp. Even at that, already feeling that something was out there, we didn't hear them until they were almost on top of us.

"I had no idea an encroaching Army could be so silent."

We came to an old sycamore log, trunk worn smooth from the elements. My uncle walked right up to it and patted it, signaling the end of our path. He turned us back the way we'd came and didn't speak again until we were halfway across the sand bar.

When he did, his voice was cold and distant.

"Two hundred thousand Chinese soldiers got within a few hundred yards of us without making a sound. We were sitting with our backs to them and didn't even know they were there until they let out the fiercest shout I ever heard and charged right for us.

"Almost every man in our camp was asleep. When the Chinese started yelling it rousted everybody out of their bed rolls, stumbling around in a fit of disarray. Jack and I both stayed low to avoid being easy targets and started firing shots as fast as we could. We didn't even have to aim, they were a human wall coming straight at us.

"The first wave of Chinese slammed into us within minutes. With bayonets flashing in the moonlight they swung through and sawed down our men by the handful. Jack and I engaged as many as we could in hand to hand combat, but for every Chinaman that tasted my blade another soon took his place.

"Outnumbered and surprised, we didn't stand a chance. After a few minutes we rallied a valiant defense, but it was short lived. It wasn't very long before men began to throw down their weapons and toss their hands into the air.

"The Chinese didn't give a damn about that though. They were mercenaries, hired by the North Koreans to kill as many Americans as possible. They killed everyone in sight, then looted the bodies for anything they could grab.

"Left with no option, we retreated back across the open shale to the banks of the reservoir. Out in the open it was apparent how thin our ranks were, even more obvious how abundant the Chinese were. To our right Buddy and Dwayne emerged shoulder to shoulder, shooting at anything that moved. A little ways down to our left was Marks. All of us fired as fast as we could, but it was a losing battle. There wasn't enough ammunition left amongst the whole unit to defeat that many Chinese.

"Marksy, we can't keep this up all day!" Dwayne shouted over the chaos.

"What the hell are we doing here Sarge?" Buddy called.

"Marks turned wild eyed towards us and said, "How the hell should I know?"

"Men continued falling around us and soon our entire unit was whittled down to less than a couple hundred men. I was working on my last two clips of ammunition when Jack shouted, "Feel up for a swim?"

"What?" I shouted. "That water's almost frozen solid!"

"Jack motioned with his gun at the oncoming crowd and said, "Swim or stand here until our ammunition runs out."

"It wasn't a question and it wasn't just an observation. It was an unequivocal fact and we both knew it.

"Marks, the only chance we got is across the water," I shouted to my right.

"Marks continued firing. "You Roberts boys are crazy bastards, you know that?"

"It's the only chance we've got!" Buddy yelled from my left. I didn't even know he could hear us, but he was on board with the plan.

"Hell, we gotta do something," Dwayne shouted.

"Marks fired off two more quick shots. "Give me two minutes!" He disappeared down the line as the four of us crowded tight, firing at the encroaching wave.

"Marks was gone less than half that before he returned, the better part of a dozen men clumped around him. "Alright," he shouted, "let's do this!"

"We continued shooting as we walked backwards towards the water's edge and the first blast of icy water spilled down my ankles and into my boots. My feet were numb within seconds as I waded back to my knees, then my waist. Around me I could hear the others gasping as the frigid water enveloped them.

"Bullets ripped into the water around us and a few Chinese soldiers stepped forward to give chase, but once their feet hit the water they gave up. We continued moving until we could no longer touch bottom, dog paddling with our weapons held out in front of us.

"Alright," Marks said in a loud whisper, "stay quiet and move as fast as you can. We're going to follow close to the shoreline and as soon as we clear the fighting we're getting out of this damn water, you got me?"

"A few 'yes sirs' went up from the group, many of them pushed through chattering teeth. As a group we swam parallel to the shore, moving as fast as our frozen bodies would allow.

"On shore we watched as the fighting fell away, the Chinese plundering anything they could get their hands on. Had we not been focused on the icy water gripping us, anger and sadness would have filled us all.

"Sarge, I've got to get out of this water soon," I heard Dwayne say and several men voiced agreement.

"Fifty more yards," Marks gasped as each of us gritted our teeth and moved forward. We abandoned moving as a group, every man going as long as he could before stumbling up onto shore.

"The cold night air blasted through our wet bodies as we emerged from the water. It felt like thousands of knives stabbing my body and I half ran, half stumbled my way forward across the sand.

"The Chinese behind us were too intent on celebrating their victory to notice us a quarter mile down the shore, our wet bodies glistening in the moonlight. Jack and I looped our arms around one another and dragged ourselves towards the woods. I ached with numbness and every muscle screamed as blood tried to rush back in.

"We stumbled through the edge of the trees and collapsed into a heap behind a felled pine. A moment later we could hear more bodies crashing into the woods, all of them falling to the ground around us.

"I made no effort to uncurl myself from behind the pine, but looked up to see Dwayne, Buddy and Marks all lying close by. Beyond them were a couple of guys I had never seen before.

"On the shore, two men lay face down on the sand, their bodies like boulders on the barren shoreline. I made a small effort to climb to my feet to help them, but Marks waved me off. "Don't. They're already gone."

"It was all the convincing I needed. I collapsed again to the ground and for several seconds I fought the urge to close my eyes, to press myself into the earth and allow the darkness to wash over me.

"Marks, we have to keep moving," Jack said. "Sooner or later somebody's going to notice those bodies and when they do, we're done for."

"Marks looked up with pain etched across his face and said, "Yeah. If we don't keep moving, the Chinese are going to find us or we're going to freeze to death."

"More moans rang up from the group as we somehow rose to our feet. A quick head count numbered us at fourteen, two less than plunged into the water a few minutes before.

"South?" Jack said.

"Marks rose to full height and nodded his head. "Yeah. The forest was thick, should help block the wind. We'll fan out and try to find shelter."

My uncle stopped walking and stared out over the lake. His eyes darted back and forth and he said, "Just like that, our regiment was cut to fourteen men. Fourteen freezing men, soaked to the bone, stumbling through the Korean wilderness.

"The next page in the album is a piece of cloth. It's about ten inches long and two inches wide. It's red with one large yellow star and four smaller stars extending out from it.

"The design is the Chinese flag, adopted only a few years before with the victory of the Communist party. The particular piece of cloth in the album isn't a flag though, but an armband. The very same armband worn by every one of the Chinese soldiers that ambushed us at Chosin that night."

# Chapter Twenty-Five

"Let's sit here awhile longer before we head back up to the house," my uncle said and lowered himself back to a knee in the sand. I nodded and settled in beside him, just a few feet from where we were before. Minutes passed as the sun slid a little lower in the sky.

"We began the night of November 27th with a unit of several hundred men. Months of fierce fighting and merging with various other regiments had our numbers in a constant state of flux. One thing I know for certain though is by the time the 27th became the 28th, we were down to fourteen.

"Marks roused the rest of the men to their feet and the dark shapes moved from the ground to upright positions. Every fiber of my being ached as I stood there, the evening breeze slicing through me.

"Jack was at my side, his face and hands so pale they were almost translucent. Marks leaned against a tree, joined by Buddy and a few of the others. Almost every man had his eyes closed and teeth gritted, fighting through the pain. Even Dwayne abandoned his customary scowl long enough to try and bite back the cold.

"Alright," Marks said, his voice no more than a whisper, "I know we're hurting, but we can't afford to be stupid here. We don't have enough men to use sentries and no firepower if we find anybody. Instead, buddy up and help each other as best you can. Keep an eye out for any kind of shelter, we'll bed down as soon as we can."

"A few nods went up from the group, but for the most part everyone was silent. Marks waited a second for men to choose partners before plodding on with Dwayne by his side.

"We walked for the better part of an hour, the sounds of the Chinese fading into the distance. For a while we all kept an eye out for any form of shelter we could find, but before long we were all just concentrating on putting one foot in front of another. It wasn't long before men began to stumble and eventually two fell to the ground.

"Sarge, we've got to stop and get warm," one of them pleaded, his shock of bright red hair was frozen into a misshapen mass. "I can't stay upright when I can't feel my legs."

"Marks leaned most of his bodyweight on a stick he'd picked up and said, "I know. We have to do something or we're going to freeze to death. Anybody got any ideas?"

"The circle was silent for several minutes before Jack said, "If I remember right, there was a lot of flint in the ground when we passed through. If you guys can fashion together some sort of wind block, we'll go find some and see if we can get a fire started."

"The scowl returned to Dwayne's face as he cast a sideways glance at us, but said nothing.

"Marks nodded once. "Alright."

"Nobody else said a thing.

"It took everything I had to keep moving, but I fell in beside Jack and together we set off. Behind us the men circled up and grabbed a few felled branches, but my expectations were pretty low for whatever they'd come up with in our absence.

"If any North Koreans or Chinese had come up on us right then, we would have just stood there and let them shoot us. It took everything I had to walk and I could tell by the muffled grunts beside me Jack was doing the same.

"I let my mind go blank as we moved along. Not until Jack touched my arm did I notice the rocks scraping beneath my boots. I stopped and watched as he picked up several and examined them.

"Flint?" I asked.

"Hell no, nothing but quartz." He tossed a piece up into the air, then grabbed it and hurled it in front of him. It flew out from him in a straight line and bounced off the ground with a spark before tailing off into the night.

"You see what I just saw?" I asked, reaching for an arm that was already moving forward. He kept his eyes trained on the spot where the spark flew and walked straight to it. With the toe of his boot he poked around for a moment before unslinging the rifle from his shoulder and smashing the butt of it into the ground several times. When he was done, he returned the rifle and filled his pockets until they were bulging.

"As soon as he had all he could carry, I knelt and filled my pockets as well. The prospect of fire brought a bit of renewed vigor to us and the return trip was a little quicker than the way there.

"As we walked, we each grabbed handfuls of whatever dried grasses and moss we found along the way. We returned to find the men had formed a makeshift wall using branches and heavy pine boughs. It curved inward around the shape of a natural clump of trees and all of the men were already huddled behind it, waiting for us.

"Nobody said anything as we formed the grasses into a small pile and Jack removed a large piece of flint from his pocket. He positioned the barrel of his rifle atop the grass and struck the flint down against it over and over. Each time a few small sparks dropped down onto the grass, but it took almost five full minutes for one to catch and begin glowing. As soon as it did, Jack dropped down and blew on it, coaxing it to life as I fed in bits of moss and twigs.

"The moment it began crackling, every man sat and watched with stunned silence. It was the first thing to go our way all night.

"Marks let out a relieved sigh and sent three men to gather as much burning material as they could. Jack and I continued working the fire into a steady blaze and as the men returned, we built two more small fires spaced across the front of the shelter.

"We kept the fires small and screened them by jamming pine boughs into the ground around them. We considered putting more across the top of the flames to thin the smoke, but decided against it.

"Our need for warmth outweighed the need to be covert at that moment."

My uncle stopped short and I could almost see relief on his face. It was as if he were there experiencing the joys of warmth all over again.

"Marks gave first watch to he and Dwayne, which was more to make sure the fires kept burning than to guard for enemies. They thought we were all dead and even if they didn't, we couldn't have fought anybody off anyway.

"Within minutes of lying down, the rest of us were

asleep. Warmth crept back in and by the time I woke up, my body was still cold but at least everything functioned."

My uncle turned his eyes to me and said, "The next page in the book is a small shard of flint. Never had we been so grateful that we knew how to start a fire the old fashioned way.

"When you get old enough, I'll be glad to teach you too."

# Chapter Twenty-Six

"Two men never woke up the next morning. The red haired boy that someone said was named Humphries and another man named Wagner.

"By the morning of the 28th, we were down to twelve."

"We removed Humphries and Wagner's dog tags, but left their bodies there. We positioned them between the fires so it looked like the camp had been for them alone and took off the best we could.

"Front to back, there was myself and Jack. Marks and Dwayne. Buddy and a man named Francis. Two boys from Tennessee named Caldwell and Sims, two more from Indiana name of Sparks and Avery. One from Kentucky named Petersen and one from not far from here named Manus.

"The bitter cold of the morning was every bit as harsh as the night before and within an hour our hands and feet began to turn pale and light blue. Men were dragging their feet and by midday most were leaning against each other just to stay upright."

My uncle paused for a moment to clear his throat and began again. His voice was low, but there was a steeled resolve in it.

"Marks, any idea where we're headed?" I asked after the better part of a day's walking. The going was slow and we hadn't made it very far, but we had been moving just the same.

"South," Marks replied, his voice strained as he leaned on the stick and Dwayne for support.

"And what's south?" Avery asked.

"Hell if I know," Marks replied.

"Hell of a plan we've got there," Buddy muttered.

"Only damn thing I know is the Chinese are north, so we're going south," Marks snapped, exasperation obvious.

"The longer the trek drew on, the weaker we became. Most of us hadn't eaten in well over a day and we weren't dressed for that kind of cold. Many were unable to raise their feet beyond a shuffle and I'm sure you could have hard us clattering along for miles.

"That day we covered at best fifteen miles, much of it ground we had passed through just days earlier. More than once we came across the bodies of fallen soldiers from our unit. The cold had preserved them intact and many of them still wore the same expression they had when they died.

"We took what we could from the men, which was mostly weapons and munitions. They were dressed no better than we were and only a few had any food to speak of on them. We had to limit ourselves to only a couple of hundred rounds of ammunition each, anything more than that became too heavy in our weakened condition.

"That night we made camp in the base of a ravine that backed into a solid rock wall. Wedged against the sides of the ravine we were able to put our backs to it and be sheltered on three sides. Using a couple of long branches and some camouflage shirts taken from fallen soldiers, we formed a roof that made us undetectable from everywhere but right in front.

"We built small fires back against the wall and curled as close to them as we could. Using sticks and thick wads of moss we formed small blocks to keep the light from bouncing off the rock behind us."

My uncle stopped again for a second and I looked up to see his eyes darting to and fro. I could see an internal war waging behind his eyes, but I said nothing.

"Jack and I were first watch that night, Petersen and Manus the second. They came to relieve us at midnight and within minutes I was asleep in a spot they had just vacated.

"It wasn't but a few minutes later that Petersen circled the fires and shook each of us by the shoulder. I awoke with a start to find him kneeling over me, a finger pressed to his lips. Firelight danced across his face, his features drawn taut.

"Without a word he moved on and when everyone was awake he motioned for the fires to be put out. Using the wads of moss and several handfuls of dirt we extinguished the flames and waited as darkness and the cold of the night washed over us.

"A few moments passed before Peterson leaned close to Marks and whispered, "Chinese patrol. No more than a dozen of them from what we can see, no telling how many are in the area."

"Marks nodded and moved forward a few feet to Manus's side. He touched him on the shoulder to let him know he was there and slid his head forward to survey the area.

"The night was still and we could hear them talking amongst each other, their boots scraping on the rocks nearby. They couldn't have been more than a couple of hundred feet away as each of us took up our weapons.

"For the first time in days the cold wasn't an issue as we waited, adrenaline pumping through our bodies.

"After a while, the sounds of the men grew softer and with an audible sigh each of us breathed a little easier. Marks and Manus stayed at the mouth of structure for a few more minutes before they both made their way back to us.

"Marks leaned on his stick and went to a knee as the rest of us circled in around him. "Look men, I know this is the last thing you want to hear but we have to keep moving."

"But sir, they went right past us. Doesn't that mean we're safe here?" Buddy asked.

"Marks shook his head and said, "We were safe here because its night and they couldn't see us. First light they'll be able to spot us right quick."

"So you think they'll stay in the area?" Avery asked.

"Marks shook his head to one side and said, "Most likely. Those were Koreans, not Chinese, which makes me think they're going to be in the area looking for stragglers and looting the dead. If we're here at dawn, somebody's going to find us."

"Marks looked around the circle, but nobody said anything. He glanced across each of our faces and said, "I damned well don't want to do it either, but we've got no choice. Five minutes. Take a piss, grab your weapon, get ready to go."

"We've already got our weapons and can't nobody piss since we haven't had water all day, let's just go now," I said. A few men nodded their heads and I even noticed Dwayne give a shrug of agreement.

"Marks leaned on his stick and rose to his feet. "You men grab those shirts from across the top, pull those sticks down from between the rocks. Somebody sees it in the morning; they'll know we've been here."

"We set off again sometime deep in the night. The sky was inky black and starless and moving was slow. We had to be sure to pick our feet up with every step and work in a single file line to make ourselves as small a target as possible.

"The Korean patrol was moving north to south in the same way we had been, so we set off at an angle towards the southwest. There wasn't much of a trail and it was tough picking our way through the dense forest. Small pockets of snow dotted the forest floor and we had to be careful not to leave any footprints as we trudged along.

"We walked for several hours through the bitter cold, nothing to guide us through the night. With each step our feet grew wearier and our weapons heavier. Avery was the first to stumble, Caldwell soon thereafter.

"Another hour passed as we continued plodding forward, the single file line ditched in favor of the buddy system again. Many were dragging their feet and didn't have the energy to avoid the snow lying on the ground any longer.

"Dawn had just broken into the sky when Jack said, "Sergeant, wait!" in a hushed whisper.

"Jack and I had been near the rear of the group and most of the men stopped and turned to us. The few who didn't turn fell to their knees and sat panting in the morning air.

"I turned to Jack to see what was wrong, but he was already moving through the brush. His steps still seemed easy and I to this day have no idea where he found the energy.

"He walked off to our right thirty or forty yards and disappeared into a pine thicket. When he dropped from sight I walked over after him, but before I got there he emerged back through the pines.

"Waving his left arm in a circle motion he whispered, "Come on" through the trees.

"Many of the men stayed where they were as I walked forward to see what my brother had found. I walked past him through the pines and when I saw it, I almost cried out in excitement.

"Using a newfound strength I joined my brother and motioned for the men to come along. I was grinning as the men rose and began making their way towards us.

"Most of them looked at us like we were crazy as they walked past and I even heard Dwayne mutter, "This better be good" as he helped Marks along.

"When the last of the men had gone, Jack and I turned and followed them through the thicket. I had figured they would go on inside, but each of them stood looking at what Jack had found.

"A cave."

My uncle paused again for another second and I had to turn my head towards him to make sure I had heard right. "A cave?"

My uncle nodded. "Yep.

"The twelve of us stood there for a moment looking at the mouth of the cave that opened from a small rise in the land. It was about four feet in height and the early morning light filtered in, revealing a wide opening inside.

"How *in the hell* did you find this?" Marks asked.

"Jack looked up to the sky and pointed at the trees. "Little trick I picked up back home. If you're in a forest and see an opening, usually means something's there. I was thinking it was a watering hole, got lucky with the cave."

"The men stared at Jack for several seconds before I said, "Um, fellas, we going to get our asses out of the cold here or what?"

"The sound of my voice seemed to break the stillness of the moment and the men filed inside.

"As the day wore on, more natural light filtered in and the cave around us got a little bit bigger. As it did, we pushed further inside, making it over fifty feet back from the opening. Back there, it was almost six feet tall in places and the walls widened to ten feet in diameter.

"We built a fire and before long light was dancing along the cave walls. Avery, Sims and Caldwell fell straight to sleep and within minutes Francis and Buddy joined them.

"Jack and I took our turn to grab wood and by the time we returned the rest of the men were asleep around the fire. We added another armload to the flames and walked back towards the mouth of the cave to stand guard for awhile.

"We sat back about ten feet from the opening with our guns propped in our laps. We leaned against the wall of the cave and it was hard to fight off heavy eyelids as the warmth came towards us.

"It wasn't until Manus shook me awake that I even realized I had fallen asleep. My eyes snapped open and I raised my gun towards the mouth of the cave. Jack was awake and watching me, a half smirk on his face.

"You boys have to come see this," Manus said, slapping me on the shoulder and grinning.

"Jack and I exchanged quizzical looks and followed Manus back into the cave to find another fire sprang up near the first one. All of the men were awake and many of them wore smiles.

"You boys ain't gonna believe what we just found!" Francis called and slapped down hard on a large stack at his side.

"Jack and I moved a little further forward to let the firelight illuminate what it was, then we both stopped cold.

"The room grew quiet around us and Marks said, "You boys know what that is?"

"I nodded and at the same time we both said, "Winn-Orr corn."

"Every head in the room turned and a few jaws dropped.

"How in the world?" Avery said.

"I looked back at them and said, "Winn-Orr is the canning plant in Birch Grove."

"Aren't you boys from..." Manus started to ask, but let his voice trail off."

I could tell when my uncle was breaking from the story because his voice changed. He went from being in the past to the present.

"Page twenty up there is a label from a can of Winn-Orr corn. Winn-Orr closed its doors in the forties and it wasn't easy tracking that label down, but we managed to do it just the same.

"What in the world those cases were doing in that cave I'm not sure. They were dated 1941 so they had probably been stashed there by somebody during the Second World War. They might have been put there by American forces just weeks before and they might have been concealed there by Koreans that had taken them from an abandoned post, I just don't know.

"What I do know that as long as I've lived since, I've never had a meal as delicious as that food from home."

## Chapter Twenty-Seven

My uncle's eyes went glassy as he remembered sitting in the cave and eating that corn. The corners of his lips played up into a smile and for a few moments the lines on his face framed a somewhat fond expression.

He rose and reached down for my hand. I gave it to him and he helped me to my feet. A small breeze crawled across the lake and washed over us and he said, "We should head back up towards the house. I don't want your folks worrying about you."

We turned our backs to the sun as it dipped a little lower in the sky and followed the path back up through the tall grass. My uncle kept my left hand in his and with the right I played at the tops of the saw grass as it blew in the wind.

A few people wandered from the house and we could see them go to their cars and drive away. Many autos still lined the dusty driveway and the calls of voices and laughter grew stronger as we got closer to the house.

We reached the deck and together took a seat on the steps. My uncle patted my knee twice and looked out over the fields.

"All told, we spent three days in that cave. We'd take turns watching the opening in two hour shifts and the rest of the time we spent sleeping or eating every last can of that corn. We all ended up with the squirts from it and by the end that cave smelled something awful, but it didn't matter. We'd go for firewood at night and for the first time in weeks if not months, we were warm and full and well rested.

"The third night we finished the last of the corn and Marks said we should be moving on. The cave had been a perfect place for us to stop and regain our strength and rest up, but it was only temporary.

"So long as we were in that cave we weren't moving. Nobody knew we were alive and the only chance we had of help was if we found it ourselves.

"The last night we took some heavy branches and mosses and formed a half wall across the front of the cave. Behind the wall we lined all the empty cans so that if anyone came in they'd knock them over and alert us. We all slept deep and sound through the night and at dawn we collected our things and moved on.

"A couple of the men tried filling cans with hot coals and carrying them to keep warm, but the tin grew too hot and they were forced to abandon them. Within an hour of waking, it was just us and the elements again.

"For two days we moved at an angle across the terrain, a renewed spirit allowing us to move much faster than before. By day we covered better than twenty miles, at night we bedded down the best we could with no idea where we were.

"On the eve of the second day we heard the sound of gunshots in the distance. We had all taken on a dazed and glassy look from the two days of hard marching, but our nerves were on edge.

"Marks drew us into single file formation and as we moved forward we could smell gunpowder in the air. Moving through the forest we came across a small cluster of Marines. Five stood on alert spread in a half circle with their backs to us, their commander behind them barking orders into a radio.

"We drew up short and waited for several seconds before Marks moved forward and called out, "This is Sergeant Marks with what's left of the 5th Division, United States Army."

"At the sound of his voice, all of the Marines turned with weapons raised in our direction. The commander on the radio jerked his head towards us and said, "Step forward with weapons lowered and identify your numbers."

"Marks had been holding his weapon in front of him in the ready position with his right hand on the butt and his left along the barrel. He grabbed hold of the weapon in his left and held it at his side and walked, hands raised on either side.

"Again, sir, my name is Sergeant Marks, $5^{th}$ Division. I have with me eleven other men, the last of our regiment."

"The commander looked him over for a second and called out, "The rest of you men come out where we can see you."

"The others in his company continued to stare in our direction with weapons raised. Each of us moved forward as Marks had. As we did the Marines would shift their aim from one of us to another.

"The commanding officer watched as we all moved forward. After a moment he said, "You men return to your positions."

"The Marines cast a quick glance at one another and turned back towards the sound of gunfire. The officer walked forward and stuck his hand towards Marks. "Lieutenant Colonel Jacobsen, $3^{rd}$ Division, United States Marine Corp. You say you're from the $5^{th}$ Army?"

"Marks returned the handshake. "Yes sir."

"Jacobsen shook his head and said, "We heard every last one of you had met your maker up at Chosin. How'd you boys get out of there alive?"

"Marks shook his head. "Damn Chinese mowed us down like we weren't even there. They had the perfect ambush set up; we never saw it coming. The few of us here had to swim out of there and damn near died of hypothermia. We've been picking our way along, moving across the country ever since."

"Jacobsen studied Marks for a moment before casting his eyes towards us. He was a solid man with close cropped black hair that was graying around the edges. His face wore the hardened lines of a man that was accustomed to this sort of thing and he wasted no movement in anything he did.

"I don't know what your plans are, but I could sure as hell use some help here."

"Where the hell is here?" Dwayne asked.

"Without turning his head Jacobsen said, "Hagaru, moving back towards Koto-Ri. The Koreans have amassed a hell of a force and are moving straight towards our rally point on the sea."

"Rally point?" Marks asked. "We getting the hell out of here?"

"Jacobsen shook his head. "No, just trying to go about this a different way. The Koreans have put all their forces through here in the south. Plan is for us to get out to the sea and board some carriers, work our way up the coast and come back in above them from the North. Try to cut them off from both the Chinese and their own internal support."

"So what the hell are we all doing here?" Buddy asked.

"We're delaying them as much as we can until our side gets everything in order."

"Everything in order?" Marks asked.

"We have to get all of our soldiers in the area evacuated out of here and we have to give our boys time to dispose of anything we can't take with us. Can't go leaving a stack of weapons for the Commies to use."

"The circle fell silent for a moment as shots continued to ring out in the distance.

"What kind of numbers we up against?" Jack asked.

"They've amassed probably twelve to fifteen thousand," Jacobsen said.

"And how many have we got?" Jack asked.

"Started with about five hundred, little over half of that remain."

"Jack looked out towards the sounds of fire and said, "Regular old Battle of Thermopylae."

"Jacobsen turned and studied Jack for a moment. "Not quite. Every last one of them died. I intend to make it out of here alive."

"Jack matched his gaze. "So what can we do to help?"

"Jacobsen snatched up the radio again and barked, "I've got a dozen able bodied Army soldiers here ready to lend a hand. Who needs the most help right now?"

"The line returned nothing but static for a few seconds before a voice said, "Lieutenant, this is Rose over on the east flank. Half my men are trapped in a ravine under heavy sniper fire. I've got machine gunners trying to get them out, but we can't find the damn shooters. Can these guys help us out?"

"Jacobsen turned his head to us and raised his eyebrows to ask if we could help them. Each of us raised our weapons and Marks said, "Just point us where to go."

"You're going to circle out of here due east for three hundred yards until you come to a ridge line. From there bear south-southeast two hundred yards until you reach a grove of pine trees. After that, just push east until you seem them.

"I'm going to get on the horn and alert everywhere between here and there you're coming, so you boys can move fast. It's over three-quarters of a mile, I'll tell Rose you'll be there in ten minutes."

"Without so much as a word, each of us took off double time in the direction Jacobsen said. As we moved the sound of gunfire grew louder and thicker around us and we could hear men yelling and crying out.

"We reached the ridge line in just over a minute and made the clump of pine trees in about three and a half. An officer emerged from the trees long enough to point us on towards the east and without a word we turned and ran in that direction.

"By the time we reached Rose and the east flank, each of us had sweat running down our faces, panting hard. We found him lying along the top of the ravine on his stomach, his binoculars focused on the opposing wall. Each of us threw ourselves to the ground beside them and edged forward.

"Sergeant Marks, 5th Division, Army," Marks said as he sidled up to Rose. "What's the situation sir?"

"Sumbitches have us hemmed in something fierce," Rose responded. "They have a major force on the far side of the ravine pushing towards us. They've got snipers and gunners over on the far wall picking us off every time we move. I've got machine guns over there on the rocks, but in this low light we can't get a good bead on where the bastards are."

"Rose handed the binoculars to Marks who studied the opposite wall. As he did, Buddy leaned towards Jack and I and said, "Looks a helluva lot like that last situation we were in doesn't it?"

"Jack and I didn't bother to respond, but we both had already been thinking the same thing.

"Marks finished looking over the grounds and said, "What do you need us to do sir?"

"Rose resumed looking through the binoculars and said, "We don't have enough ammunition left to just fire blind at that side of the ravine. We do that; they'll just wait us out and mow us down.

"We need someone to paint 'em for us."

"Paint them?" Dwayne asked.

"A man to Rose's right tossed a box across Rose's back that landed and sent bullets rolling in all directions. ".30 caliber tracer rounds," he said. "Fire from an M-1 just like a regular bullet."

"I'll give my guys in the ravine the sign, and they'll draw out enemy fire," Rose said. "We need your best shooters up here to spot that fire and make an accurate return. From there, our gunner above can take care of them. Slow and tedious, but doing it piecemeal is the only option we've got."

"A few low whistles went up from around us.

"Why can't the gunner just shoot when he sees the return fire?" Sims asked.

"Again," Rose said. "We don't have enough ammo. We have to know that where he's firing is where they are."

He didn't wait for a response before turning to Marks. "Who's your best shooter?"

"Marks looked down the line. "They're all pretty damn good, sir."

"I've got pretty damn good," Rose said. "I need a deadeye."

"Roberts," Marks said, not clarifying which one of us he wanted. We both rose from the dirt and circled around.

"Not you," Marks said, motioning towards me. "Just him."

"For a second I was offended before realizing he was right. I unslung the rifle from my shoulder and ejected the round in the chamber. The man to Rose's right, Dixson, gave Jack and I both a handful of shells and we loaded them in.

"Rose moved back a few feet from the edge and knelt down in the dirt. Using his finger he drew a rough outline of the ravine below and outlined where we were, where the men were and where he believed the shooters to be hiding.

"Now I've told the boys above to be ready, we'll be going live in just a second. Get into position, and I'll give my guys below the signal."

"Jack crawled up to the spot Rose was just in and got situated. I laid my rifle on the ground beside him, a half dozen tracer rounds in the dirt by my knee.

"For a moment everybody waited in tense silence as Jack got himself ready before nodding. "Give the word."

"Rose passed the command on through his radio and a moment later the opposite embankment came up. A half dozen muzzle flashes lit up the brush like firelights at dusk.

"I looked back and forth between Jack and the ravine several times before he squeezed the trigger. The second he did a bright yellow light burst forth, shooting through the air like a flare gun. It hit right where some of the flashes were coming from, followed by a burst of machine gun fire from overhead.

"Nice," Marks muttered.

"Again," Jack said, ignoring the comment as he swapped out rifles.

"Kneeling beside him, I loaded a fresh round into the chamber and placed the gun back beside him. Again the opposite wall lit up with fire as Jack cited in and let fly.

"For the second time in as many minutes, the machine fun above cut down a Korean sniper.

My grandfather breathed out and I could tell he was again breaking from the action in his head. He used the same detached voice he used that meant he wasn't back there any longer, but he wasn't really with me either.

It was if he was a bystander in both worlds.

"All told, Jack traced out five different snipers. By the time he was done, the rest of the Marine regiment was able to walk out of that ravine.

"When they got there, Rose shook his hand and Marks clapped him on the shoulder. Buddy gave him a bear hug and the rest of our group joked about how the Army boys came along and helped out the Marines.

"Even Dwayne managed to give him a nod."

My uncle motioned back towards the bag sitting on the ground and said, "Why don't you go grab that for us?"

I sprang to my feet and jogged to the book hidden inside the knapsack as my feet made loud clomping sounds along the floorboards. Lifting the whole thing from the ground, I carried it to my uncle.

He placed it across his lap and opened it back to our previous spot before flipping through the pages we covered down by the water. I saw the homemade camouflage, the Chinese armband, and the corn label all pass by in a blur.

My uncle turned his eyes up towards me and said, "The next page is a .30 caliber tracer round for an M-1."

As he spoke he flipped the page over and revealed a shell not much different than the one I had seen before.

Turning back towards the water my uncle paused for several long moments, taking in the sights around us.

"The next page is where things start to get interesting."

## Chapter Twenty-Eight

Interesting.

The dictionary defines interesting as anything that's engaging or exciting and holding the attention or curiosity. According to that definition, every word my uncle had uttered up to that point could qualify as interesting.

I've often wondered why my uncle chose to use the word interesting when describing the events that were to come. It wasn't until I was much older that I understood what he was trying to say.

Common English syntax has taught me that there is a secondary form of the word, one that my uncle had in mind when he said things were about to get interesting. Instead of using it as a descriptor, it can be used in terms of a state of affairs.

When my uncle said things were about to get interesting, he was politely telling me that things were about to go to hell.

"That day in the ravine pretty well summed up our entire road from Hagaru to Koto-Ri," my uncle said as we sat and watched the sun slip a little lower in the sky. "At least, what I assume the rest of the road from Hagaru to Koto-Ri consisted of."

I turned my head towards him and started to mouth a question, but his upraised hand stopped me.

"Let me get to it," he said. "Jacobsen was right about the impending force of the Korean Army bearing down on us. He was very wrong however about the numbers they had.

"We'd plant ambushes, use explosives, do anything we could to slow them down. Each day they'd return with a fresh wave of soldiers even heavier than the one before.

"Worse yet, every day our delaying action became a little less delaying. The first couple of go-rounds we'd entrench by night and maintain those positions by day. Within a week we weren't even bothering to entrench ourselves. We'd take up positions behind whatever cover we could find and always be prepared to move on less than two minutes notice.

"We'd heard rumors before about the rivalry between the different factions of the military, but the Marines assimilated us in as their own. Caldwell said it was because Jack saved their asses that first day; I tend to believe it was because we had an enemy facing us that was far greater than some petty rivalry.

"The second day we were there we lost Francis and Avery, the third day Sparks, the fifth day Petersen. By the end of the week there were only eight of us left from the entire 5<sup>th</sup> Division, from all those boys we had joined up with at Fort Campbell.

"Our losses were on par with the losses of the Marines around us. Each day a handful more soldiers fell and each day we'd collect their dog tags and move on the best we could. The Koreans looted and pillaged the bodies where they lay and more than once tried to use them as bait to lure us out of our positions."

My uncle paused for a second and exhaled. His elbows rested on his knees and he dropped his head and stared at the ground between his feet for a full minute before continuing with the story.

"The eighth day saw the rising of the coldest sun I have ever felt. It was there and gave a faint light, but there was no warmth in it. I couldn't help but remember being told to drop everything we didn't need so many months before and thinking I'd give anything to have all that winter gear with me.

"We had been in a steady backwards motion since we joined the Marines, each day our flight a little faster as the Koreans drew in closer.

"Our attention was so focused on covering our rear, we didn't realize that by midday we had backed ourselves into a corner. Our path was following a ridgeline moving east, never realizing it ended in a sharp canyon. The only options for us were to move due north and try to outrun the encroaching Koreans or to maneuver the canyon.

"Many of our men were wounded and the rest of us were exhausted, near starvation and freezing. Jacobsen convened with his officers and decided the only reasonable action we could take would be to head north. He would leave behind a series of machine gunners, fanned out from the corner of the canyon to the northwest. By arranging them in a sweeping pattern, it would afford the most time to get everyone out.

"Jacobsen asked each of his Lieutenants to pick their best gunners and to have them report to him as soon as possible for instructions. Rose picked two boys from his outfit and had them report while the rest of us helped get everyone ready for the evacuation."

My uncle paused again, his second time in the last couple of minutes. He hadn't done that the entire time he had been telling me the story and I could sense this must be something important.

"Jack and I had been helping a group of wounded soldiers along when Marks flagged us down. He asked us if he could have a word in private and we both knew it couldn't be good.

"When we were out of earshot, Marks looked at us and asked, "Either one of you boys ever fire a machine gun before?"

"We shook our head in unison, neither saying a word.

"Jacobsen has asked for a tenth gunner team to finish out the fan. He says he can't very well call on a single Lieutenant for another team and has asked that it come from us.

"There are only eight of us for crying out loud!" I objected.

"Marks nodded his head. "I know it. Damn it I know it. Problem is, I can't turn down an indirect order from a much higher ranking officer and we can't have word getting out that the Marines had to save the Army's asses.

"You boys feeling up to this?"

"Jack stared past Marks towards the horizon as I kicked at the ground with the toe of my boot. A full minute passed before Jack asked, "So how does this work?"

"I knew full well there was no way we could or would turn down that assignment, but him saying it out loud was one of the hardest things I ever had to hear.

"Marks looked from Jack to me and said, "One gun per team. One does the shooting; the other does the spotting and ammunition shagging."

"Ammunition shagging?" I asked.

"Machine guns chew through bullets like you wouldn't believe. In the event you run out, he runs to the other teams and gets more."

"Aren't we all running low on ammunition?"

"Marks ran a hand over the back of his scalp and turned away for a moment. He looked back at us and said, "Look, I'm not going to sugarcoat this for you. It's a shit draw and I hate that I have to leave my two best soldiers behind like this, but it's all we've got.

"All I can tell you is fire at anything moving and when that's over, run like hell."

"Each of us nodded again, somewhat thankful for the matter-of-fact manner Marks gave us the news.

"So where are we positioned?" Jack asked.

"Marks turned again and pointed to a spot no more than fifty yards from where we were standing. "You're on the corner of the ravine. You will be the last ones out and have the furthest to go to get there."

"Jack looked up to the sky for a moment and I cursed under my breath. Nobody said anything else for a long while.

"Just bring us the damn gun," I finally said. "We'll do what we can."

"Marks nodded and shook each of our hands, then saluted us both. We returned the salute and walked over where we were to be positioned.

"A Marine brought us our machine gun and hundreds of rounds of ammunition. He shook each of our hands and thanked us for what we were doing and moved to join the others heading north.

"You do the shooting, I'll do the running and spotting," Jack said once the Marine was gone. I have no idea why he decided to do it that way, but I didn't say anything against it.

"The next half hour or so we spent readying ourselves for the oncoming Koreans. I checked and rechecked the gun, familiarizing myself with the bolt action and the in feed of bullets. Jack walked back and forth between us and the nearest gun team, between us and the best route north.

"Once we were both comfortable with everything, we waited. Moments passed with each of us lying there, waiting for what we were certain would be our death. I thought of a hundred different things I could have or maybe should have said to my brother, but I didn't say any of them. We both lay in silence, knowing what the other was thinking.

"Sometimes you can't find the words.

"Sometimes you don't need them.

"It took about an hour for the Koreans to catch up with us. We were well concealed between two large trees with a clump of low growing brush in front of us.

"The first group of soldiers to come through was no doubt scouts, just a handful at best. They strolled along with their weapons loose in front of them, paying very little heed to their surroundings. Two of them broke off and veered to the right, towards where Jack and I lay.

"A bundle of nerves, my finger began to tighten on the trigger, but Jack laid a hand on my arm and said, "Not yet. If we fire before the main force is here, we'll alert them to where we are."

"But isn't that the idea? To make them slow down and buy us some time?"

"Jack shook his head. "Yeah, but if we're going to do this let's do it right. A dead Korean is better than a slow moving one."

"We watched as the two scouts in front of us walked past where we lay and went to the edge of the cliff. They stood side by side with their backs to us, each of them looking down over the edge.

"Stay right here," Jack whispered and rose from beside me. Turning my head I watched as he crept over towards them before breaking into a full sprint.

"They heard the thudding of his boots as he ran and spun around just as he reached them. Without warning he dove feet first and caught them both square in the chest with a boot. Neither one made more than a muffled grunt as they tumbled backwards over the cliff.

"Jack lay on his back where he had landed for a few moments, then picked himself and jogged back, shaking his head as he went. He dropped back down beside me and stared over the ground as if nothing had happened.

"I peered out over the sight of the machine gun and whispered, "One of these days you're going to have show me that move."

"I looked over to see a half smile cross his face. "You liked that huh?"

"We both smiled out at the quiet forest, waiting for the Koreans to show up.

"Within minutes, they had.

"The main body of the Korean advancement was arranged six or seven across in rows marching through the forest. I'm assuming they had similar detachments fanned out in a wide arc, but all I could see was the group right in front of us.

"Let them get as close as possible," Jack whispered beside me. "We need to mow down as many of these bastards as we can while we still have the element of surprise."

"I nodded and watched as row after row came into sight. Beside me Jack placed both his and my M-1 on either shoulder and slid the barrels forward so they were facing the oncoming Koreans.

"We waited for them to draw a little closer, but we never had the chance. Off to the right one of the gunners started firing and the sound jolted the Koreans to life. They jerked around towards the sound and many raised their weapons.

"As soon as I heard the sound of gunfire, I squeezed the trigger as round after round burst forth from my gun. With each passing bullet the gun kicked in my hands and I squeezed it a little tighter. Beside me Jack fired quick rounds from each our rifles, then reloaded and fired again.

"As I held the trigger and swept the gun from side to side, I could see Koreans catching bullets and jolting to the ground. Many of them moved in jerked motions and looked as if they had been electrocuted as one after another fell.

"Some scrambled backwards for cover, others dove behind bodies already down, many stayed where they were and tried to find out where the shooting was coming from.

"The gun clicked several empty sounds and I grabbed another sleeve of bullets from the ground and slammed it into the feed. Sweat dripped from nose and my shirt clung damp to me as adrenaline coursed through my entire body.

"The first sleeve of bullets caught the Koreans by surprise and almost every one found its mark. By the time I got the second sleeve loaded many had taken cover and it took much greater care to hit a target. Jack continued to fire off single shots and every so often I could hear him grunt meaning he'd gotten another one.

"The second sleeve went almost as fast as the first one as I continued to fire at anything moving in front of me. As I broke to load the third sleeve Jack said, "Shit, where'd the other gun go?"

"We both pulled up for just a second and could tell there was no longer any machine gun fire coming from the right. I slid the sleeve into the gun and said, "I'll stay here and cover you, you go see what's going on."

"I slid back down to the stone slab I was using as a base and fired shot after shot as Jack swung wide to the right. The Koreans were beginning to return heavy fire and all around me leaves and branches shattered as bullets ripped through them.

"A minute or two later I heard the sound of machine gun fire pick up again and I knew that either the other team had gotten more ammunition or Jack had taken over for them. In unison we fired rounds into forest, holding the Koreans at bay."

My uncle paused as the front door swung open and another partygoer I had never met sauntered out and headed towards his car. He cast the two of us a look of disgust and made a point to bump each of us as he walked off the front porch, but said nothing.

My uncle shook his head and waited until the man was in his car and said, "We stayed like that for over an hour. I figured when Jack never came back that he must have taken over for the other gunners. The problem with that was I didn't have anybody left to shag bullets for me.

"The first four sleeves went by fast, the next two I was pretty careful with. By the last sleeve, I only fired if I knew I could score a direct kill.

"The afternoon soon started to give way to evening and Jack slid in beside me. "Those two over there didn't make it. Looks like random shots got them; otherwise the Koreans would have taken the gun."

"I continued firing slow and steady, my eyes trained forward the entire time. "How you looking on ammunition?" I asked.

"Getting low, you?"

"Damn near out."

"Jack grabbed the M-1s and fired another couple of rounds. "I'm not hearing much activity from the other gunners down there. Either they've been hit or they've gotten out of here. I'm going to go back down there for a few more minutes and drive back what I can. You finish your sleeve and then let's get the hell out of here."

"It's a plan," I said and snapped off another round.

"Jack disappeared into the trees and a few moments later I could hear the gun pick up again. I finished the last of my sleeves and rose to go, but my upper body wouldn't move.

"Lying there all that time motionless with the last sleeve, my body temperature had dropped. The sweat that was coating my arms had frozen solid to the rock slab beneath me.

"My shirt and arms were frozen to the rock and my hands were frozen to the gun.

"Jack finished his firing beside me and I heard his gun grow silent. A few moments of inactivity passed as I tried to wrench myself free from the rock, each time the skin on my forearm pulling a little more.

"What the hell are you doing? Let's go!" Jack said from behind me.

"I turned my head towards him and said, "You go on ahead, I'll be there in just a second."

"I could hear the sound of Korean voices growing closer and looked up to see their shapes looming in the growing darkness. I tugged again at the ground and my right arm tore itself free, leaving most of the skin behind. Warm blood ran from my forearm and I tried as much as I could to use it to free my left arm from the ground.

"With another loud and forceful grunt I managed to pull my left arm free, leaving behind another chunk of flesh. No such luck releasing the gun though, the unwieldy implement frozen tight.

"I retreated as fast as I could, the voices of Koreans growing closer with each passing second. The machine gun was heavy and awkward as I tried to run with both hands gripping it.

"Jesus, what happened?" Jack asked.

"I told you to leave me be," I said as I continued to struggle with the gun. "My hands are frozen."

"Jack grabbed me and said, "Stop for a second." I did what I was told and watched as he unzipped his pants and removed himself.

"I knew what he was going to do, but wasn't the happiest about it. I knew I would never make it away from the Koreans stuck to that gun, so I held my arms out and closed my eyes as he relieved himself.

"The warm urine soaked between my fingers and within seconds I was able to pry my left hand free. Using my left to rub warmth into the right I wrenched my fingers free of the cold steel.

"Now get rid of that thing and let's go!" Jack whispered. Turning on the ball of my foot I slung the gun as far over the cliff as I could.

"We paused just a second to listen and when no sound returned, we ran hard towards the north. My feet ached and the cold air clawed at my lungs, but we continued to run as hard as we could."

My uncle paused for a moment and licked his lips. "How those Koreans had swung around in front of us I'll never know. Jack and I discussed it later and figured the other gunners must have bailed early or been killed because within half a mile we were face to face with hundreds of Korean soldiers.

"They stood with torches lit and guns aimed at us as we rounded a bend in the path almost like they knew we were coming. Both of us pulled up and looked around for some avenue of escape, but there was nothing.

"We both stopped and raised our hands high above our heads. Neither said a word and as we stood there the Koreans began cheering. Many fired rounds into the air and I thought we were done for.

"A man I assumed to be their commander, a man in khaki pants and a tall helmet, walked forward and looked us up and down. He wore a smug smile on his face and spoke in Korean as he leaned in and sniffed me, then made a face. I have no idea what he was saying, but at the end of each sentence he and his men would laugh.

"After a few minutes of this he pointed at us and two men with rifles stepped forward. The first slammed the butt of his gun into Jack's stomach, bending him in half as he gasped for air.

"I started to say something in protest but before it got out the second man's gun slammed into my jaw. Two teeth flew from my open mouth and blood began running down the back of my throat."

Pointing to the page in front of us, a single tooth pressed into the middle of it, my uncle said, "This isn't one of the teeth I lost that night but rather one I'd lose a little while later. That blow loosened most of them on the right side of my mouth and it was a wonder I managed to keep any at all.

"Looking back, our only options were to face the Koreans or throw ourselves over the edge of the cliff and hope for the best. Sitting here now I guess we made the right decision. Sure took a hell of a long time for us to realize it though."

# Chapter Twenty-Nine

My uncle reached down and pushed back the sleeve of his shirt. He bunched it with the sleeve of his dress uniform and slid them both several inches up his forearm. He turned his exposed wrist over for me to see and said, "See these scars here?

"That night the Koreans bound our wrists with the coarsest rope I've ever seen. It was small enough to pull tight and thick enough to withstand whatever struggles we gave against it.

"The Koreans stood and laughed at my bleeding face and Jack doubled over for a few seconds before their commanding officer barked some orders. Men scurried back and forth and within seconds others were jerking us upright and forcing our hands behind our backs. They made us stand straight with eyes forward and put a gun to the base of our skull to ensure we did just that.

"The other men returned and bound our hands behind us. They took pleasure in tightening the ropes as much as they could and twisted the braids into our wrists as they went. By the time we pushed off I could feel blood dripping down the back of my hands.

"For our part, no matter how hard they tried neither one of us uttered a sound.

"The bulk of the Koreans went on ahead, with only a few in the rear to walk with us. They took turns prodding with their guns or kicking us, though we neither said anything.

"We walked onward several hours into the night like that, the Koreans pushing forward after the fleeing Marines. It wasn't until the moon was bright overhead that we stopped for the night. By the time we did I was nothing short of exhausted. My shoulders ached from being forced back so far. My hands were going numb from being exposed and I could feel the blood dried and crusted to my fingers.

"That first night they placed both of us on either side of a tree and tied us in place. They pounded stakes into the bark a foot or two above our heads and pinned our wrists to them so that we had to stand the entire night with our hands overhead.

"They posted a guard to stay with us that rotated every hour or so. Each time a new guard would come along they'd spend a few minutes working us over. Swift kicks or punches to our exposed ribs or stomach before heading off to take a nap. They knew there was nothing we could do, no use in missing valuable sleep over two prisoners that wouldn't last the week anyway.

"By the time daylight came my hands were pale blue. They cut our hands down from over our heads and again forced them behind our bodies and retied them. I didn't even mind them chewing into the skin this time as the blood was welcomed warmth.

"That day too we marched onward with Korean guards pushing us along. They didn't seem as interested in tormenting us as they had the night before and by midday they seemed to have pretty well tired of it.

"We walked along side by side for the entirety of that day as well, neither of us saying a word. We were both beyond exhaustion and the only thing I could do to keep my mind occupied was concentrate on squeezing as much life as possible back into my hands and the throbbing pain in the side of my jaw. I kept running my tongue over the hole where those two teeth had been and could feel at least three more were loose to the touch.

"The second night they put us on either side of a tree and forced us to sit. They wrapped a long rope several times around the both of us and left us be. I guess by that point they figured if we didn't at least sleep a little, we'd die before we could be any good to them.

"That night I didn't notice the cold or the pain as I slid into a deep and instantaneous sleep. It was probably more like passing out, but either way I didn't move an inch until the blast awoke the camp just before dawn the next morning."

My uncle paused for a second and cleared his throat and I turned my head towards him. "The blast?"

My uncle bobbed his head. "Whenever the military has to evacuate an area and can't take something with them, they destroy it so the enemy can't use it.

"That morning we were awoke by one of the loudest blasts I've ever heard. The ground trembled beneath us and I could feel tremors from the base of the tree running the length of my spine.

"My head shot up and my eyes snapped open as I thought our forces had come for us, but that hope was soon replaced by the sinking realization that our men were hopping on a ship and heading elsewhere. Nobody knew where we were and nobody was around to even bother looking."

Uncle Cat paused for a moment, then said, "When the blast went off the camp sprung to life. The commander stormed around shouting orders and soldiers ran back and forth. Nobody seemed to notice us sitting there against the tree and for a long time I hoped they'd just run off and leave us.

"The commander screamed more orders at his men and marched himself back into his tent. The camp continued to bustle and after a few moments he reemerged and pointed to the two of us on the ground.

"A sinking feeling filled my stomach as a man marched towards us and pulled a long knife from his sheath. He came right at us and raised the knife over his head and in one motion slashed through each of the ropes binding us to the tree. Sheathing the knife, he grabbed each of us by the shirt collar, hauled us to our feet, and took us to the commander's quarters.

"The flaps of the tent hung open and we stepped just inside and stood with our shoulders touching. By doing so we blocked the sun coming into the room and the commander had to stop and squint up at us.

"He said something in Korean and when neither of us responded he said, "Am I to believe you're not answering because you don't speak Korean or because you're ignoring me?"

"His sudden use of English caught us both a little off guard, but still neither of us spoke.

"I hope for your sake that it's because you don't speak Korean. Ignoring me would be very bad." As he talked he stood and moved around the desk and perched himself in front of it, one leg on the ground and the other hanging limp in front of him.

"Jack gave his head a half cock and slid his eyes towards me. I did the same and motioned towards the

Korean with my eyes. My jaw was still throbbing and I didn't trust what my voice would sound like.

"We don't speak Korean," Jack said in no more than a whisper.

"The man nodded. "As I'm sure you know, I am the officer in charge here, General Tsan."

"He paused and watched for some form of recognition from us, but when we gave him nothing he continued.

"What you might not know is why I haven't killed you yet. The answer is two very simple reasons. First is you could be a very good source of information for me. Second, you have both survived this far meaning you must be strong men. Part of our job here isn't just to stop you, but to persuade to join our side."

"Your side?" I croaked out without thinking.

"A faint smile crossed the general's lips at the sound of my voice and he said, "Communism of course.

"But before we get to that, I intend to use you for the first purpose I mentioned. You two want to start by telling me what that was just a little bit ago?"

"A full minute passed with neither of us saying a word. The general looked from one face to another before picking up a long steel blade from his desk. "I will ask this once more. What was that explosion?"

"I weighed in my head what the consequences were for the information were we to give it to him. There was nothing he could do with the data after the fact and there was a whole lot he could do to us for not telling him. I opened my mouth to speak but apparently Jack had reached the same decision.

"The Marines were clearing their trail," he said.

"Clearing their trail?" the general asked.

"Ridding themselves of anything they couldn't carry on board or move." As Jack spoke he maintained a low voice that dripped with disdain and kept his eyes locked on the back wall.

"The general nodded. "I had figured as much. You Americans think your gear is so superior that we'll go diving for your scraps like dogs."

"There was nothing resembling a question in there and we both remained silent.

"The general studied us for another moment and said, "I like you two. You have a certain confidence about you that as an opposing general I loathe, but as your future leader I enjoy."

"My brow furrowed at his last statement, but he continued as if he didn't notice.

"As of this morning, I am having you two sent to join up along the trail back to Hagaru. From there you'll head north into one of our indoctrination camps. If everything goes well, I'll see you both back here in a few months wearing the other flag with red, white and blue in it."

"He snapped something out in Korean and the man with the knife reached in and pulled us out. He shoved us towards the back of camp, then passed us along to two young soldiers. Neither one was even as old as we were, but the automatic weapons in their hands made them appear much more senior.

"Both of them circled around and pressed a gun to our back. Using the tips of their barrels they spurred us forward for what turned out to be the better part of the day. Each time we tried to pull forward a little to get past the gun point, they would speed up and jab us even harder.

"Just before nightfall we came upon an enormous cluster of people camped by a river. The rising moon cast a pale light over the scene and as we approached we could see many people huddled together and Korean soldiers standing sentry around them with guns in hand.

"Our two handlers gave us one last shove into the mass of people before joining the ranks of the other soldiers standing guard. They spoke to no one as they took their spot and nobody moved their heads from the surrounding areas to acknowledge their presence.

"Jack and I stumbled forward into the group and stood together surveying the crowd.

"You see anybody at all we know?" I asked as I scanned faces.

"Not a soul," Jack said as he did the same.

"A few minutes passed as we continued to scan the grounds before a voice said, "Boys, why don't you come join us?"

"We both turned our heads to see an old man sitting cross legged on the ground as several older women and a few children crowded in around him. Most were pressed tight against one another and a few had even managed to find sleep.

"Jack and I glanced at each other before making our way towards him. We moved slow and took up seats on the outside of the group.

"The old man reached forward and said, "You boys lean in here and we'll help you out of those ropes. I can see from here they must be cutting into your skin."

"I glanced down to notice the dried blood still caked on my hands from the walk the day before. I extended my wrists towards him and his delicate old fingers deftly untied the Korean knots. Jack leaned forward and did the same and within minutes we were free from our physical bindings.

"Thank you mister," Jack said, rubbing each of his wrists.

"The old man leaned forward again and said, "Name's Mercer. Reverend Mercer." As he spoke he extended his hand and each of us shook it.

"Roberts," Jack said. "I'm Jack and this here is Cat."

"Mercer looked from one to another of us and said, "You boys must be freezing."

"Jack ignored the statement and looked around the camp. "Who are all these people? Where did they come from? Where are they going?"

"The reverend dismissed the questions with a wave of his hand. "There will be time for all of that. Trust me; there will be plenty of time. For now, you boys must be freezing."

"Mercer reached into his jacket and pulled two large handfuls of straw. He handed one to each of us and said, "Use it as stuffing to keep warm. Use anything you can as stuffing. Leaves, grasses, rags. Straw works the best though."

"Jack and I looked at the wads of straw in our hands and I asked, "If this stuff is so valuable, why are you giving it away?"

"I'm not, I'm recycling it."

"Recycling?"

"Mercer sighed. "Let's just say the original owner won't be needing it anymore."

"Jack and I each nodded as Mercer nestled himself down lower with the people around him.

"Like I said, there will be plenty of time for everything tomorrow. Tonight, you boys get warm and get some sleep."

My uncle stopped again and his breathing slowed a beat. I could tell he was back to the present and I looked up to see his eyes darting back and forth across the water.

"Neither one of us really knew what to make of Reverend Mercer that first night. We talked it over a little and decided he probably knew what we were about to go through better than us and did as he suggested.

"That evening I collected several large handfuls of straw along with some Aspen leaves and dried grasses. It wasn't like sitting next to a crackling fire, but it did help insulate.

"Jack and I moved to as close to the center of camp as we could and found a free spot. Our decision to sit in the middle had nothing to do with stealing warmth, but spoke more to the fact that it gave us ample warning in every direction should the guards decide to get any ideas.

"We sat with our backs to each other and despite itching a little bit from the straw, I did warm enough to find some sleep."

Uncle Cat reached down and with his scarred wrist still exposed flipped the page.

"Page 23," he said, "is nothing more than ordinary straw.

"Yet another very simple item that saved my life that night, and many nights thereafter."

## Chapter Thirty

"The next morning we were awoke by the sounds of gunfire. Jack and I both jumped to our feet as the people around us remained on the ground and tried to shake themselves awake. Faint grey light streaked the skies and it was tough to see everything that was going on around us.

"You boys calm down," an old woman said as she hefted herself to her feet. She had to be in her early sixties with thick grey hair hanging in curls. Her cheeks were plump and red from the cold air. "That's how they wake us up every morning. Kind of a daily reminder that we're waking up here with them instead of at home in our beds.

"As if we could forget."

"She finished climbing to her feet and dusted herself off. "Josephine Moore. *Sister* Josephine Moore."

"Ma'am," I responded, dipping my head down. "This is my brother Jack and I'm Richard, but you can call me Cat."

"Josephine nodded. "I'm glad to know you but awful sorry we met. They just bring you boys in?"

"Yes ma'am, last night," Jack said.

"As we talked another blast of gunfire went into the air and the ground began to scurry with activity.

"The first burst is to let folks know it's time to get up, the second is to let us know it's time to get moving," Josephine said.

"People began milling by us, many of them still entrenched in sleep. Their eyes were half open and they stumbled forward without lifting their feet from the ground.

"We stood a moment and watched the people file by and I turned to Josephine and asked, "Who are all you people? Why are you here?"

"As I spoke Reverend Mercer approached and said, "Come now, we can discuss this on the road."

"We joined the massive throng of people moving along and for a while we marched in silence. Guards walked with us every fifty feet or so and often they would shove or prod along a prisoner they felt wasn't moving fast enough. Sometimes they did it just for fun.

"A few miles into the journey the guards allowed themselves to fall behind and once they did, Mercer began to speak.

"'The first and last hour or so of each day the guards walk beside us," he said. "During those times the most officers are around and they have to be seen poking us along, pushing us for better time. During the middle of the day, most of the officers ride ahead to scout or meet or do whatever it is they do.

"Once they're gone the soldiers tend to fall back behind us. So long as we keep up a steady pace, they don't seem to mind too much."

"And what are they doing in the rear all that time?" Jack asked.

"Josephine cast a sideways glance at him and said, "Just about everything you can imagine they would. Drinking, gambling, beating prisoners for sport. It starts pretty mild, but the more they drink the more intense it gets."

"For a few long minutes silence filled the air.

"So who exactly are all you people?" I asked.

"We are here as a part of a missionary group from Park City, Utah," Mercer said. "Sister Moore and I came out four years ago to bring the word of the Lord to the people of South Korea. There were eleven us then, there are four of us left."

"Where were you folks located?" Jack asked.

"Spent the first two years traveling from village to village," Josephine said. "It was tough going, especially for a group as large as ours. Every day was a struggle to find food and shelter and let's just say the people were less than receptive to our being here."

"It's not that they were bad people," Mercer said, "they were just a product of their environment. Many of them have spent their lives living in fear of one enemy or another. When we came along with our funny language and clothes, they assumed we intended to harm them."

"We lost five people those first two years to instances of people assuming and reacting," Josephine said. "Folks would open fire or lay booby traps and we would walk right into it. All we could do was bury our friends, pray for their souls and continue to plug along."

"Silence again settled in for a second before I asked, "So what happened? I'm assuming it got better or you wouldn't still be here."

"As Sister Moore said," Mercer said, "that was our life for the first two years. After that though, something magical happened. We came across a village due south of Seoul known as Pi-Kon. The people there were so exhausted from living in fear and perpetual uprising that they decided to trust us.

"They let us into their village and their homes and within days the Lord took over. People listened to His teachings, learned from His word and began to live in the way the Bible advocates. We were able to build a church and a school there, permanent homes for our staff to live in.

"The last two years have been good."

"We waited a moment to see if he would continue the narrative, but when he said nothing I prompted, "So what happened?"

"Mercer tossed his hand out in a sweeping motion. "This happened. We were a peaceful village and hoped we could be left free of this awful conflict. As history has shown though, war touches everything."

"Josephine snorted. "Destroys might be a better word."

"Mercer nodded. "Just the same, the war found us. When the North Koreans came we were in church, all of us. We were deep in prayer and they burst through the door and demanded we exit to the streets. No questions were asked, no belongings were gathered. They herded us outside and told us to start walking. Anybody that disobeyed was shot on the spot."

"How long ago was that?" Jack asked.

"That was two weeks and half a village ago," Josephine said. "We began as a hundred and fifty. We're now a dozen or so over fifty."

"I surveyed the group and said, "How can that be? There must be three or four hundred people here."

"Other villages," Mercer said. "Errant captured soldiers like you, people they come across on the roadways. They don't care. Anybody that isn't North Korean is shuttled along."

"Sounds just like Hitler in Germany," I said, shaking my head at the thought.

"Josephine nodded and said, "Odds are that's the model they're using. Eradicate the world of everyone else and then you've only got yourself to worry about."

"We spent the rest of the afternoon moving forward, each side asking the others questions about the state of things and how we came to be where we were. For the most part the guards left us alone and the pace remained steady.

"Many of the people with us were much older and by late afternoon were being helped along. Each time somebody would stumble one of us would take them by the arm, speaking words of encouragement as we went.

"The cold remained stiff and bitter and we took turns moving to the outside of the pack to take in more insulation. At first I was reluctant to take my turn, but after several hours in the icy breeze I too was stuffing handfuls of dead leaves into my fatigues."

My uncle paused for a second and one by one extended his legs forward to stretch them. His knees gave small popping sounds as they reached full extension and were returned to their place on the front steps.

"As the afternoon wore on the sky grew a dimmer shade of gray. The sun never really came out at all, but it was light. You know the sort of day I'm describing.

"We continued to push down the path, each of us with an elder draped across either shoulder. I myself was helping two women that didn't weigh much more than ninety pounds apiece. As we walked I would by accident lift them from the ground for several feet at a time and I couldn't help but think that they didn't have much time left.

"In helping the women along I hadn't been paying a lot of attention to the group as a whole and looked up to find a small group of soldiers had found their way back to us. There were four of them huddled close and they had the nervous mannerisms of somebody that was up to something.

"We hear you boys just got in last night," one of the men said. He was thin and wiry with a patchy red beard jutting from a well defined jaw bone.

"That's right," Jack said, glancing at them and returning his gaze to the front.

"He looked at Jack and then me and motioned towards my face. "That would explain your jaw. Thing hurt as bad as it looks?"

"Truth was it hurt like hell and had I not been plodding through frigid temperatures, it might have been unbearable. "Not too bad," was all I said though.

"A second man swung a quick glance from side to side. "Listen, we're fixing to make a run for it here and were wondering if you wanted in."

"I didn't say a word, deferring to Jack. He set his jaw and pretended to ponder for a second, but I could tell his mind was already made up.

"No thanks," Jack said and shifted the man on his right shoulder a little bit.

"Red Beard snapped his stare towards Jack and said, "Why not?" in a hostile whisper.

"Jack shook his head and said, "I don't have enough information. I don't know how the guards operate, what kind of weapons they have or even where the hell we are. If a move's to be made, the time has to be right."

"The second man looked at Jack and said, "We have all that information! We can do this!"

"Jack shook his head. "No you can't and you know it. All four of you are thin and ragged from walking. I don't know how long you've been here, but if I had to guess I'd say at least a month. You've just been waiting for some nice strong legs and backs to come along in case you need help."

"A third man, a black man with a bald head said, "What about loyalty soldier? We need you!"

"Jack shook his head. "Right now, these people need us more."

"Red Beard spat on the ground in Jack's direction and turned his fiery eyes towards me. "You with him?"

"I am," I said, and nothing more.

"The group passed a collective angry glance in our direction and the second man said, "For your information, we don't need you. We're doing this with or without you; we just thought we'd extend the invitation. Thought we had some brothers in arms back here."

"I heard Josephine smirk beside me, but nobody said anything. Another moment or two passed before they moved on ahead again. Silence fell over the group and for a hundred yards or so nobody said a word.

"Thank you," Mercer said.

"Jack nodded. "We did it as much for ourselves as for you folks. Don't get me wrong, we're happy to help as much as we can, but those men reek of desperation. Desperation often leads to foolishness."

"Josephine sighed. "The guards have a system for anybody caught trying to escape. Anybody leaving will be shot, as will two others. They demonstrated once the first day to make sure we all got the point. They won't hesitate to do it again."

"I looked up into the afternoon sky and said, "It's getting on towards evening now. Guards ought to be joining us soon. They won't try anything this late will they?"

"My guess is they've been waiting for this time," Jack said. "They know they have the shortest amount of time before dark and they know the terrain here is pretty flat. This is the best chance they've got."

"Jack had no more than finished the words when a crashing sound in the weeds to the right stopped the procession in its tracks. Everyone crouched down and tried to see what was going on as a second noise sounded out into the cold air.

"Jack clasped me on the forearm and with eyes motioned out towards the left of the trail. I squinted past him and saw all four men, bounding for the woods.

"What the hell was that racket?" I whispered.

"Probably threw some rocks or something," Jack said. "Anything to divert attention for awhile."

"Wouldn't they have just been better off sneaking out, not alerting anybody at all?"

"Desperation often leads to foolishness," Jack echoed.

"We stayed crouched down, the people around us tucked in tight as Korean guards sprinted up from the rear. The sound had caught many by surprise and as they ran by their hats sat at angles on their heads and they fumbled with their weapons.

"It took less than a minute for one of the guards to spot the fleeing men and figure out what had happened. He began shouting in Korean and waving his arms as a group of guards sprinted off after the soldiers.

"The entire procession huddled together and waited, each of us hoping for the best and expecting quite the opposite. A few minutes later, the sound of gunfire split the late afternoon air.

"Tears ran down the faces of women around us as men sighed and shook their heads. I met Jack's eyes for a moment before looking past him to the soldiers walking back across the field towards the procession.

"This can't be good," I whispered and several heads turned to follow my gaze.

"The tears and shaking heads stopped as everyone stared at the ground and prayed for the march to continue. The group of guards walked towards us and once they got close enough began shouting in Korean.

"They shouted for several minutes and when they stopped everyone stood waiting, unsure of what to do. Without warning each of the guards walked forward and grabbed two people and drug them from the group.

"Women screamed and children cried as one by one the men pulled them forward and shot them between the eyes. Eight people, just like that. Four men, two women, two children, all over the stupidity of a group of desperate soldiers."

My uncle reached down and flipped the page to reveal a thin black glove on the next page.

"Page 23," my uncle said. "As we walked on the people in line paused to pay their respects. I remember being touched by the act of humanity in such a dire time and I bowed my head and sent up a prayer for them as we went by.

"A few minutes later a woman handed me a black pair of gloves from one of the men. It wasn't until then that I realized what the people were really doing. They were looting their own dead."

Uncle Cat paused again and exhaled , his eyes fixed before him. "To this day I cannot decide what the most inhumane action I witnessed that day was. Seeing a group of soldiers put their own desperation ahead of eight innocent people, seeing the North Koreans gun all twelve down, or seeing a group of people claiming to be followers of God looting the fallen."

## Chapter Thirty-One

"We marched on for almost a week, each day a little harder than the one before. Every night the Koreans gave us a small loaf of bread and that was our sustenance for the day. Most of the time the bread was moldy, but we ate it anyway.

"Our only form of water was to eat the snow from the ground around us. As the days passed the snow crystallized more and more and before long we were eating pure ice. The harsh granules chaffed our lips and throats and it wasn't uncommon for lips or gums to be bleeding.

"A couple of nights we were lucky and came across abandoned school houses or churches and were able to stay there. The cold, hard floors weren't a vast improvement from the ground outside but having walls to block the wind helped a great deal.

"We'd huddle close and pack the room as tight as we could and by morning we'd almost be warm again. If the soldiers wanted to they could have torched the place and sent a couple of hundred of us up with it, but I think that would have been too easy for them. They knew most of the people would stay inside just to be close to a fire.

"Each day some of the weaker ones from the group would fall behind, never to be seen again. Some would tire of trying and sit down along the trail and wait for the cold or soldiers, whichever came first. As we walked we could hear the occasional gunshot pierce the air, but there was nothing we could do about it.

"For our part Jack and I continued to help two people at a time. We tried to spread it around as much possible, but there was too much weakness to help everyone.

"As we walked, more and more people joined us. Soldiers, South Koreans, missionaries, even a few Spaniards and Frenchmen. Where they all came from I don't know, but came they did. By the end of the week our group had swollen to over four hundred."

The door creaked behind us and my mother poked her head out. She saw us sitting on the front porch and asked, "You two have a nice walk?"

I turned, gave a half smile and nodded my head, but said nothing. My uncle kept his gaze on the lake ahead and said nothing as my mother returned the smile and headed inside.

"On the morning of the sixth day, the soldiers summoned us with their familiar revelry of gunfire.

Freezing, starving, and exhausted, we all stumbled to our feet and waited for a call to march that never arrived.

"In its place came a small squatty man with the insignia of a general in the North Korean Army. He wore sunglasses despite it barely being light out and strode with an air of importance that was sickening. He smiled the smug smile of a man in charge and without understanding a word he said I could tell it was dripping with arrogance.

"He addressed the group as a whole, speaking in a tone just above conversational and making everyone strain to hear him. As he spoke he waved his arms from side to side and motioned to and fro.

"A South Korean named Sun-Jin that had been walking with us whispered, "He's saying that we have reached our destination. It is time to break the group up into Koreans, soldiers and everybody else."

"Each of us turned our head toward Sun-Jin and I asked, "Where the hell we all going?"

"We are all going to our, what is the word, induction camp," Sun-Jin said.

"Induction camp?" Josephine asked as her eyes searched across each of our faces.

"I'm not sure if this is the right word I am looking for," Sun-Jin said. "Place where they will teach us about Communism."

"Jack and I raised our heads and Mercer said, "You mean indoctrination.""

"And you mean brain washing," I added.

"The sound of a gunshot erupted from behind us and we all crouched and snapped around towards the sound. The general stood with his pistol aimed in the air and a smirk on his face. He said a few more lines and fired again, then disappeared through a crowd of guards.

"He says the first shot was to get our attention and the second was for us to get in line. He also said if it takes too long or anybody tries anything, the next shot he fires will be into somebody's head."

"Sun-Jin had barely finished speaking when someone enveloped me in a bear hug from behind. I could hear Josephine sniffling against into my shoulder and could see Mercer reach out and shake Jack's hand.

"We don't have time for proper good-byes, so this will have to do," Mercer said as he in turn shook my hand. "I won't forget the way you boys stayed to aid these people and I won't forget the effort you put forth in helping them along. Many here wouldn't have made it without you."

"After hugging Jack, Josephine pulled herself back and stood next to Mercer with tears running down her face. All around us people hugged and cried and headed in their respective directions.

"You boys watch over each other," Josephine said, her voice cracking as she spoke. "We'll be praying for you."

"Jack and I both nodded and Jack said, "You folks take care. Take care of yourselves and of these people. They need you."

"Josephine cried harder as Jack and I waved to them and turned towards the group of soldiers moving off to the left. Compared to the other groups around us we were pretty small, maybe sixty men ranging from the ages of eighteen to forty.

"Most were in far worse shape than Jack and I, looking as if they'd been marching for months or years. Their clothes were tattered and hung from them like they'd lost most of their body mass. Their hair was long and matted and many wore patchy facial hair.

"It was only a matter of minutes before the other groups began moving off. The missionaries and non-Koreans were the first to go and we could hear the women wailing as they disappeared from sight. The Koreans went after them, following the same road for a short distance before forking to the east and disappearing from view as well.

"We were the last group to move, left standing in the road for the better part of an hour. The men milled about and many began to grow restless. It wasn't until a small plume of dust rose in the distance that we knew why we'd been made to wait."

My uncle paused again and cleared his throat. He coughed a couple of times and sat breathing heavy for a moment thereafter. Once he regained his composure, he continued.

"The plume of dust rose from a troop of North Koreans coming to escort us into camp. We watched as they grew closer, two lines of fifteen each. Combined with the soldiers already with us they had just about as many as we did, all of them holding automatic weapons.

"Why they thought they needed that much firepower, I do not know.

"The two lines split apart as they arrived and flanked us on either side. The soldiers that had been on march with us brought up the rear and together they herded us with a three sided box.

"The pace began at a brisk walk, but before long the soldiers resumed their light jog. We had to match pace to keep up with them and more than a few of the men didn't make it. They went down and were trampled by the men around them or finished off by the guards behind us.

"The jog lasted for a little over a mile and by the time we made it there the guards outnumbered us. Six months prior I could have ran ten miles in the summer sun with ease. That day a mile almost did me in.

"The road continued on as we veered off to the left. We made our way down what was little more than a footpath for about a hundred meters before finding ourselves facing a large wooden gate.

"The gate was solid, with barbed wire wrapped along the top of it in three rows. As the gate swung open I could see the wall around us extending for a vast distance in all directions.

"The guards formed us into a single file line and marched us in with them flanking either side. As we marched I could see American soldiers sprawled everywhere. Many of them were even more ragged than the men with us and their faces were drawn and gaunt with hunger.

"The smell of raw sewage hung in the air and I could see men relieving themselves and vomiting within feet of each other. Behind me a man whispered, "Welcome to hell," and I couldn't help but nod my head in agreement.

"The guards marched us straight through camp and filed us into a large open faced tent. Row after row of folding chairs was lined inside and they motioned for us to fill them and sit down.

"What the hell's going on here?" I whispered to Jack as we sat down.

"Jack furrowed his brow. "Not sure."

"From behind us a projector kicked on and a grainy film popped up on the rear wall, the only one in the tent. It showed people working and playing together and the announcer spoke in perfect English.

"It was an advocacy filmstrip for Communism.

"When the film began a few of the men booed, an act that earned them a sharp crack with the butt of a rifle. Nobody else said a word and for several minutes we were forced to watch the fake families living happy lives in a society of Communism.

"When it was over the lights sprang back to life and another North Korean officer stood before us. He seemed to be a copy of the ones before him and I couldn't help but wonder if they had a warehouse somewhere for manufacturing tiny, arrogant officers.

"Good morning," the officer said, smiling to the room. His English carried a slight accent, but not as bad as I would have expected. "My name is Major Han, welcome to the Ah-San education facility." He paused for a moment to see if the name elicited any response and when it did not, he continued.

"The purpose of the Ah-San facility is not to serve as a prisoner of war camp, but rather to educate you to the joys of Communism and detain you until this skirmish is over. Once it is, you will be returned to your country so you can spread the good news of our way of life.

"As you exit this tent you will be given some information about Communism for you to learn. In a few days time we will convene as a group and review the material, that way we know you are learning it."

"A soldier in the back said, "And if we don't?"

"The major looked at him with a bemused expression and nodded upward. A guard stepped forward and cracked the man across the skull with the butt of his rifle, the sound a loud pop in the quiet tent. The soldier rolled forward and fell to the ground unconscious, blood flowing from the back of his head.

"Major Han returned the smile to his face and said, "We are an education facility, but we will not hesitate to do what is needed to aid in that process. I hope in the future little incidents like these will not be necessary."

"Without another word, Han turned on his heel and strode from the room. The guards positioned themselves at the end of each row of chairs with stacks of pamphlets and as we left they handed one to each of us."

My uncle motioned with a gnarled finger towards the album and said, "Go ahead and flip to the next page."

I did as told to reveal an old and frayed pamphlet, faded and water stained. I couldn't make out any of the writing across it but could see the faint outline of red lettering along the top.

"That too, is an original," my uncle said. "Lord knows I didn't mean to bring it back with me, I just happened to find it much later.

"Page 24 is how the North Koreans planned to win the war. Not by bullets or bombs, but by indoctrination."

## Chapter Thirty-Two

Placing a withered hand on my shoulder, my uncle drew himself up from the front porch step. He kept his gaze on the lake before him for a few moments before turning and making his way up the stairs to the porch. He motioned me back to our chairs and said in a soft voice, "Bring the book."

I scooped the open book up in both arms and followed him as he settled down into his rocker. When he was ready I placed the book across his lap, drug my chair a little closer and climbed up into it.

My uncle waited for me to find my seat, then turned his attention back to the album. He reached out with aged hands and traced his fingertips over the page before turning to the next one.

My eyes furrowed as I stared at the objects in front of me, looking like several pieces of corn. I stared at the white, hard kernels trying to make sense of them before uttering, "What *are* those?"

"Jack and I walked out of that education tent without any idea where to go next. Each of the men in there with us filed out and moved in a different direction, no one destination seeming to be any better than another.

"We stood shoulder to shoulder and surveyed the camp as weak and wounded soldiers wandered by. A few looked us up and down or muttered in disgust, but most didn't even lift their eyes enough to know we were there.

"The men around us were worn and frail, looked like they had been locked away in a World War II concentration camp. Many were rail thin, with bones jutting out at odd angles. They were dirty and smelled horrible.

"Many gave us the impression that their spirit had been broken.

"I remember thinking I would rather die in Korea than ever get to that point.

"We should make a loop of the place," Jack said at my side. "Get an idea of where things are and what to avoid."

"I knew we were both already thinking of looking for the best way out, but neither said it aloud.

"Retracing our entry, we walked to the front of the camp and worked our way in a counterclockwise loop around the camp. As we walked, guards around the perimeter watched and called out to us in a language we couldn't understand. Most of the time whatever they said was followed by smug laughter, so I can imagine they were having fun at our expense.

"Inside the walls, the camp was even bigger than we realized. It was more or less one large square, lined by a tall wooden fence with barbed wire around the top. There were two gates, one on either end, and they too were solid wood with barbed wire.

"There was a line painted on the ground fifteen feet inside the wall that was meant to keep prisoners from trying to escape. There were a few bodies lying between it and the wall, left as a reminder to any others that might think of approaching the wall.

"Every fifty yards or so was a small hut with a couple of guards watching over the grounds. Each one carried an automatic weapon that looked ancient, but I have no doubt they worked well enough for some unarmed prisoners.

"It took Jack and I a half hour to make our way back to the front gate. The lap of camp seemed like a waste of energy at its completion, every angle the same as the one before it. Guards, walls, starving soldiers in every direction.

"We noticed a group of men huddled near a small fire and moved in that direction. The fire didn't draw us in as much as the men around it. We walked up behind them and stood on the outside of the circle for several minutes.

"The men in the circle talked amongst themselves, too low for us to really hear what was going on. After awhile I looked a question at Jack, who furrowed his brow and shook head and motioned with head for us to go.

"As we turned to walk away a voice snapped out, "Hey! Who the hell are you two?"

"I froze mid step and cast a glance at Jack, who calmly turned and faced the group. "Corporal Jack Roberts, 63rd Regiment, 5th Division. This here's my brother Cat, Corporal, 63rd, 5th."

"A lane parted through the crowd and we could see a trio of men sitting tight next to the fire. They were older than most of the others in camp and wore the expressions of those that had been through worse before. They seemed oblivious to the cold and didn't have quite the same gaunt façade as most of the others.

"The man in the middle said, "5th? We heard that group got put down up around Chosin." He was a wiry man with thinning blonde hair that was graying fast. A scar ran from his right eye to his jaw line and it tugged at the corner of his mouth when he spoke.

"We took a few steps towards the fire and Jack said, "It was. Ourselves and a dozen others were the only survivors."

"The three men exchanged quick glances and the one in the middle said, "So how the hell did you boys end up here?"

"I deferred to Jack, who said, "Spent a couple of weeks picking across the countryside. Ran into the 3rd Marines fighting their way back to Koto-Ri and joined up to give them a hand. We stayed behind to offer machine gun cover on the retreat, got taken alive. Ten days of hard march brought us here."

"The three men exchanged looks again and the man on the right leaned in and whispered something to the others.

"Where exactly is here?" I asked.

"The three men fell silent in their conversation and looked up at us. Nobody said anything for a few moments until the man in the middle said, "Ah-San prisoner of war camp. They prefer to use the term education facility, but that's only so it sounds better in the newspapers. They don't want the rest of the world finding out what they're doing in here."

"He stopped short and Jack prompted, "Which is?"

"Any damn thing they choose," answered the man on the left. He was a pale man with watery blue eyes and a bald head that gave way to a horseshoe of hair above the ears. "They beat us, they mistreat us, they starve us. Sometimes the guards shoot us for sport."

"And what do we do in return?" I asked.

"The man on the right scoffed and said, "Whatever the hell they tell us to. We memorize and recite their propaganda and we abide by their rules…"

"His voice trailed off and Jack took a step forward. "Until?"

"The three men sat stone faced and stared at us. I moved up close behind Jack and we met their gaze full on. "Until?"

"The man in the middle looked at us and said, "You two meet us right back here at sundown."

"I started to ask what for, but Jack grabbed my arm to stop me. I looked up with confused eyes to protest, but he twisted his head from side to side.

"We'll see you gentleman here tonight under one condition," Jack said.

"The man on the right scoffed again and spat at the ground. He was the most rotund of the group and I could imagine that in a different world he would be a fat man. He had a moustache like a walrus that covered the better part of a red face. His thinning hair was plastered to his head and his mannerisms suggested he was a man that was used to throwing his weight around. "Way I see it, you boys ain't got much ground to be making demands here."

"The man in the middle said, "Shut up Marv," without looking at him and added, "what condition would that be?"

"Jack stared at him and said, "We need to know who we're speaking to and where we can find some food."

"The man studied us for a second before running a hand over his chin and nodding. "Son, you have got some cojones. Lucky for you, I like that in a soldier. Might even come in right handy around here."

"He paused and looked from his left to his right. "This here is Major Marvin Atwood, on my right is Lt. Colonel Raymond Phelps and you're speaking to Colonel Harold Spires. These men you see around us here are the last of our division, United States Army 3rd Infantry."

"Phelps tossed us a handful of something that looked like corn seed and said, "You boys ever seen millet before?"

"I caught a couple of the seeds and examined them. "No. Looks and feels kind of like field corn that's been left on the stalk too long."

"Spires nodded and said, "That's just about right. Stuff's hard as a rock. You can't chew it, so you've got no choice but to swallow it whole. Body can't process it, so it prods and pushes it's way right back on out.

"Most of what they give us to eat around here is this stuff or week old moldy bread. You eat the millet you have diarrhea so bad you'll be dehydrated within days. You eat the bread you'll get food poisoning and vomit yourself into dehydration even faster."

"So what do we do for food?" I asked.

"And what's this concern with our health and hydration?" Jack asked. "There are plenty of men around here who are a lot worse off than we are."

"Spires and Phelps looked at one another and Spires smiled. "I like you boys more already. You come back this evening at sundown and we'll talk about your health and hydration."

"And as far as food goes," Phelps said, "Korea has decided to rid itself of anything foul or impure. As such, they'll give anybody presenting them with three ounces or more of dead flies some real bread. You come in with more than six ounces and they'll give you some soup to go with it."

"I curled my face up a bit and looked at Jack, thinking to myself *they pay for dead flies?* Jack stared at them for a moment and said, "Thank you sir."

"I followed suit and said, "Thank you sir" and started to raise my arm to salute, but Jack caught it just inches into its path. He motioned for me to follow him and we left the fire, the group closing the circle behind us.

"What was that all about?" I asked as we walked away.

"Jack waited a moment before answering. "My guess is they would like to not have the Koreans know who the officers are around here. You can tell by the scar on Spires face he's already been interrogated, but they probably don't know who the other ones are."

"And knowing where the officers are is a bad thing?" I asked.

"Knowing who the officers are, where they're assembled and that they're having secret meetings at sundown could be very bad for all of us," Jack said and strode forward.

"I followed for a minute, our path taking us to the small stream of sewage running along the western edge of camp. As we grew closer the stench grew almost unbearable. "Where the hell are we going?"

"To get something to eat," Jack said.

"It only took me a minute to figure out what he meant. We were going to the flies."

My uncle stopped himself and I shifted my gaze up to look up at him. It seemed like an odd place to stop and I waited for him to continue.

He didn't though, just stared out over the water and tapped at the kernels of millet on the page before him. The sun slid a little lower in the sky and the smell of dusk filled the air, the only sounds the muted conversation from the house and my uncle tapping on the page before him.

# Chapter Thirty-Three

"When you grow up in the country the way we did, you can't help but have a strong stomach. Tending livestock, hunting, fishing, it doesn't matter. You develop a natural deference to sights and smells.

"I had skinned catfish, butchered deer, shoveled horse manure and pulled leeches from my own skin. None of that held a candle to what we walked into that afternoon."

My uncle paused for a second and sniffed the air, then snorted and shook his head.

"We walked to the western edge of camp to where a small stream had formed, winding its way across the frozen ground. As we got closer we found it wasn't a stream at all, but a steady flow of urine, feces and vomit. The three had mixed together to form a blue and green liquid that collected in stagnant pools, small pieces of something awful floating in them.

"Isn't it too cold for flies?" I asked as we walked towards the incredible stench. With each step my nose burned a little more, tears forming in the corners of my eyes.

"Jack stopped and said, "Out here, yeah. We need to find someplace warm enough for them. You can't have a mess like this without flies."

"We got as close as we could to the flow and turned to the right, walking along with our gaze darting to and fro. Every so often we came across a soldier relieving himself or vomiting. We paid them no heed and they did the same for us as we walked on, searching for our meal ticket.

"As we walked on a little further, Jack stopped short. "You hear that?"

"I pulled up and stood still, barely able to hold a thought beyond the smell in my nose. It started low, but after a moment I heard it to. Steady and persistent, like the humming of an idling engine.

"Flies, and lots of them.

"A canvas tent stood several hundred feet ahead and we moved towards it. We closed in fast, the hum growing louder as we approached. I drew a few feet ahead of Jack, almost running, envisioning the soup and bread I was about to receive.

"I moved forward and reached for the tent flap and without thinking drew it back. As I did so Jack reached forward to try and stop me, but it was too late.

"The sight before me caused me to add my own vomit to the stream."

I hadn't expected that and my head snapped around to him. My eyes bulged a bit as he stared out over the water and I could see a wave of nausea wash over his face.

"The tent was filled with sick and wounded men, piled upon one another in the tiny tent. Many had open sores over their legs, arms and faces.

"The air in there was moist and sour and flies clung to the walls of the tent in heavy clumps. Many more lined the edges of the wounds on the men, the victims too weak to remove them or too tired of fighting an unending battle to bother.

"A few men cracked their eyes open and looked up, responding more to the light and rush of cold air than us.

"Two men with wispy hair and ragged beards squatted beside a prisoner. When they saw us they glanced at each other and back again.

"Let me guess, you boys are new and hungry," one of them said.

"My voice was still lost to the sight around me and all I could do was nod my head, my throat locked and dry.

"The man on the left said, "You boys look young and like you have some strength about you, so we'll arrange a trade. We've got more men in here right now than we can handle. Most of them are suffering from dysentery and the ones who aren't will be soon if we don't get them separated."

"Jacks eyes darted back and forth. "How many?"

"The second doctor looked at us each in turn. "Just like that, huh?"

"You said you wanted to arrange a trade," Jack replied. "We're hungry."

"The two doctors moved forward and the first one stuck out his hand. "Rothchild, call me James." He was a tall, thin man with a bald head accented only by a few wisps of light brown hair. He wore wire rimmed glasses and his eyes carried the red tinges of a man that didn't sleep much.

"The second shook each of our hands in turn and said, "Bill Quincel." He had the matching red eyes of Rothchild, his wisps of hair blonde. His skin was leathered with age and he wore the expression of a man that had seen a lot in his years.

"You boys start with this half of the room," Quincel said. "Take as many as you can over to the main tent and place them close together. They'll need the warmth of one another and most don't have the energy to move themselves."

"It's a hundred yards or more over there and there's a dozen or so men here, so we don't expect you to get them all. Take as many as you can and we'll be in your debt," Rothchild said.

"I shot a look at Jack, who caught my eye and snapped his head towards the first patient. Without a word he grabbed the ankles of the first man in line and waited for me to grab his wrists.

"Looking at the mass of men lying on the ground I looked at Jack and shook my head, then hefted the first man to my shoulder. He was sweaty and clammy to the touch, motionless as the crook of his stomach settled against my shoulder.

"I'm not making any more trips than I have to," I said and swung the tent flap open. The air stung cold after being in the tent and my pace was quick as I shuffle-stepped across the yard.

"I didn't turn around, but I could hear Jack crunching along as well.

"I passed through the open sides of the tent and placed the man along the back wall where we had watched the film. A few moments later Jack placed another man beside him and together we adjusted them to keep them as warm as the situation would allow.

"One of the men cracked his eyes open and looked up at us for a moment, but closed them again. Once we had them settled, both remained motionless.

"We walked back side by side with the gaze of many onlookers following us.

"Jack swung the tent flap open and we both grabbed another patient. The doctors both looked up in surprise as we hoisted them to our shoulder and walked out again.

"A few more glances came our way as we placed them beside the others. We walked back again and within minutes each added a third and then a fourth to the pile.

"You getting tired yet?" I asked.

"Jack cast a long glare in my direction. "Nothing a bowl of soup and some decent bread can't fix."

"I snorted a laugh as we reached the tent and made the last couple of trips. By that last go-round even the frail men were feeling very heavy.

"We arranged the men around one another, the ones that seemed to be in the best shape on the outside. A few soldiers had wandered over to watch and a few gave words of encouragement, but nobody offered to help.

"Sweat was dripping from my nose and down my cheeks by the time we made it back to the tent. The doctors had spread the other men out on the ground, each of them with enough room to lay flat.

"As we walked in Quincel sat back on his haunches and scratched his forehead with his thumb. "Damn. That was impressive."

"Rothchild rose to his feet and walked to the wall of the tent where a wooden crate sat. He reached into the bottom of it and pulled two small cloth sacks from it and tossed one to each of us.

"What's this?" I asked.

"Rothchild motioned to the room around us and said, "Six ounces of flies for each of you. Enjoy your meal, you've earned it."

"I hefted the bag in my hand. "Six ounces huh?"

"Quincel smiled and said, "Over time flies dry out, so we managed to get around that by inserting flecks of metal into them. Ups the weight, slows down the drying process."

"So where do we take these things?" I asked.

"Quincel motioned back over his shoulder. "Go to the guard tower just past the main tent. There's a scale in there where they'll weigh the flies. Once they make weight, you'll get your food."

"Quincel nodded. "Thanks a lot guys, we appreciate it."

"You guys need a hand again," Jack said, "come find us."

My uncle stopped and flipped the page. On it was several small glints of silver with some black crumbles spread around them.

He smiled and pointed to the page below us. "These were originally flies with bits of metal inserted into them.

Over time the flies have crumbled away, but you can still see the metal there.

"Like most of the objects in this book, these too saved my life."

Uncle Cat stopped and returned his gaze to the water in front of us.

"How did flies save your life?" I asked after a few seconds, still unclear what he was trying to tell me.

My uncle tapped the page and said, "When you see flies, you see an annoyance or think of a bothersome buzzing. When I see flies I think of food, strength, and the energy it gave me to do what needed to be done."

I paused for a second, allowing the words to hang in the air. "What needed to be done?"

My uncle didn't bother to answer. He just gave me a knowing look and focused again on the horizon.

# Chapter Thirty-Four

My cousin Suzy swung the front door open and ran across the porch. We could hear her sniffle as she passed and tears streamed down her face. Her face was red and puffy, a steady stream of muttering sliding out as she went.

She bounded down the front stairs in two steps and ran to the tire swing hanging in the front yard. Without stopping she jumped and wrapped her legs around the rope, landing atop the tire. I watched her as she shoved her thumb in her mouth and rested her head against the rope, the tire swaying in the breeze.

Aunt Jane stepped out onto the porch behind her, the sound of her heavy shoes thudding against the floorboards. Her face was drawn and angry as she walked to the edge of the porch and stood stone still for several seconds.

She exhaled and turned back to the house. She saw me watching her and said, "Children are to be seen, not heard," and walked on inside.

Throughout the ordeal my uncle's eyes never left the horizon, the setting sun sparkling against his face. He waited several seconds for the door to stop reverberating behind us and said, "That afternoon we ate the soup and bread, which was just a step above gruel and hard tack. To someone that had been carrying people for two weeks solid on moldy bread, it tasted like Christmas dinner.

"The doctors had been dead on with their measurements. When we gave the guards the small bags of flies they had laughed at such a paltry collection. It was all I could do to stay quiet as their eyes bulged at the scales reading six ounces each time.

"After eating, we went back to the tent and asked the doctors if we could steal a corner of space for the afternoon. Rothchild conceded that if we were willing to haul their water each day, we could stay in the tent as much as we liked.

"The tent was at least fifteen degrees warmer than the air outside and it was easy for us to agree to the terms. The air was damp and musty, but it was warm and that was most important.

"We moved to the corner and curled into balls side by side and slept away the afternoon. Once or twice I could hear the doctors moving among us or feel a rush of cool of air from someone stepping in, but never enough to pull me from my slumber.

"I'm not sure how long I lay on the ground, curled on some matted grass, that afternoon. It seemed I had just laid down when Jack shook my shoulder to rise.

"Mph, what time is it?" I asked as I rolled to a seated position and rubbed my eyes.

"Getting on towards dusk," he said, pulling back the edge of the tent flap and staring out across the grounds.

"How long have you been awake?"

"Jack shook his head and said, "Little while is all. The last patient that came through here kicked me on his way out. Never did fall back asleep."

"My gaze swung over the room to find several sleeping patients, but no sign of the doctors.

"Where'd Quincel and Rothchild go?"

"Went to get dinner, they won't be gone long."

"I raised myself to a knee and shook my head clear. Jack continued peering out from behind the flap and said, "When we go over there, don't give up anything. Say as little as possible, keep your face as still as you can."

"These guys are up to something big, aren't they?"

"Jack nodded. "Yup. I just can't tell if they want our involvement as help or as a diversion."

"We waited for the doctors to return and looped our way back over to the fire. The guards were watching as soldiers moved about, drawing their rations and preparing for the night.

"A few minutes after dark, we stole up on the 3rd infantry encampment. Men were grouped tight and as we approached the crowd spread and drew us inward, closing back up fast around us.

"Phelps, Spires, and Atwood sat three across in front of the fire in the same formation they had been in before. They looked like they had not moved at all in fact.

"We said sundown," Atwood said, motioning for us to sit across from them. "It's a full ten minutes past."

"Jack and I returned his stare, but said nothing.

"Spires nodded. "That's good. We wanted to see if you two had the sense not to make a direct line for us with the guards watching.

"First test passed."

"First test for what?" Jack asked, neither of our faces revealing anything.

"Atwood leaned forward and pointed a beefy finger across the fire. "Before we go any further here, we need to know you boys are in. This is the kind of thing that could end badly and we need to know you two aren't going to get any of us killed."

"Jack's voice remained a steady dead pan. "First test for what?"

"Phelps looked at each of us in turn and said, "We've been here for three weeks now. We were in Chon Ma for two weeks before that. With each passing day we lose a little more weight, get a little weaker. We need to do something and we need to do it soon."

"His words hung heavy in the air and the men around the fire edged a little closer, some fidgeting a bit.

"What he's saying is we have a plan. We need the personnel to pull it off," Atwood said.

"Spires swung an open hand around the fire and said, "You two have been here less than a day and I am sure you can see that many of the men are on their last legs. Most have been in camp as long as or longer than us and just don't have what we need."

"And that is?" I asked.

"Spires stared at us and said, "As of six weeks ago the United Nations knew about nine different camps across North Korea. This wasn't one of them."

"There are Red Cross programs, prisoner exchanges, things in place to aid with the soldiers we know about. If nobody knows we're here, we're all sitting and counting days until we die," Phelps said.

"I think you can tell where we're going with this," Atwood said.

"Jack nodded and said, "Few questions spring to mind right off."

"Spires raised a hand. "Let us get this out, then we'll work on details.

"I don't know if you've heard or not, but every morning a group of men are sent to the river to fetch water for camp. The detail goes out in a group of seven, pulling a wagon that rests just behind the main tent. On the wagon are a dozen large wooden barrels which get filled with water and drug back each day. Once the wagon is back in camp, it's a free for all until the water's gone."

"Now the Koreans don't care which seven guys haul the water, just so long as seven are there every morning to do it. We're not sure how or why they decided seven, but we figure it's because you need at least that many to keep the wagon moving once it's full," Phelps said.

"Spires added, "Our plan is once the morning comes, to plant a crew of our own seven guys to serve as the water detail. It shouldn't be hard to convince the other prisoners to let them in and we can bribe them if we need to."

"Spires stopped short and silence fell around the fire.

"So what do you need from us?" Jack asked.

"Tonight when you leave here, make a trip past the main tent," Spires said. "What you will find are the barrels strewn about on the ground, laying as they did this morning after the rush for water."

"Jack remained stone faced and nodded his head slightly. "You want to plant us in the barrels."

"Atwood nodded his head and said, "We want you two to hide in the barrels overnight. The next morning our guys will carry you to the river. They'll submerge you just like they're filling the barrels normally and you two will swim away."

"Phelps took over and said, "Given the time of year and what we know about the river, it's going to be hard going. Some of the edges are frozen solid and some of the other parts haven't frozen because of fast currents.

"The wagon goes to the same spot every day, which is about a quarter mile from the rear gate. The current is running back towards the road you came in on. You'll remain in the water until you're out of sight, then be able to follow the river to the original road."

"From there the road runs due south back into South Korea," Atwood said. "You'll run parallel to it across the 38$^{th}$, find allied forces as soon as possible, and send them back here for us."

"The men finished speaking and silence again fell over the group. I couldn't see any faces beyond the five of us tight around the fire, but I could feel the others edging closer with anticipation.

"You two haven't said a word through all this," Spires said, "so let's hear your thoughts."

"Jack stared motionless back for a full five seconds before cocking his head towards me. "What do you think?"

"I hadn't expected Jack to pull me in like that, though I figure he did it to make us appear solidified to the officers. I gave a non-committal shake of my head. "Any time a plan can be summed up nice and neat that fast, I get a little worried."

"Jack nodded. "I agree."

"We both turned our faces towards the officers and Phelps said, "Let's hear your questions. The plan isn't set in stone. You know your own capabilities better than we do and you have better knowledge of the surrounding areas."

"A second of silence passed and I asked, "First of all, why us? You guys have hundreds of soldiers around here, many of them from your own company. Is this thing legit or are we just sacrificial lambs?"

"As I spoke Jack turned his head in my direction and when I finished we both looked back at the officers with the same stony faces as before.

"You're right," Spires said. "You don't know us, we don't know you. Like I said before, we've all been doing this for six weeks or more now. Look around this fire. These men are freezing, starving, exhausted. They're in no condition to make the kind of journey we're asking you to make.

"You two are fresh into camp. You've both still got a little body fat on you which tells me you have energy to work with and the cold won't get to you as much others.

"Judging by that little show you put on today carrying sick prisoners, you've also got strength and determination.

"We've got over four hundred soldiers around here and no way of getting out unless we find some way to get word to our forces. The only chance we have at that is finding the two most able bodies we can."

"We've been looking for two for the obvious reasons," Phelps said. "Two can help each other, keep each other warm and aid each other if injury occurs. If one goes down, another can finish the mission."

"He fell silent and for a moment the only sound was the low crackling of the fire. "I assume you've got some idea as to how you propose we swim through icy water in this cold and still make it south alive?" Jack asked.

"Atwood reached down by his side and grabbed a small package and tossed it to Jack. It was small and light weight and made a loud crinkling sound to the touch. "Two weeks ago they brought in another load of medical supplies to the doctors. Most of the stuff was old and outdated, but it came in these plastic bags. We've been saving them ever since."

"We'll give each of you winter fatigues to place inside the bags and secure to your bodies. You'll wear what you have on now inside the barrels and to swim downstream. Once out of sight you can emerge from the water, change your clothes and sink everything back into the river," Phelps said.

"What kind of guard detail we looking at?" I asked.

"Six men carrying an automatic weapon and a handgun," Spires said. "They take the crew out with two men on either side and two in the rear. It's a lot colder along the water, so they stay back a bit and watch before circling up and following the men back. Most of the time they're smoking cigarettes and playing grab ass with one another, not real worried about a few haggard soldiers filling water barrels."

"Jack looked again to me for a long moment. I met his eyes, but said nothing.

"Jack turned back to the officers and said, "When do we do this?"

"Spires raised a hand towards the sky and said, "Right now we're three days past full moon. Twelve days from now we'll be at new moon. Less moonlight, easier for you to move unseen. Twelve days for you both to eat as much as this place will allow and sleep as much as you can."

"And no more stunts like what you pulled today," Atwood said, agitation again showing in his voice.

"Jack moved his gaze across to Atwood and said, "That *stunt* today helped two dozen soldiers. It also gave us a decent meal and a warm place to sleep for the afternoon."

"Some of us aren't afraid to get our hands dirty," I said, Atwood's demeanor beginning to wear on me. The comment found its mark and Atwood grew red and balled his hands into fists, but said nothing.

"You two stay as far away from the guards as you can," Spires said. "Don't volunteer for water duty and no more walks along the perimeter. You guys need food, come and find us and we'll have someone go get it for you."

"We're not used to handouts," I said. "That's not the way we were brought up."

"Phelps smirked. "Trust me, by the time you're done you will have earned a few bowls of soup and loaves of bread."

"Quiet fell over the group again and Jack turned his head to me and motioned for us to be going. We both stood as the officers did the same.

"Spires reached out and shook Jack's hand then did the same with mine, pushing small pieces of paper into our palms. Phelps did the same.

"Maps," Spires said. "Surrounding areas, routes south."

"Study them, know them, and as soon as you have them committed to memory, burn them," Spires said.

"Jack and I left the fire and took a short walk around the grounds. We stayed away from the edges of camp and out of any firelight as we made our way back to the doctor's tent.

"Both of the doctors were lying down for the night when we arrived. Without opening his eyes Rothchild said, "I hope you boys make it. I don't know much longer the rest of us here can last."

My uncle paused again and lay the book on the floorboards. He reached down and slid the next page across to reveal a small crude map, the location of which I had no idea.

"We did as Spires said and burned those first maps the very next day. Each day they would give us new ones with better detail to study before we burned them as well.

"This particular map is the general layout of the area surrounding the water drop point, what they like to call a bird's eye view. They gave us at least one copy of it every day with new features reported by whomever they sent to fetch water."

My uncle snorted and said, "It's funny how much different things can look when you're in freezing water and hiding from guards with automatic weapons though."

## Chapter Thirty-Five

Suzy remained in the tree swing, the tire drifting back and forth, each time rotating a little more. I could now see the plain back of her pink dress with frilled collar and her golden curls splashed down onto her shoulders.

My uncle sat watching the lake as once again the fishing boat made a final pass of the evening. I stared at my cousin in the swing and the men in the boat for several long minutes until the anticipation got to me.

I had to know.

"So what happened?" I asked.

My uncle slid his gaze towards me, allowing it to lead his head as he turned in my direction. "What happened?"

"With the escape? What happened?"

Uncle Cat smiled a warm, wrinkled smile and said, "You're getting ahead of yourself again. There's more story to tell before we get to that point."

I opened my mouth to say something but caught myself before the words came. I remembered what my uncle had told me just a few hours before and opted to wait and see how the story played out.

"The next couple of days were about as standard as life gets in a prison camp, if such a thing exists," my uncle said. "Each day we fought the masses for the doctor's water and each afternoon and evening we were allowed corner space in the warmest place in camp to sleep.

"Twice a day someone from 3rd company would bring us soup and bread, ducking it inside the tent flap and retreating back without a word. We tried helping with the process, but a strongly worded note from Spires put a halt to that right quick.

"For most men in camps, life is a daily trial of staying alive. It is a perpetual fight to see the next morning. For us, it was an exercise in patience and boredom.

"Patience to remain calm, knowing what lie just a few days away. Boredom, trying to fill the time until it got there.

"Things went well for almost a week. We helped the doctors move soldiers about whenever we could. We ate, we slept, we pretended not to notice the sideways glances of the other men in camp.

"After that first week though, things changed in a big way."

My uncle paused again and lifted his gaze straight ahead. He clenched his eyes closed and for a moment it looked as if he was gritting his teeth. When he spoke, his voice bore a slight strain to it.

"On the eve of the eighth day the horn sounded, summoning the prisoners to the interior of camp. The horns blared for five solid minutes after which the guards encircled camp and moved inward, pushing every soldier they encountered along with them regardless of condition.

"When everyone was assembled, we were all ordered to sit. Most of the men could barely stand and whether intended it or not, the order was a blessing.

"When everyone was seated, Major Han strutted from behind the tent onto stage. He wore the same clothes as the previous encounter; the only difference in him being his arrogance seemed even larger than before.

"He stood in front of the group and removed a piece of paper from his pocket. We had all seen the Communist pamphlets hundreds of times and knew on sight what it was.

"Speaking without a microphone he said, "It seems that with each passing day, we find more and more of these being tossed aside. We find them lying on the ground, against the prison walls, my guards even tell me they've seen men using them as shit paper."

He paused for a moment as the look of arrogance lapsed into anger and back to arrogance again.

"What we are going to do about this is have ourselves a little pop quiz this afternoon. I will pick two people from the audience. I will ask one a series of questions and for every question he answers wrong, his partner will be beaten. They will then switch places and we will continue."

"The smirk grew into a full grin as he paced across the front of the tent, reveling in having all eyes on him.

"Why don't we go with a couple of new recruits this time? Someone fresh into camp, see if they've been doing their studies as instructed."

"He paced back and forth again, rubbing his chin and trying to appear deep in thought. "Ah yes, I know, how about those two boys I hear put on a little show of strength the other day? Carrying soldiers back and forth across camp and such?"

"The hairs on the back of my neck stood up and my heart began pounding. I had skimmed through the pamphlet once and cast it aside, more worried about the maps than anything Han gave me to learn. I shot a glance at Jack, who remained motionless, eyes focused forward.

"Han scanned the tent and said, "I will give those two boys until I count to three to present themselves front and center, otherwise I will instruct my guards to start shooting people. Trust me, you don't want that."

"Jack beside me exhaled and whispered, "We've got no choice" but before we could stand two men on the other side of the tent rose.

"Phelps and Spires.

"Han looked at the two older men standing and scoffed. "A valiant effort indeed, but the two gentlemen I'm looking for we're rumored to be carrying men thrown over their shoulder. I doubt either of you could carry a pillow right now."

"Phelps and Spires stood with eyes ahead, neither saying a word.

"A dark cloud crossed Han's face and he said to the group, "While the efforts of your friends here are noble, I will not stand for someone making a mockery of me. Now either the men I am looking for will stand and be questioned or I will begin the shooting, starting with these two!"

"As he spoke he pulled out his handgun and aimed it at Phelps and Spires. All around us the familiar sounds of guns being locked and loaded sounded as North Korean soldiers raised their guns to their shoulders and moved closer.

"Jack grunted at my side and together we both stood before the group. Han continued scanning the crowd, his eyes wild with anger until his gaze landed on us.

"Ah, there you are," he said and a small smile danced upon his lips.

"I slid my eyes to the left to see Phelps close his eyes and slide back into his chair. Spires looked at us and shook his head from side to side.

"Han stood and looked us over for a full minute before the smile grew larger across his face and said, "Bring them. Because of their little stunt here today, they'll be receiving an extra special quiz."

"The words had just finished leaving his lips when guards seized us from all sides. Many of them wore smirks and from their demeanor and positioning so close to us I couldn't help but think that they already knew what was coming.

"A guard grabbed both of us on either side and another prodded us with the barrel of his gun. The men around us watched in silence as we were led from the tent, across the grounds and out the rear gate.

"As we exited Han and another officer jumped into a small green Jeep and sped towards the command post to the east of camp. It stood in the center of a cluster of small buildings, in the foreground of several longer barracks.

"The guards marched us out the back gate and pushed us to a jog. As a group we moved across the open ground and less than ten minutes later stood in front of the command post.

"The buildings around us were all painted brown with words written in Korean in bright yellow. We stood in the cold morning air, breathing and sweating for several minutes until Han's voice called, "Bring them here."

"The guards shoved us up the three wooden steps and through the open door into a small room littered with maps and reeking of stale cigarettes. Han stood in the center of it with two other men and motioned towards a descending staircase. "If you would be so kind."

"I glanced at Jack and the look on his face said he didn't like this any more than I did, but there was little we could do in a room with seven armed men.

"We followed the steps down into a large earthen space, barren except for a large fire pit blazing forth. The fire illuminated everything and made the mud walls sweat from the heat.

"Han sauntered down behind us carrying a very large knife, the stainless steel of the blade glinting in the firelight. "I won't insult your intelligence enough to continue to pretend that this has anything to do with pamphlets," he said and placed the blade of the knife in the fire, the handle resting between two large stones on the outer edge.

"In a place like this, things that *aren't* happening can be just as important as things that are. Take this past week for instance. Your first day here you boys were carrying prisoners around like they were feed bags. Ever since you have barely emerged from your tent.

"Han lifted the knife from the fire and inspected the glowing blade, then placed it back where he had gotten it.

"One of my guards saw you two talking with that group we brought in a couple of weeks ago. Since then you haven't gone back, yet everyday one of them is seen bringing food to your tent and just now two of their leaders tried to take your place."

"Han picked the knife up again and said, "If you cut a man, you run the risk of him bleeding to death before he can tell you what you need to know. By heating the blade first, you can sear the skin on contact. Twice the pain without any of the nasty side effects, like death."

"Han passed the blade in front of us to make sure we saw the blade glowing bright. "Now what's it going to be? You two going to tell me what's happening, or am I going to have to get physical with my friend here?"

"Neither of us said a word.

"Han's eyes passed from me to Jack and settled back on me. He looked me up and down and started to speak, but before he could Jack spit on the ground at his feet. My eyes shot open with shock, the only person in the room more surprised than I being Han himself.

"How's that for an answer?" Jack asked.

"Han stood with mouth agape for another moment or two before motioning to the guards behind him. He kicked dirt over the spit as guards tied Jack to hooks in the wall behind us. I screamed out in protest but was restrained by several guards as Jack remained silent, not resisting in the slightest.

"Han thrust the knife back in the fire and looked up at me. "The way this works is I will ask you questions. For every one you don't answer, he gets a little better acquainted with my friend here."

"He pulled the knife from the fire and held the gleaming tip close to Jack's face. "How you feel about that? Leaving that pretty little face of yours in the hands of this man?"

"Jack's face remained stone still. "Do what you have to, he doesn't know anything and he will not say anything. *He will not say anything.*"

"I knew that last part was aimed right at me and I set my mind to remaining silent no matter what happened.

"Han looked at me and smiled. "We'll see about that. Now, why don't you start by telling me what those boys around the campfire wanted with you two?"

"I breathed in and said with as much hatred and gravity as I could muster, "What campfire?"

"Han's eyes went from my toes to my head and he shook his head to one side. "Have it your way then," he said and ran the knife from the base of Jack's ear to just below his jaw line. "Each time you defy an answer, I take this line another inch across his jaw. You stay silent; I'll cut him from ear to ear. Little something I like to call a Korean Grin.

"Now, again, what did those men want with two piss ants like you?"

"I stared straight into Han's eye and said, "I don't know what you're talking about."

"Without hesitation Han took the knife and increased the incision to just right of Jack's throat. I could hear the skin popping and hissing as the hot metal seared it and the smell of charred flesh hung heavy in the air.

"Jack's eyes burned with hatred and his mouth twisted into a shape that screamed with fury, but he made not a sound.

"Let's keep going, shall we?" Han asked. "Why is it on your first day here you two were carrying soldiers all over the place and now you never leave the tent?"

"A hundred different insults sprung to mind, but I feared what he would do to Jack if I said any of them. "Just got tired."

"Han shook his head and with one fluid motion extended the cut another two inches beneath Jack's jaw line. "Acting like I am stupid is even worse than lying to me," Han said. "Last chance to free your friend from his misery. What do you all have planned here?"

"I stood rail straight and looked at him. A few seconds passed and I said, "I have no idea what you're talking about. We've only been here a week."

"Han shook his head and walked to Jack, grabbing him by the jaw. He pushed Jack's head towards the ceiling and finished the cut, connecting his incision and Jack's left earlobe. As he pushed his head upward a few small places pulled open and blood ran down Jack's neck and seeped into his shirt.

"Jack was pale and bathed in sweat, but somehow he remained silent and upright.

"Major Han walked over to me and held the gleaming knife inches from my face. "I would put this knife directly across your throat as well, but somebody has to help his sorry ass back to camp. I want you to look at him and see the pain you caused him. I want you to smell his burned flesh in the air and see his blood on the tip of my blade.

"Next time I see you two, it's your turn."

"Without another word, Han spun on his heel and marched upstairs. Most of the men followed him out, only two remaining behind with Jack and me.

"I walked to my brother and untied his hands, the ropes chewed down into his wrists. He panted hard and sweat poured from his face. He didn't even try to stop or help me.

"I hoisted his right arm across my shoulders and helped him up the stairs, carrying most of his weight as his body fell limp against me. Once outside, I hoisted him to my shoulder and covered the ground back to camp as fast as I could.

"The guards on the perimeter were waiting at the gate as I stormed by with Jack on my shoulder. Many soldiers stared as I passed and some called out to ask what had happened, but I paid them no heed as I went straight to the doctor's tent."

My uncle stopped again for a second and exhaled. As he did so he opened his eyes and for the first time I noticed his hands had been clenched into tight fists.

"I burst through the tent flap and dumped Jack on the floor at their feet. Quincel was the first to reach him and said, "That sumbitch Han and his Korean Grin."

"Is he going to be alright?" I asked.

"Quincel bent low over Jack and ran his finger over the cut. "He should be, though it'll be a few days before we know for sure. This one doesn't look to be too deep; he hasn't nicked any major veins or arteries."

"Quincel stood and crossed to the corner for supplies. I saw Jack crack open his eyes and I fell to my knees beside him and grabbed his hands in mine. "I'm so sorry Jack. I was just trying to do what you wanted to me."

"Jack's eyes parted a fraction more and his head moved an inch from side to side. "Do not apologize," he whispered. "You did what I told you to, what I would have done."

"His eyes then closed again and Quincel returned and began daubing iodine over the wounds. I stood and moved off to our corner of the tent and sat with my hands draped over my knees to keep watch.

"I didn't move or eat or sleep for two solid days thereafter."

With that my uncle fell silent for several long minutes. I could hear a few laughs from inside and a few leaves rattle in the breeze from the tree overhead, but everything else was silent.

"This picture was taken by Mama some time later when we finally made it back," Uncle Cat said, turning the page once again. "The wounds had heeled by that time but you can still see the thick scar tissue running from ear to ear caused that day.

"That sick bastard Han and his damn Korean Grin."

# Chapter Thirty-Six

"Those next few days were some of the hardest of my life," my uncle said. He hadn't broken for his customary pause and the sudden sound of his voice startled me for a moment.

"For two solid days I sat in the corner and watched vigil over my brother. Every so often Quincel or Rothchild would ask me to dab ointment on his wounds or change a bandage, but otherwise I remained motionless.

"Several times the officers sent men from the 3rd infantry to summon me to the fire, but each time I turned them away. After a half day they realized I wasn't budging and began sending food, but I didn't touch that either.

"If Jack couldn't eat, I wouldn't eat.

"After Jack told me I did what I had to do, he fell into a fitful sleep that lasted an entire day. He would thrash and moan and sweat would run from him, but there was nothing we could do but watch and wait.

"On the second day Jack opened his eyes and drank some water before falling right back asleep. This time it was more relaxed and peaceful and when he awoke again on the morning of the third day, he had made it through the toughest part.

"That morning when the infantryman from the 3rd came to bring us food, I told them I would meet with the officers at dusk."

Uncle Cat paused for a second and bobbed his head up and down with the rhythm of his rocking chair. I could never tell if he was debating something or just gathering his thoughts, but either way I gave him time to do it.

"That evening Jack took the first food he'd had in days, managing to keep down most of his bowl of soup. Once Jack ate I too had some bread and soup and the food did wonders for my tiring body.

"I left Jack sleeping in the tent and stole into the night air, careful to make a wide arc and to let nobody see me going near the fire of the officers. It took me twice as long as usual to get there and when I did I found them arranged just as before.

"Nice of you to join us," Atwood snorted as I approached.

"I had more important things to tend to," I said. There was more I could have added, like a couple of cheap jabs at Atwood, but I decided to let them pass.

"How is your brother?" Phelps asked.

"He's coming around. He slept through the night last night and he managed to keep food down this evening. Doc thinks he'll be fine soon enough."

"Spires nodded his head. "I'm guessing you know why we asked you here."

"I stared into the fire for a moment and said, "Yeah, I know. This isn't about my brother; it's about what we can do for you."

"There are over three hundred men here—" Atwood started to say, but Spires held up a hand to silence him.

"You're right," Spires said. "We need to know if you are still up to the task. We also need to get your input about finding a suitable replacement for your brother."

"The mention of a replacement caught me by surprise and for a moment I stared back with my mouth agape. Jack and I had been together since birth and the notion of doing this without him made the hair on my neck stand on end.

"Before I could respond I heard the soft crunch of boots on gravel and a familiar voice said, "Who the hell you thinking of replacing?"

"I didn't have to turn around; I already knew who was behind me. Instead I watched the look on their faces as my brother emerged from the shadows and took his place beside me.

"The utter shock on Atwood's face was one of the most satisfying things I've ever seen in my life.

"Jack moved a little slower and stiffer than usual and as he sat beside me I heard him grunt softly. I waited for him to situate himself and together we both stared at the three of them.

"Neither of us said anything.

"The three of them sat for a moment before Phelps asked, "You sure you're up to this? It can take a man weeks to recover from something like that, if not longer."

"Jack gave them a sullen look. "I'm here aren't I? None of us want to be locked up any longer than we have to be. If my getting in that barrel means this doesn't happen to anybody else, then that's what I'll do."

"Spires nodded again. "How long before you'll be ready to go?"

"Moving just his eyes, Jack looked upward and said, "New moon isn't far off. I'll be ready by the time it gets here."

"Spires slid his gaze from Jack to me. "In his condition, a large part of the responsibility here falls to you. You up for it?"

"The question offended me, but I held it in. "Just so long as that son of a bitch Han gets what he has coming to him."

"Atwood smiled. "Listen to the young man with the big words."

"Without thinking I muttered, "You want to be next?"

"Atwood's face grew several shades of red. "Boy, if you were half the man I am..."

"I *am* half the man you are," I said, motioning to his midsection, "which is why I'm going instead of you."

"Phelps and Spires both cracked a smile and Spires said, "That's enough" as Atwood swelled with rage.

"Phelps fished into his pocket and pulled out a long sleeve of yellow material and tossed it across the fire to Jack. Jack unfurled a kind of plastic film, thin and very light weight.

"This here is called Ioban, they use it in surgery. You pull the back off the yellow film and press it to the skin like tape."

"He pulled up a pants leg to reveal a long and jagged scar. "I took a piece of mortar in the leg in Paris, ripped one hell of a gash. After sewing it up the doc gave me this to put over it. Helps hold the skin together, keeps it from getting infected."

"Jack glanced at it. "Will I still be able to move?"

"Just like putting a piece of tape over it," Phelps echoed.

"Jack folded it back up, put it in his pocket and said, "Thanks."

"The five of us sat looking at one another for several long moments before Jack said, "Is there anything else you boys want or can I go get some rest?"

"Phelps nodded. "That's a good idea."

"As each of us stood Spires said, "This should be the last time we see each other. Good luck gentlemen."

"We both met his eye and nodded. Without another word, we walked away."

My uncle paused again and flipped the next page in the album. It was little different from the rest of the pages in the book in that time had worn it to a deep yellow.

It was very different from the other pages in that I couldn't see a thing on it.

"Uncle Cat, what is it?" I asked.

My uncle raised a finger and outlined an edge. As he did so I could notice a slight difference in the shades of yellow and it dawned on me what the page held.

"Ioban," my uncle said. "After what it did for Jack in those next few days, it earned a place in the book."

## Chapter Thirty-Seven

My uncle raised his hips from the chair and leaned forward, resting the album on the ground at his feet. He interlocked his fingers and extended his arms as far out as they would reach and drew himself up, swinging his arms in a wide arc so they reached above his head. The vertebras in his back cracked one after another and he let out a loud and satisfying sigh.

He moved forward to the edge of the porch, placed his left hand on the support post and leaned forward until his shoulder pressed against it. Tilting his head to the side, he rested his head against the post and stood for a few moments taking in the sights around him.

"One of the men in the 3rd had served as an interpreter before being captured. In the days leading up to our departure the officers decided to send him with the water patrol each day in hopes he might catch something.

"Turned out they were right.

"On the day before we were to hide, he overheard the guards laughing about the job Han had done on Jack. One of the men had been present for the scene and said it hadn't sat well with Han that Jack didn't make a sound. That next day, he intended to try again.

"The interpreter ran to the officers the second he returned to camp. They summoned us back to the fire and it was decided that we would depart that night, a day early.

"Jack's recovery had been coming along, though there was no way of knowing for sure just how far. He never made a sound one way or another and shook me off each time I asked. They only things I had to go on were his eating and sleeping, both of which were almost back to normal.

"The docs continued to clean his wounds and rub salve on them and by the time we found out we were going ahead of schedule there were only a few small cuts that still bore a scab.

"That afternoon the 3$^{rd}$ brought us each double rations of food and two of the plastic bags Phelps had promised us, along with two sets of winter fatigues. Men wore the clothes over so as to not be seen carrying clothes through camp, then stripped down and left the heavier clothes behind.

"We each ate one ration of bread and soup early in the afternoon, slept until just before dusk, then rose and finished the food. We folded the winter fatigues into the plastic bags and pressed them to our chests as the doctors secured them by wrapping surgical tape around our torsos.

Once we put our own fatigues back on, you couldn't even tell they were there.

"We just looked like we were full and healthy again, the same as we had been six months before.

"I went first that night, stealing through the back flap and circling the main tent through the darkest of shadows. I found the barrels lined up as promised and climbed into the first one left standing upright. It was a tight fit and I had to force my legs and hips down tight before I could pull the lid back on over my head.

"The barrel was moist and cold and smelled of mildew. The wood was thick with frost where the previous day's water residue had frozen and after having slept in the tent, the barrel felt frigid. A few moments later I heard Jack climb into his barrel.

"After that, it was an interminable wait for morning."

My uncle paused for a moment and lifted his head from the post. He focused on something in the distance and for a second his gaze seemed to harden, but just as fast it softened and he shook his head.

"Sleep was impossible that night. I passed the time by fighting to make sure my body didn't freeze up crammed inside the barrel. Every few minutes I would clench and unclench a particular muscle group several times, trying to keep blood flowing as best I could. By morning my feet were numb, but otherwise I wasn't in too bad of shape.

"The inside of the barrel was dark and it wasn't until I heard voices outside that I knew morning had arrived. One of the men came and knocked twice on top of my barrel to let me know we were moving and a few seconds later I felt myself being lifted onto the wagon and positioned just so.

"They lifted Jack and I onto the wagon first and put the other barrels around us in case the guards decided to take a glance in any of them.

"The sudden movement jolted my stiff and aching body and new pains shot down my lower back and legs. As the wagon began moving each bump in the road brought another stab with it and I had to bite my lip to keep from making any sounds.

"After several minutes the wagon stopped and I could hear soft talking as one by one the barrels around us were removed. My adrenaline began to pump and my body became taut as each passing second brought me one step closer to escape.

"All of the other barrels were filled and back in position by the time they got to us. I heard a voice whisper, "Here we go boys. The waters running fast and cold today so take a deep breath and brace yourself. Once in the water, you'll need to get about a hundred yards downstream before you're out of sight."

"Another voice added, "And remember, Han's coming looking for you today and he's going to send the hounds of Hell when he finds out you're gone. You boys hit the grounds running and get somebody back here as fast as you can."

"I felt myself being lifted and carried through the air, and heard the first voice say, "Good luck gentlemen." I swallowed in two gulps of breath before being plunged into the iciest, coldest Hell I have ever known.

"The lid pulled off and bright light flooded in as freezing water rushed around me. For a second my entire body locked up as the freezing water jolted my system.

"Only after a moment did my mind take over and force the rest of me into action. Bracing my feet against the bottom of the barrel I pushed as hard as I could and torpedoed out through the water. Spreading my arms in front of me I pulled in long strokes and frog kicked as hard as my legs would allow.

"I closed my eyes tight and could hear nothing as I counted off strokes through the water. The pain of the cold water pawed at my body and after awhile I realized I was screaming into the frigid water.

"When my lungs could take it no longer I flipped myself onto my back and poked my face above the surface.

My mouth was the first thing to exit the water and I took in several long pulls of air before raising my nose and eyes and looking back to the beach.

"I was over eighty yards from where the men were finishing loading our barrels onto the cart and I pulled my face back beneath the surface and swam on. I kicked and kicked for another fifteen or twenty strokes until I felt a hand grab my arm and pull me to the surface.

"That's far enough," Jack whispered as he crouched in the water beside me. "Any longer in this water and hypothermia's bound to set in. If not for the adrenaline, we'd already be ice."

"We both crawled from the water and into a small clump of pine trees where we peeled off our wet fatigues. With unresponsive and blue fingers we peeled the surgical tape from our skin and using two old t-shirts the doctors had given us dried off as best we could. We then pulled on the winter fatigues and put the wet clothes back into the bags.

"Placing a couple of large stones in each of the bags we sealed them up with the surgical tape and tossed them into the river. They floated for a few feet atop the swift current before disappearing to the bottom.

"The fresh clothes didn't warm us up much at all as we stumbled alongside the river. Silent and drawing in painful breaths of air, it was a good ten or fifteen minutes before we loosened up enough to move to a light jog.

"Our boots were the only thing we didn't have a fresh pair of and the outside of them became stiff and frozen from the cold air. The soles were much heavier than usual and every so often we had to stop to rest the burning in our legs.

"We continued moving all afternoon and through the night. We followed the road until it forked south, always staying close enough to know where we were but far enough away so as to not be spotted.

"Neither of said anything as we moved through the cold air, both of us conserving our strength and energy. If Jack was feeling the effects of his wounds he didn't show it. Except for the Ioban splashed across his neck, it was near impossible to tell that anything had happened to him at all.

"As the first grey streaks of light began to stripe the new day Jack said, "We should hole up for a couple of hours and get some rest. I think we have enough of a jump on them to buy us a little break."

"I nodded my head. "If I don't rest soon I'm not going to have any energy left when it matters."

"We kept moving for a few more minutes before I asked, "Any ideas about the best way to bed down?"

"Jack remained silent for several seconds as we picked our way through the forest floor. After awhile I noticed I was walking alone and turned to find Jack squatting down and studying the earth by his feet.

"Jack cast an eye to the treetops and said, "What are your thoughts on sleeping up there?"

"I gave him a look that relayed I thought it was crazy, but remained silent.

"Jack extended his hand to me, in it a single eagle feather he had lifted from the forest floor.

"I'm thinking it might be the safest," he said. "Whatever we find down here is going to be obvious. A hollowed out tree, a bear den, anything of that sort. We'd be sitting ducks, easy targets for sure. Up there, at least we'd have a fighting chance."

"I shot a skeptical look at Jack and surveyed the treetops above us. "A fighting chance? How the hell we going to fight from up there?"

"He ignored the questioned.

"I was thinking there," he said, pointing out a large tangle of tree branches thirty feet above the ground. "You can stay in that one; I'll stay in that one over there." This time he pointed to another tangle twenty yards back in the direction we had just came. "Rest with your back against the tree and your legs out over the tangle. That bunch should definitely support your scrawny ass."

"I to this day have no idea how he spotted those two nests, I really don't. All I could think to say was, "How long until we move again? How will I let you know if I spot trouble?"

"Jack squinted into the distance and said, "Right now the sun is about two hands above the horizon. When it gets to be right over head, start working your way down. If you spot any trouble, give me a whippoorwill. I'll be listening for it."

"Jack left me standing on the forest floor and made his way towards his tangle. I watched as he began ascending his tree and after a few moments snapped myself awake and went towards my own.

"The branches were frozen solid and quite rigid and it made for easy climbing. I reached the tangle with minimal difficulty and surveyed the area around me to find I was concealed from the ground.

"The branches were more than enough to hold me up for days.

"I pulled a few tight around me so they formed a wind block and curled myself up as tight as I could. My feet were numb and I still felt deep-rooted chills from our swim almost a day before.

"Despite all that, exhaustion won out. Within minutes I was sleeping."

My uncle raised his head from the post again and looked at the ground. He began toying at the floorboards with the toe of his shoe and for a moment he resembled a cowboy on the porch of some old west saloon instead of a man trying to stand upright unaided.

Tossing the top of his head back towards the rocking chair my uncle said, "The next page over there is an eagle feather.

"That too is not the original one, but that's not important. I thought of carrying the one Jack gave me with us but I figured if I were to lose it somebody might see it as a sign of our passing.

"To this day though I have never seen an eagle in flight, on a coin, or even a feather stuck in a hat without thinking of myself perched in that tree.

"In a roundabout way, that eagle feather too is part of the reason I'm here today. If Jack hadn't found that eagle feather we would have never found that place to bed down. If we hadn't found that, we would have never made it through what we were about to go through."

# Chapter Thirty-Eight

"The sun was still just above the horizon when a low but persistent whippoorwill sprung me from my sleep. Judging by the angle of it I had only been out a couple of hours, but the sound of Jack whistling woke me up just as well if he had been shaking me.

"I waved my arm to let Jack know I was awake and sat for a few moments blinking away the sleep. After the fog lifted I poked my head from around the tree trunk and saw Jack had already begun climbing down from his perch.

"I swung my legs from the bough of branches and followed suit, scaling the limbs two and three at a time. When I was about ten feet from the ground I swung free and dropped, pain shooting through my cold feet.

"What is it?" I asked as Jack stood waiting for me.

"They're coming," was all Jack said and took off at a jog.

"I stood and peered in the direction we had just come, then turned and sprinted to catch up with Jack. By the time I caught up with him I was panting and grunted, "How the hell you know that?"

"I could hear them clamoring through the woods," Jack said. "I figure we're still about a mile in front of them, but if we stayed in the trees till noon we'd be done for."

"Within seconds of sitting in the tree I had been asleep and hadn't heard another sound. Didn't matter though, if Jack heard it that was good enough for me."

My uncle pushed back from the post and repositioned himself so his back was resting against it. He moved side to side a few times to scratch his shoulders before coming to a stop and resting his gaze on the horizon.

"From mid-morning until dusk, we kept moving. We'd jog for awhile, walk awhile, then jog some more. Twice we came upon water and drank enough to keep us going without cramping up.

"The only time we could relieve ourselves was into the water after we had drank from it. The ground was dry and frozen and urine would have been obvious, let anyone looking for our sign know we'd been through there.

"At dusk, the trail seemed to run out from beneath our feet. I hadn't been paying real close attention and almost jogged off the edge of a cliff before Jack pulled me back.

"Where the hell are we?" I asked, not expecting to run out of ground any time soon.

"Jack look around in the dim light and he said, "Come here, I'll show you."

"He led me around a small bend in the forest and through a thicket of trees. As we crossed to the other side I could heard birds calling and the cold air caught in my throat as I emerged on the other side.

"Men, dead and frozen, lay piled around us in all directions. Many of them were disfigured beyond recognition but I could tell from their uniforms they weren't ours.

"What the hell happened here?" I whispered to myself, surveying the hundreds of dead and the many more birds feasting upon them.

"*We* happened here," Jack said, taking his place beside me.

"I turned my head to look at him and furrowed my brow before it clicked. My jaw gaped as I understood what he meant.

"This is where we were captured. Most of these men are dead because I killed them," I muttered.

"You did what you had to do," Jack said, pointing to the left. "If not, they would have done that to us."

"I followed his finger to see a small group of soldiers swinging from the trees. There was three of them hanging with a fourth on the ground in a heap.

"Those are our boys aren't they?" I asked, my voice just a whisper.

"Yep," Jack said and nothing more.

"I took a step towards them, unsure what I was going to do but Jack stopped me with a firm hand. "Don't. They're long gone and we can't save them. All we can do is let whoever's behind us know where we've been."

"Remaining motionless I stared at the men's bodies swaying high above the ground as I heard Jack's boots crunch away from me. Several long seconds passed as I stared at the scene in front me, then turned and followed him out.

"We took the ravine due east towards the coast through the night, at last completing the escape we had tried to make thirteen days before. The trail was cold in front of us and it looked like nothing had passed through in well over a week.

"Through the night we continued moving, being sure to keep a wide berth around the ravine's edge as we moved through the forest.

"As the night wore on the temperature continued to drop and the cold bit at our ears and faces. I tried pulling my hands into the sleeves of my fatigues to keep them warm but soon abandoned that for thrusting them into the front of my pants. It made moving harder but helped my hands a great deal.

"At the first sign of daylight I asked Jack if we should be stopping soon for rest. We had spoken very little through the night and his face was drawn and pale.

"I had just finished my sentence when Jack pressed a finger to his lips and dropped into a crouch. He pressed himself behind a large tree and motioned for me to do the same.

"Confused, I mouthed a question to him and he pointed to his eyes with his interior two fingers, then in the direction we were going. I dropped to a knee and peered out around the base of the tree and saw what had spooked him.

"A fire."

Aunt Jane pushed her way from the front door and clomped her away across the front porch and down onto the first step. She put her hands on her hips and yelled, "Susan Brady, get in here and say good-bye to everyone. We're leaving soon!"

Suzy climbed down reluctantly from the tire and walked up through the front yard grass. Her thumb was still stuck deep in her mouth and as she walked by her mother and up the stairs she let out another long and low shudder.

Aunt Jane waited as she walked past, her hands on her hips, before following her in. She wore the same stern expression as before and again she glared at me as I watched the scene play out.

Once they were inside and we were again alone I turned to my uncle and asked, "A fire?"

My uncle nodded his head and said, "A campfire. Small and discreet, but a campfire nonetheless.

"I looked up at Jack and whispered, "Now what?"

"Jack peered out around the tree and replied, "Stay here, I'll go check it out."

"I had no intention of doing anything of the sort, but did as told until he was a little ways ahead of me before following him. We were still about seventy-five yards from them and we picked our way from tree to tree. Neither of us made a sound as we closed in on them and stopped twenty-five feet from the fire.

"There were three men sitting around it, all of them American and all looking like they had seen better days. They were thin and wore battered clothes to match their matted hair and beards.

"I peered out from behind a rock and whispered, "American?"

"Jack turned to find me just ten yards behind him and for a moment he gestured from me to return to where we were. I gave him a quick shake of my head as he just stared back at me.

"The moment passed and he mouthed, "American," then pointed to himself and motioned towards the camp.

"I moved forward to where he was sitting and waited as he emerged from behind the tree and walked forward. His arms were raised by his sides as he moved very slow.

"He had almost reached the campfire undetected when he said, "My name is Jack Roberts. I am an American soldier."

"The sound of Jack's voice startled them into movement and all three stumbled over themselves reaching for their guns. Seeing them fumble and wrestle for their weapons was almost humorous.

"Jack stood with his hands raised and waited as they gained their feet and stood with weapons raised.

"Who the hell are you and where did you come from?" one of the men asked.

"I already told you my name is Jack Roberts. We were working our way to the coast and spotted your fire."

"*We*?" another man asked.

"My brother and I," Jack responded. He tossed a thumb over his shoulder. "He's back a little ways behind me. It was my turn to scout ahead."

"The man took several small steps towards the woods where I was I hidden and said, "What, you got some kind of ambush set in place for us here or something?" He swung the gun from where I was to Jack and back again.

"Jack looked at the man and in one fluid motion raised his right arm and snatched the gun away from him. He continued the path of the gun over the man's head and swung it down across his calves, lifting him from the ground and causing him to land hard on his back.

"The other two stood with eyes wide as Jack said, "I tried being nice, but you boys wouldn't hear of it. As I told you, I'm an American soldier. My brother and I are trying to get to the coast to find help."

"The man who had not yet spoken lowered his weapon and said, "You'll have to forgive us. We've been on the lam for several days now and have gotten pretty paranoid."

"Jack leaned down and extended a hand to the man he had just upended. "Don't worry about it. We're on the run too. I know how it goes."

"The man on his back accepted the hand and said, "I'm Fred Dunn, these here are Lewis Walker and Scott Greer."

"As he introduced them I walked from the woods and stood beside my brother. Jack nodded to them and said, "You already know me, this is my brother Cat."

"Each of us nodded to one another and I asked, "So you boys are on the lam from what?"

"The men set down their rifles and resumed their places around the fire, the warmth feeling like a Godsend.

"We were scouts for the 11th Ground," Walker said. "One day a little over a week ago we were riding ahead when we heard gunshots roaring behind us. Damn dumbass Captain didn't bother to listen to a word we said and walked the company right into an ambush."

"Did they get wiped out?" I asked.

"Naw, there wasn't enough Koreans around to take out a whole company," Greer said. "Just enough to take down a few soldiers and keep us from getting back. Company took off in one direction, we took off in another. Been moving around for a week now hoping to happen across somebody, but so far you two are the first ones we've seen."

"Silence fell for a moment before Jack asked, "Ideas where anybody's at? Where you're headed?"

"The men looked at each other and Dunn said, "We heard there's another carrier working its way up the eastern seaboard. We were kind of headed in that direction, but no telling where at along the coast it'll be."

"So how bout you boys? How'd you come to be here in the woods, alone and weaponless?" Greer asked.

"I cast a look at Jack who said, "Ah-San education facility."

"The men looked at one another and Walker said, "Never head of Ah-San. You sure that's where you were?"

"I nodded my head. "That's exactly why we left. Nobody knows it exists. There's no aid, no possibility of exchange—."

"Just the possibility of more of this," Jack said, raising his chin and displaying his scar.

"The men winced and Dunn said, "So what's your plan? Any idea where you're headed?"

"We were headed back this way towards the coast when we were captured," Jack said. "Seemed like a fine idea to continue going that direction."

"The three men exchanged glances and Walker said, "You boys are more than welcome to join up with us. We're headed that way and there's strength in numbers."

"We need to be moving soon," Jack said. "We know as of yesterday Ah-San had sent a group out after us and they were getting pretty close."

"How long you boys been running?" Greer asked.

"This morning makes two days," I said.

"You boys had anything to eat or any sleep since you left?" Dunn asked.

"I started to reply but Jack said, "We're fine." His voice wasn't angry, but carried a finality to it that echoed in the silence. I could have used some food, but I wasn't about to cross my brother.

"Walker opened his mouth to say something, then thought better of it. He paused for a second and said, "Let us dowse this fire and we can all move out."

"Jack and I stood by the warmth a few moments longer and then moved to the far edge of camp. The men moved about gathering their things while we made impatient gestures and noises trying to speed them along.

"We're going to end up regretting this," I whispered to Jack as Dunn emptied his canteen onto the fire. "Fool might as well be sending smoke signals to the Koreans. If they didn't see that plume rise they'll for sure smell it in the air."

"Jack nodded in agreement. "Best we can hope for is they bedded down for the night and we gained some distance on them."

"The three of them stuffed things into their packs and hoisted them to their shoulders. They ambled towards us and under my breath I whispered, "We going to try to lose them?"

"Jack turned his back to the camp and muttered, "Not unless we have to. They have weapons."

"The group set out, Jack and I setting the pace with the others doing their best to keep up. Several times we could hear them grunting and complaining, but we pushed forward without paying them any heed.

"By midday Jack and I had each assumed one of the packs from the men as we continued to move. They were careful not to relinquish their weapons or anything valuable though. I think they sensed we were pulling away and wouldn't hesitate to leave them if necessary.

"Late in the afternoon we ran out of ravine and began working our way due east through heavier forest. The trail was thick and wide from the passing of so many soldiers a short time before, but it was clear nobody had been through in quite some time.

"By nightfall I could smell the salt of the ocean and hear the sound of waves breaking in the distance. Jack and I had divvied the remaining gear from the third pack and were shouldering the entire load, but it was still everything the men could do to keep up with us.

"Look, I haven't heard so much as a sound from behind us all day," Dunn said. "We have to slow or you're going to kill us."

"We slow down you're going to kill us," I uttered under my breath.

"Jack grunted a quiet agreement by my side and I could see the strain of listening to the men bicker was wearing on him. Pain he could deal with, annoyance he wouldn't.

"Just a little further," Jack said. "We're about to find out if we were really smart or complete idiots."

"Complete idiots?" Greer asked. "What the hell you talking about?"

"Without a word Jack moved forward. We walked for another fifteen minutes or so and just as Walker began to lob another complaint, Jack said, "We're here."

"I had no idea where we were and couldn't see a thing, but I stood by Jack's side and let him know I agreed with whatever he said.

"Here?" Dunn said. "I don't see a damn thing *here*."

"He started to walk forward but Jack stuck an arm out and stopped him.

"You see that?" Jack asked, motioning out into the darkness before us.

"Everyone squinted into the night and Greer said, "I don't see a damn thing. Nothing but black out there."

"Exactly," Jack said and squatted to the ground. He ran his fingers over the earth at his feet and held them up so we could see the dark smudges covering his hand.

"What the—" Walker began to say, stopping himself before he got it out.

"Ash," Jack said. "All you see is black because that's all there is."

"Fire?" Dunn asked.

"Jack shook his head. "Blast charge. When they left, they piled up everything they couldn't take and blew them up so the Koreans couldn't use them."

"Dunn dipped down and ran his fingers over the ground. "So what's this leave us with?"

"Jack made a slight clucking sound with his voice and said, "Tells us a couple of different things. First, it tells us that there were Americans here, but there aren't any more. Second, there must have been one hell of a lot of Koreans around because going by the size of this blast we left a ton of munitions behind."

"His voice carried a tone that signaled he wasn't done and Greer prompted, "And third?"

"Listening to Jack explain the situation, I knew where we was going. "Third means we're no closer to finding help."

"And it means we have to find a new route and get moving," Jack finished.

My uncle pushed himself away from the post and returned to his chair as I did the same. The book lay open on the ground at his feet and he motioned towards it and said, "Lean over there and flip to the next page."

I hopped from my chair and fell to a knee, pulled up the corner of one page and turned it to the next. It was splashed with smudges of black, highlighted in grey and white. Large, thick swaths of color that leapt back and forth across the page with no real pattern to follow.

Uncle Cat pointed to the page and said, "Soot, just as black and foreboding as the patch we came across that night."

There were many questions I wanted to ask about the soot, but I held back. I knew he'd get to it in due time.

## Chapter Thirty-Nine

Uncle Cat remained motionless for several long minutes, his face impassive as the late day sun bathed him in golden sunlight. Every crack and crevice of his hardened features showed in the brilliant light, yet his eyes and lips gave no indication of activity whatsoever.

I sat and stared at the course swirls of black on the page before us and wondered how they had come to be there. Questions passed through my mind as I stared so hard at the abstract designs they started to fit into a design. I relaxed my eyes and let the shapes meld together and just before they reached clarity, my uncle spoke.

"The site of soot stretching in every direction did two very different things for the men running through the Korean countryside that evening.

"It gave Jack and I renewed energy. We now knew we were no closer to help than we had been and needed to keep looking for aid.

"It made the other men even more tired. The thought of being no closer to a final destination seemed to weigh on them and within an hour of leaving the blast site, they demanded a stop.

"Alright, I know you two can do this forever, but we can't," Dunn said, stopping and having a seat on a felled log.

"Walker joined him and said, "Freddy's right. We've been moving all damn day and ain't gotten nowhere."

"Greer walked over to their side and rested his forearms across the top of his gun barrel. "Yeah, maybe it's time we took over for a while."

"Jack and I were several paces ahead of them and turned to survey the three men before us. All wore expressions mixed of exhaustion and arrogance and had weapons within arm's reach.

"I turned my head to look at Jack and said through my breath, "Are they serious with this right now?"

"Staring back Jack said, "Looks like it."

"Together we turned and moved a few steps back towards them.

"Look, we didn't mean any harm or disrespect. We're just trying to find aid and get our soldiers out of Ah-San," Jack said.

"Walker held up a hand. "And we understand that. Nobody's trying to accuse you two of anything. We're just saying we're going to lead for a while and our first act as leaders is to stop here and rest for the night."

"We'll head out again at first light," Dunn said. "Once we've all slept and had something to eat."

"Jack and I each swung our gaze around the clearing they had chosen and I asked, "Are you sure you want to stop right here? Maybe we could find someplace a little bit further off the trail?"

"Greer pushed his arms forward to be sure we noticed the Garand they were resting on. "Nope. We like it here."

"I shot a look at Jack and raised my eyebrows. He ignored my glance and said, "Alright gentlemen, we'll rest here and move out again in the morning."

"A smug expression crossed Greer's face as exhausted relief washed over Walker and Dunn.

"You boys get us some firewood, we'll start setting up camp," Greer said, motioning for us to unload the packs we'd been carrying all day for them.

"I walked a few steps towards Greer's outstretched hand and dropped the pack at his feet. "You think that's a good idea? This time of night? Fire can be seen for a mile, smelled even further."

"Greer glared hard at me and said, "Of course it's a good idea. How the hell are we supposed to heat our food? Keep warm?"

"I matched his glare. "I forgot you've gone almost twelve hours without eating, must be rough. Maybe you can get the Koreans to hold back from killing us while you finish your meal."

"You two keep talking about these Koreans like they're behind every damn tree. We've been plugging through this forest for days now and haven't seen the first sign of Koreans."

"Before I could reply Jack stepped in and pushed the other pack into Greer's chest. His face was sullen as he looked at him and said "If these fools want a fire to lie beside we won't stop them, but we don't sure won't join them."

"Walker stood and ran a hand through his beard. "Now where are you two running off to? No need for everyone to go getting themselves worked up here, we're all just tired."

"Jack turned his eyes to Walker and said, "We'll be nearby and we'll be here ready to move at first light. You boys enjoy your night."

"He turned on his heel as he finished speaking and jerked his head towards the forest. I followed him and once we were beyond earshot he said, "These guys are a complete liability, but they do have food and weapons. If they're still here come morning we'll get something to eat and a hard day's march out of them. If we don't find anything by tomorrow night, we'll split off on our own."

"I nodded my head as he spoke and cast an eye towards the clearing. "What are we going to do in the meantime?"

"Jack lifted his gaze and said, "Same as we did last time. We're going to get ourselves a little ways off from them, well beyond their firelight, and find a tree to rest in."

"We made a wide circle of the camp and found a clump of trees that gave us what we were looking for. Seven or eight tall trees grew intertwined and afforded a few large resting spots beside one another while still allowing us to look down on the camp.

"By the time we began climbing the trees we could smell smoke in the air. Once we reached our perch, we could see firelight flickering in the distance.

"We sat and watched for several minutes as the three of them moved about the fire, casting their shadows to and fro as they laughed and ate their food. Each of us sat and shook our heads at the sheer audacity they had. About the time they lay down, we too drifted off to sleep.

"The next time I awoke was a couple of hours later. I'm not sure how much later but the fire had died to a third its original size and the sky wasn't quite as dark as when I'd climbed the tree.

"I awoke with a start to find Jack sleeping. Something didn't feel right and I crept to the edge of my resting place and peered down into the camp. At first everything seemed to be in order, but I soon saw below what was wrong.

"Shapes.

"Several large dark shapes loomed around the clearing, closing in as their shadows grew extended from the dying firelight.

"I gave a very soft whippoorwill and saw Jack's eyes pop open. I gave him the same index fingers to eyes gesture he had given me and pointed towards the clearing. He blinked twice and looked down to see the scene unfolding.

"Hidden away, side-by-side in the treetops we watched as a dozen figures emerged from the darkness and surrounded the three sleeping men. We didn't hear a single sound as they converged and with quick and ruthless efficiency killed each of them where they lay, using their bayonets instead of bullets to conserve ammo and noise.

"What do we do now?" I whispered to Jack as the soldiers plundered the camp and melted back into the shadows of the night.

"Jack watched the camp clear of Koreans and said, "We wait and we pray. We climb down now we'd never have a chance. We stay here until we know they've moved on, then we pick a new path and keep going."

"I nodded as he spoke and turned my attention back to the three motionless masses lying around the fire. "Damn fools."

Silence fell over the front porch and I looked up find my uncle still in the exact position he had been in before telling the story. His mouth was pulled tight and his eyes squinted into the sun, but otherwise his face had not moved a bit.

"There wasn't a thing we could have done. We were weaponless and powerless to help them in way; any effort we would have made would have only killed us as well."

He started to say something else, but stopped himself and said again, "Damn fools."

## Chapter Forty

"Neither one of us slept another wink that night," Uncle Cat said. "Jack leaned back against the base of his tree and stared off into the distance, moving as little as possible and conserving every bit of energy he could. Now and again I noticed the part in his lips shift and felt like he was mouthing words, but I couldn't hear a thing.

"I sat on the edge of my perch and watched just as I had when the Koreans first showed. Little by little the campfire died away and new shadows emerged on the walls of the clearing. Each time one did I stared hard and long and tried to determine if it was real or not, but saw no actual movement.

"Several hours passed before dawn broke across the Korean countryside. I remember I kept wishing we were home in Ohio because it would already be daylight, and I could be hunting or fishing or anything instead of hiding in a damn tree.

"We waited a full hour past sunup to make sure nothing was around and climbed down from our perch.

Neither of us had seen or heard a thing for several hours and felt certain the area was clear.

"Walker, Dunn and Greer lay in camp just as they had upon bedding down the night before. The only sign that anybody had passed through were several large blood stains on each of the men's blankets.

"Creeping around the edge of the camp we entered at the closest point possible to the men and surveyed the situation. All three bodies were already cold and a quick check found the Koreans had taken most everything worth having with them.

"All told we found two cans of beans, a knife and a length of rope. I was able to grab a change of socks from Dunn's pack, but nothing else of use.

"We moved in and out of the camp in less than five minutes and left the men where they lay. The blankets they wore were inviting, but if the Koreans passed back through it would have alerted them to our presence.

"Without the burden of having to wait for three slower men, our pace quickened a great deal. I'm not sure if it was the rest or having witnessed what happened to the others that seemed to put a little extra charge in our step, but either way we moved fast through the forest.

"After an hour of hard pace I ventured the first words of the morning and asked, "Where we headed?"

"Pusan," Jack said.

"Pusan? Isn't that a hell of a long ways south of here?"

"Jack shook his head. "Not anymore. It took us so long before to get this far north because we had a large company and were crisscrossing our way up. I figure we hump hard all day, we can be there by tomorrow night."

"And what are we hoping to find in Pusan?"

"Our only hope is that we still have a presence in the area. That our original plan to free up the 8$^{th}$ worked and that they're still there."

"Many questions popped into my head, but I held back from saying anything. The plan was pretty thin, but I knew it was the best we could hope for. Jack wouldn't lead us into danger on purpose and after finding the seaboard void of any help, we didn't have much choice.

"We continued moving hard through the forest for the entire morning and into the afternoon. Mid-day we used the knife to open one of the cans of beans and took turns scooping out handfuls and eating them cold with our fingers. A few minutes later, we were moving again.

"It was the first bit of real food I'd had in quite a while and the strength they provided was astounding. I spent the afternoon running my tongue over my teeth and remembering their taste as mile after mile clicked by beneath our feet.

"Nightfall set in and still we pushed on with no sign of Koreans or civilization. On into the night we moved, our pace slowing as we became careful of our every sound. We had to make sure we were never in a place where our silhouettes could be seen against the night sky or where we might leave footprints in a pocket of snow.

"By morning, we had again been moving for almost a day without break. The can of beans we had eaten long before was a distant memory and my stomach was a tight knot, every so often letting out an involuntary growl.

"Just before the sun rose I said to Jack, "What are your thoughts on opening that last can of beans?"

"Jack nodded. "I agree, we either need to eat or rest."

"I returned the gesture. "I don't really think we have time to rest, do you?"

"Jack shook his head and said, "We might, but I'm guessing those men at Ah-San don't."

"So we eat?" I asked and drew the can of beans from the pocket of my fatigues.

"Jack removed the knife from his belt and said, "We eat, but not those. I have another idea."

"He took the knife and cut a branch from a tree about four feet long and a little over an inch in diameter. Running the knife down each side he stripped away the small twigs lining it and cut a deep notch in one end. He jammed the handle of the knife into the notch and wrapped the rope around it, securing it into place.

"It looked like an old Indian spear by the time he finished.

"I hate to break it to you, but we haven't seen any deer since we left Ohio there Tecumseh," I said.

"Jack smirked and said, "I was thinking of something a little smaller, a little more accessible."

"I gave a half shake of my head. "I haven't seen any squirrel or rabbit either."

"Maybe if you'd shut up long enough to listen..."

"His voice trailed off and I stood silent, listening into the distance. At first I hadn't noticed it, but after a few moments I heard it as well.

"Running water."

The screen door swung open again and an elderly couple I had never seen before hobbled from the front door. The old man used a walking cane much like my uncle's and the woman clung to him as they descended the stairs and made their way to the line of cars parked in the driveway.

My uncle swung his eyes to them as they loaded into their ancient Plymouth and drove away, rooster tails of dust rising behind them.

Leaning back in his chair my uncle rested his arms on either side of him and said, "It wasn't large enough to be considered a river, more like your average creek. It was maybe fifteen feet across in some places, in others as narrow as five.

"Remaining well concealed in the trees we worked our way downstream until we found a small riffle at a bottle neck in the creek. It was at most four feet wide and fed a large round pool that was a bit deeper and fairly calm. Large trees sloped in on either side and fuzzy green moss clung to everything.

"Stay here," Jack said. "No point in us both being out in the open."

"He turned to leave but I grabbed his arm and said, "I'm a better fisherman than you are, I'll do it."

"Jack stopped and looked me full in the face for several seconds, but said nothing.

"Seriously. I'll fish," I said. "You climb onto one of those branches overhead and look out. I have an extra pair of socks I can put on afterwards, no point in us both having frozen feet again."

"Jack turned the homemade spear in his hand and gave it to me butt first. I took it from him and set it on the ground and began to remove my boots as he climbed into the closest tree.

"I waited for him to get into position and survey the area. He peered long and hard in either direction and motioned it was clear for me to venture out.

"Morning light filtered between the limbs as I stepped barefooted onto the large grey rocks and worked my way around to the pool. The water was clear and deep and I could see several fish lying along the bottom.

"I stepped to the edge of the water, cocked the spear by my ear and waited for several seconds. I picked out a nice fat one resting near me and in one swift motion shot the spear hard into the water.

"My aim was a little off and the blade of the knife struck hard into the soil as the fish darted to the side. I heard Jack snort above me and smirked back at him without looking his way.

"When fishing in water you need to remember there is a mirror effect beneath the surface. You can't aim right at what you see or you will always be a few inches north of your target. In my hunger and haste, I had foolishly aimed right at its head.

"I pulled the spear from the water and raised it again to my ear, realigning my aim. I shot the spear back into the water and the knife found its mark just behind the fish's ear.

"Grinning wide I lifted the fish and held it up for Jack to see.

"What the hell is that thing?" Jack asked.

"I brought the fish closer and looked at it. "Breakfast."

"Jack chuckled as I pulled the fish from the knife and flattened it on the rock beside me. Gripping the spear just above the knife handle I sawed its head off and lay the body atop the rock. I tossed the head into the water upstream and using two handfuls of water washed the blood from the rock.

"The fish in the pool did not seem to notice what had just happened and continued to float along the bottom. Standing erect I raised the spear to my ear and found another plump target. I speared it just in front of the gills so hard I almost took its' head off. I removed the rest of it, washed the blood away and lifted the two large fish from the rock beside me.

"How many you think we need?" I asked in a low voice.

"I looked up to see Jack's eyes grow wide as he motioned for me to get back into the woods. Without thinking I grabbed the spear and dove into the trees, bullets strafing against rock and water as I went.

"Crashing into the forest I peered around a tree stump to see two North Koreans making their way from rock to rock towards me. I watched for a moment as they came closer before slipping to the tree Jack was in and tossing him the spear.

"I don't think they know you're up there," I whispered. "Stay here and I'll lure them in."

"Jack started to protest, but I left the tree and crept to the edge of the water. I grabbed several large stones from the bank and crept my way towards the oncoming Koreans.

"I chose a spot behind an old tree stump and waited as the first Korean rounded into sight. I let him pass and waited for the second one to show before taking aim with my first rock.

"Throwing as hard as I could, I threw a rock that hit him on the shoulder. It caught him off guard and twisted his body sideways, his feet sliding from the log he was on into the water below.

"He came up sputtering as his partner turned to see what had happened. The second motioned towards me as I threw another rock that landed in the water just inches in front of him. He fell back again, water spraying up around him.

"The first guard turned towards me and raised his gun as I sprinted towards the tree Jack was in. I could hear him crashing along behind me and waited as he drew closer and closer.

"When he was only a few feet away I slid my foot out from around the tree so he would see it and waited. I could hear his pace slow to a creep. I held my breath and knew we would only get one chance. I prayed Jack wouldn't miss.

"He didn't.

"The next sound I heard was a guttural moan followed by the clattering of a gun to the ground and a man falling. I swung out from around the tree to see the first Korean lying on his back with the homemade spear sticking up from his forehead. His eyes stared open into the sky and blood ran in thick rivulets down his face.

"Jack hopped from the tree to the ground beside me and we each took a leg and drug the man around the tree and out of sight. I pulled the spear from the man's face and Jack grabbed his gun and together we waited.

"A minute later the second man made his way down the path, dripping water everywhere. Jack raised the gun but I stopped him and cocked the spear.

"As he walked by us, I stepped forward and thrust the spear into the man's ear. His face froze in surprise for a moment as his body went slack and fell to the side.

"Jack raised an eyebrow and I said, "There may be more. No use alerting everyone."

"We drug the second man beside the first and removed a hand gun and his rifle from him. I untied the knife from the spear and gave it to Jack and took a knife from the first Korean. The new weapons gave me a sense of hope and no longer did I feel so vulnerable in the forest.

"We walked back upstream to where we had been and I put my boots back on. The last thing we grabbed before heading out again were the two fat fish I had caught just a few minutes earlier.

"As we left I looked at Jack and said, "I don't know about you, but I'm not that hungry or tired anymore."

"For the first time in days, Jack smiled. "Yeah, me neither."

My uncle stopped and leaned forward with great care. Resting his left hand on his knee he reached down and flipped the page before us. On it was a miniature spear, barely eight inches in length.

My eyes bulged at the tiny object on the page. "Uncle Cat, is *that* the spear you used?"

My uncle chuckled for a second and said, "No son, not quite. Like I said, we tore that spear apart as soon as we were done there and took the knife with us. Years later we built this one from an old pocket knife blade and a stick. It's small and looks kind of funny, but it's an exact replica of the one we made."

# Chapter Forty-One

My mother pushed her way through the swinging porch door and walked out in the oncoming evening sun. Her black dress sparkled in the bright light as she raised a hand to her eyes to shield them from the encroaching rays.

"You found a friend out here Austin?" she asked as she walked behind my chair and ran her hand over my hair. Her voice still wasn't the sing-song I was used to, but it was much better than what it had been that morning.

"Yes ma'am," I said and looked from Uncle Cat to my mother.

"He isn't bothering you out here is he Uncle Richard?" she asked.

My uncle raised a hand and smiled. "Oh no, not at all. I'm probably bothering him, he's been so nice to sit out here and listen to an old man ramble all afternoon."

Mama cocked an eyebrow and said, "Oh really? We can't seem to get a word in with this one jabbering away all the time. You sure you've got the same guy?"

Uncle Cat only smiled and said, "I don't know who he is, but he's been right good company out here just the same."

My mother kissed the top of my head and headed towards the door. Over her shoulder she said, "If he gets to bothering you, just send him in," and disappeared back into the house.

Without turning to look at me Uncle Cat said, "We'll be done out here soon enough, but not just yet. We've still got story left to tell."

Remaining hunched forward on his elbows, my uncle leaned forward with a great sigh and passed the top page from right to left. I remember watching the calm methodic manner in his movements, several seconds passing before I shifted my eyes down to the page before me.

On it was a clear tube with a long sharp needle on the end. Several numbers were written in black along its side and it was cased in a plastic wrapper.

"Uncle Cat, what is that?"

My uncle smiled with one side of his mouth and said, "I guess I should be glad you don't know what that is either. That son is a syringe."

I furrowed my brow and asked, "What's a syringe?"

I'm not sure if my uncle didn't hear me or chose not to answer, but for several long minutes he stared straight ahead. I couldn't tell if he was lost in thought or lost in another time, but either way I knew he wasn't there with me.

After several deep sighs and a few heavy blinks he came back and said, "Neither one of us were that hungry, but we ate those fish anyway. We were both subsisting on pure adrenaline and it seemed foolish to let the fresh catch go to waste.

"I have no idea what kind of fish they were, something somewhere between a catfish and a bass. It had the mouth and body type of a bass, but the scale-less skin of a catfish. As we walked, we'd peel back the skin with the knives and gnaw away at the raw flesh. Despite both saying we weren't that hungry, once we got going it didn't take long for us to finish them off.

"We worked our way back upstream to our original path and crossed back headed south. The day was well on its way by that point and we wanted to put as much distance as we could between us and the Korean guards lying downstream.

"Moving through the woods, we stayed the same course through much of the day. By late afternoon we were encountering fresh tracks and signs of recent passing, but didn't see anybody.

"A few hours before dusk we began to climb. The terrain changed from flat forest to rising rock and we had to choose our steps with care to keep from setting off any rock slides.

"We moved on into the night, the world a new shade of cold as the terrain grew rockier and afforded even less shelter from the wind. At midnight, our ascent ended.

"The trail was narrow, resembling more of a goat path than anything. Jack was leading and he stopped so fast I almost knocked into him.

"Together we had reached a ridge that tapered down into Pusan. The moon was just a few days past new and cast a thin pale light over the scene before us. The lights of the city could be seen flickering in the distance and scads of campfires dotted the land surrounding it.

"So which side is which you reckon?" I whispered to Jack.

"Jack nodded with his chin towards Pusan and said, "I'm guessing we've got the city and all these fires out here belong to people who aren't happy about it."

"Standing shoulder to shoulder we surveyed the landscape for several minutes before I asked what we were both thinking, "What are we going to do?"

"Jack exhaled and lifted his gaze to the sky. "I'm thinking we've got five, maybe six hours before daybreak. We'll say five and a half before first light."

"So five and a half hours to go or get off the pot?" I asked.

"Jack ignored the question and studied the terrain before us, his eyes darting back and forth in the soft moonlight.

"What are we looking at?" I asked.

"Trying to assess distances," Jack said. "Way I see it, we've got three options. Left, right or straight up the middle."

"I swung my gaze from right to left along the horizon and said, "Right now we don't know who's who, so we have to assume the outlying fires belong to Koreans."

"Jack nodded. "Yup, and I don't know about you but I've only got so much left in the tank here. Shorter sounds better."

"For Jack to be so candid surprised me. I tried to find the words before settling for a simple grunt and head bob.

"I followed Jack as he descended the ridge, each of us choosing a path amongst the rocks and grasses. The front side of the slope had a much softer slope than the back, and for a longer time we were out in the open.

"We stayed in a deep crouch and darted across as much as our bodies would allow.

"By the time we reached the bottom of the ridge, we were both panting hard. The exertion mixed with heightened apprehension had my entire body tense and I could feel sweat forming in the small of my back. After days and days of fighting off freezing conditions, it was a good feeling.

"Once we hit forest again we were able to be a little less careful in our movements, using the trunks of thick old trees to conceal us as we worked our way forward. Every so often we'd stop and listen for any sound of enemy, but each time we found nothing.

"As we moved a thought hit me and I whispered, "Jack, if this is all forest, how were we able to see all those fires from atop the ridge?"

"Jack moved on for several steps without answering. His ignoring me grew annoying and after a minute I asked again. Without turning, he pointed straight ahead. "You'll see in a minute."

"He was right.

"Whatever ire I might have had at Jack disappeared on the spot, replaced by worry as we reached the edge of the forest. In front of us spread nothing but wide open plane, dotted with tree stumps in every direction.

"I don't remember Pusan being this open," I said.

"Jack shook his head. "It wasn't. See all these stumps out here? Looks like the Koreans stripped it clean."

"Confusion crossed my face. "Why?"

"Trying to lay siege to the place, starve them out. No trees means no way to sneak in supplies."

"What about the sea?" I asked. "Don't they realize it's a port town?"

"Jack nodded. "I didn't say I understood it, I just said that's what it looks like they've done."

"Resting against a pair of trees we stared out over the cleared grounds, collecting ourselves for a moment. "So what are we going to do?" I asked.

"Staring hard over the plain Jack said, "It looks like most of these trees they cut about two feet off the ground. That's way low for us to run, really too low for us to crouch too.

"We're going to have to Army crawl it."

"My eyes bulged a little as I locked in on Pusan in the distance. "That's got to be a few miles or more."

"More like four or five," Jack said. "We've got maybe four hours of light too so we're going to have to get moving."

"I started to protest, but realized there was nothing to say. He was right, if we didn't get moving we'd have to wait in the woods another twenty hours and risk being seen. Also, every day we stayed meant a little more moonlight we'd have to contend with.

"Stay behind me, move from stump to stump as much possible," Jack said. "If you need to break just shake my foot or make a tiny whistle."

"Nodding my understanding, I dropped flat to my stomach and waited as Jack slid forward in front of me. I watched as he slid his right forearm and knee forward and followed with his left. When he was a few feet in front of me I did the same, my body realizing in minutes just how hard this was going to be.

"An Army crawl is a way of crawling without ever lifting your stomach from the ground. Soldiers have been using it for hundreds of years to move undetected or to get under heavy obstacles. It's not a natural position and puts enormous stress on your limbs. Every step is a task, forcing your body forward along the ground.

"Jack moved from stump to stump, carving a path like a snake up through the leveled forest. For a while I did my best to follow his movements, but soon my path was more of a straight line. I just didn't have the energy to exert moving side to side.

"Inch by inch we crawled through the darkness of the night. For the first hour we didn't see or hear a thing, but soon thereafter we started finding a few of those fires we had spotted from above.

"Afraid to so much as breath we crept by the small pockets of men, certain that the rifles strung across our backs wouldn't go very far should they discover we were there. Most of the fires held small clusters of tents, but were void of movement.

"Several hours into our crawl my body began to give out on me. Days of little food, less sleep, heightened anxiety and constant pressure were taking their toll. Dust and grasses mixed with the cold air in my nose and mouth and clawed at my lungs. The material on my fatigues grew thin with wear and I could feel my skin scraping against the barren earth.

"The night sky began to lighten little by little as forward we continued to push. The lights of Pusan grew closer, but not fast enough. As dawn approached, it became apparent we weren't going to make it.

"We pushed hard for a while longer before Jack stopped and allowed me to crawl forward beside him. Our breath was raspy and hoarse and for several minutes we lay with our chests heaving in the night air.

"We ain't going to make it are we?" I asked.

"Jack swung his head to each side as he gulped in air. "We don't have a choice."

"I lay on my side and looked back towards the woods, but couldn't see a thing through the darkness.

"How much further you think we have to go?"

"We've been going hard for several hours now. Less than two miles," Jack said as we both stared at Pusan. It seemed so close, like some cruel twist on a Christmas tale of lights leading folks home.

"We're going to have to run, aren't we?" I asked, already knowing the answer.

"Jack exhaled and said, "Yup. We're going to have run crouched from stump to stump as best we can while we still have some darkness. After that, it's a sprint to the finish."

"I waited a few more seconds to regain my breath and said, "Let's do this."

"Jack climbed to a knee and said, "Side by side from here on in. Everybody that sees us will be seeing us from the side; we want to give them as small a target as possible."

"Together we rose to a crouch and began moving forward. In that position it was little more than a fast walk, but it still felt like we were flying compared to lying flat and crawling along the ground.

"We kept that pace for almost half an hour until the first silver light began to paint the sky. Again I was glad for the extra cloud cover as we continued moving forward.

"How much further you think it is?" I asked as we moved straight for the city.

"Half a mile," Jack said as stared straight ahead and continued to move in a hurried crouch. Several more minutes passed by, and then it happened.

"We were spotted.

"Through our own panting we hadn't heard the voices off to the right of us or noticed the men circling their fire. If we had we probably would have dropped to a crawl and hoped to slink by, but as was they spotted us moving through the felled trees.

"We might not have heard their voices, but we heard the gunshots. Thin and spotty at first, but picking up and becoming heavier.

"At the first sound of fire we both raised to full height and sprinted forward with everything we had. I drew my hands into tight fists and pounded my feet into the ground, my head bobbing up and down as I ran as hard as I could for Pusan.

"More shots rang out and I noticed bits of earth kicking up around us. The city grew closer and I could see a high wall built around it with wire stripping the top. A large gate was fifty yards to the left of us and as we ran I yelled, "There!" and pointed with my right arm.

"Together we changed course and pounded forward. As the shots continued I could see soldiers popping up above the wall in front of us and Jack screamed, "We're Americans!" over and over.

"We were almost one hundred and fifty yards out when it hit me. A bullet crashed into my left leg and sent me tumbling to the ground. It ripped through my calf a few inches below the knee and hot pain seared through my body as I went down hard, sending Jack sprawling over me.

"Jack landed face first and came up bloody. "You hit?"

"Yes," I said through angry gritted teeth. "Just go, I'll be right behind you."

"Jack slid beside me and saw the blood running from my leg. I told him over and over to go on, but he ignored me and hoisted me to feet. He threw my left arm over his shoulder and together we ran forward like two men in a three-legged race competition.

"My left leg dangled in the air as I leaned on Jack and bounced on my right as fast as I could.

"Americans atop the wall returned fire while Jack and I ran for the wall. As we covered the last few yards the gate swung open and we both dove through, landing in a twisted heap of flesh, metal, and blood.

"The gate swung closed behind us and for a long time I lay there, breathing as fast as my lungs would allow and feeling the fire burning in my leg. Shots continued to ring out from around us, but I didn't have the energy to look up at them.

"I began to hear the voices around me and I opened my eyes to see a group of Koreans peering down. Without thinking I grabbed the sidearm from my waist and brought it out as they raised their hands and stepped back.

"An American officer stepped in between us with raised hands and said, "Easy son, those are *South* Koreans. They're on our side."

"I lowered the weapon and fell back, my head resting on the ground as I continued to gulp in air. "Jack, you crazy bastard, are you alright?"

"A painful moan preceded his voice. "Aw hell, nothing that won't heal." He rolled forward and I felt him tearing away the leg of my trousers to inspect my leg.

"How bad is it?"

"Looks like it passed through," he said. "Lucky you're so damn skinny."

"I looked around to see a large group of Americans and South Koreans staring down at us. A man in sharp dress with Captain's insignia on his arm emerged from the crowd and I raised my arm to salute.

"He smiled and said, "That won't be necessary. You boys alright?"

"Jack fought his way to his feet and said, "Corporals Jack and Richard Roberts, 63rd Regiment, 5th Division, sir. He's been shot through the leg."

"The Captain eyed Jack's Ioban wrap and bloodied face. "You don't look much better. Captain Earl Hix. This is the 85th Regiment, 8th Division.

"Welcome to Pusan."

"Thank you, sir," Jack said and for a moment all was quiet.

"A sergeant appeared by the Captain's side and asked, "Did you boys just say you were from the 5th?"

"I nodded and said, "We were one of a handful to make it out of there alive. We were separated from the others though; don't know where they are now."

"Well hell," the sergeant began to say, but the Captain raised a hand and cut him off.

"First we get these boys wrapped up and fed, then we'll talk. He turned his attention to us and said, "In my quarters in two hours?"

"He asked it as a question, but we both took it as an order. "Yes sir."

"The Captain melted back from the group as fast as he had arrived and the other men around us began to follow suit. A small group of medics arrived in a Jeep and helped us onto it, took us over to medical to be taken care of."

My uncle stopped there for a second and motioned for me to come around to his left side. I jumped from my seat and swung around as he lifted his pant leg and pointed to two scars on either side of his calf. They were both round in shape and a little larger than a nickel, scar tissue formed around their edges.

"This is where the bullet entered, and this is where it exited," Uncle Cat said, pointing first to the outside of his leg and then the inside.

He rolled his pant leg down and I leaned back on my knees, looking up at him.

"When the bullet entered my leg it grazed my tibia, the larger bone running down the front. A small spur of it broke off and to this day it's still floating around in there. That's why I have to use this thing," he said, motioning towards his cane.

"Every so often the spur will get itself positioned just right and begin rubbing against the muscles and tendons in there. When it does, my leg forms fluid around it to try and act as a cushion between them.

"When that happens my leg will swell up several times its own size and I'll have to take a syringe like the one on the page here and drain the fluid.

"For a while I went to a doctor about it, but he kept pushing me to get surgery. I wasn't about to do that and it seemed stupid for me to keep paying him to drain it, so one day I just started doing it myself."

My uncle paused for a moment before saying, "There were a lot of different ideas we had for this page. We could have showed pictures of scar tissue on our arms and legs from Army crawling, but we both had scars from being tied up, frozen to rocks, things of that sort and it would be hard to differentiate.

"We could have chosen a map of Pusan and the surrounding areas but in the end we thought this would be best.

"This one simple object manages to summarize both the journey and the destination. The pain I went through in being wounded and the pain Jack went through in seeing me to safety."

## Chapter Forty-Two

The sun sat no more than a few inches above the water and was so bright I had to shield my eyes or look away. Without blinking my uncle sat and stared straight ahead, his eyes impervious to the blinding light as it rolled off the water and washed over us.

Truth be known, I don't think he even knew it was there. He sat for several minutes, rocking back and forth in his chair and tapping the edge of the album. Nothing was said between us, but every so often he would absently touch his left leg.

"The medics took us to sick bay and went right to work tending our wounds. They cleaned my leg and dressed it, covered the thick scratches on my forearms and knees. They removed the Ioban from Jack's neck, cleaned it out and took care of the scratches on his face. When they were done they gave us both heavy doses of antibiotics.

"As they worked some young Korean nurses brought us bowls of rice and hot tea and we ate it down while the doctors fussed about us. An hour and a half later the same person from the medic's tent drove us over to see Captain

Hix, still in our borrowed winter fatigues and fresh bandages.

"The doctors gave me crutches as I left sick bay and I gave them an honest shot for about fifty feet before tossing them. It took more effort to support my own weight on them than it did to hobble along and deal with a little bit of pain.

"The Captain had commandeered a small home to serve as his quarters, a structure about the same size as the enlistment station from what seemed like ages before. There were men running back and forth from it and for a couple of minutes we stood outside and watched.

"A few moments passed before a young private with thick black hair poked his head out and said, "The Captain would like to know if you plan to join us or should he come out here to speak with you?"

"Jack and I exchanged a glance and we made our way into the house. For all the activity we had witnessed from outside it was quite subdued and I could even hear soft music playing in the background.

"Captain Hix was seated behind a large desk and motioned to two wooden chairs as we approached. Several men lined the walls in chairs of their own and every eye was on us as we approached.

"So, I already know your name, rank, and division, so let's start there," Captain Hix said. He had thick hair that was once black but now predominantly silver and parted on the side. His face was smooth and bore a few lines around his mouth and eyes but was otherwise free from blemish. "The 63$^{rd}$, 5$^{th}$ huh?"

"Yes sir," Jack said. "Most were wiped out up near Chosin, a handful of us were able to make it out."

"Captain Hix leaned forward and said, "Way I heard it, it was more like *all* of you."

"Jack bobbed his head. "Just about. Dozen of us were able to swim out of there and work our way across the countryside. Along the way, we ran into a bunch of Marines making their way eastward and decided to give a hand. The two of us got separated laying down some delay fire, taken captive."

"Captive?" Hix said, surprise in his voice. "Where'd they send you? One of the numbered camps? Amkon?"

"I shook my head and said, "No sir. Ah-San."

"Hix furrowed his brow and shot a look at one of the men sitting to his right. "Ah-San? Do we have anything on an Ah-San?"

"The man twisted his head and Hix asked us, "Are you sure? We don't have anything on the books for that one."

"Jack nodded his head and said, "Yes sir, very sure. That's why we're here."

"At Ah-San we came across a Colonel Harold Spires and the 3rd Army infantry," I Said. "He, along with Lt. Colonel Phelps and Major Atwood kind of run things for our side there."

"Hix shot a look along the left side of the room and leaned forward. He rested his elbows on the table in front of him and said, "I'm listening."

"We were only in camp a few hours when they sent for us," Jack said. "Said they had been scouring the incoming prisoners and we were the first that looked like we might be able to handle the job."

"As it was, they knew that nobody knew about Ah-San," I said. "If they didn't get somebody out to pass word along of they were as good as dead."

"So they planted us in their daily water barrels and deposited us in the river a little over five days ago. We've been working our way here ever since," Jack finished.

"Concern painted Hix' face and he turned to an aid on the right side of the room, "When was the last confirmed word from Colonel Spires?"

"The aid rifled through some papers and said, "Over a month ago, from up north of the 38th."

"A man to the left of Hix tapped a map on the wall above his head and said, "You think you two could show us where this place is?"

"I nodded as Jack said, "We can show you and take you there."

"The man returned my nod and for a moment the room fell silent. Hix leaned back in his chair and asked, "How many men are there?"

"Several hundred," I responded, "at that camp. There are also two more camps in the area, one for Koreans and one for non-military personnel. And those are just the ones we know of for certain."

"We came in with a train of over five hundred," Jack said. "No way of knowing how many are up there total."

"The men around us exchanged glances as Hix asked, "And the treatment there?"

"Jack leaned his head back and pointed to his throat. "Major Han, the man in charge there, left me with this parting gift right before we took off. Major Atwood told us it isn't uncommon for the guards there to engage in shootings or beatings for sport."

"Not to mention they're living in complete squalor," I said. "There's a river of shit flowing through camp and the main foodstuff is millet. Men are dying by the day."

"Any kind of aid? Medical attention?" another man asked.

"I shook my head and said, "There are two doctors in a single tent there. Quincel and Rothchild. Little to no supplies, stuff they have is outdated. We gave a hand all we could, but it's grim."

"Hix stood and began to walk from behind his desk to the map on the wall. "As you boys saw this morning on your way in, we're pretty well bottled up behind these walls." He started to continue but paused and said, "Speaking of which, how the hell did you two make it that close to the gate?"

"We topped that ridge last night just after midnight," Jack said. "Crawled the rest of the way here."

"A few whistles went up from around the room and Hix said, "That's near six miles from here."

"I held up my bandaged elbows and said, "We'd gone the whole way too if we hadn't run out of darkness."

"Hix nodded and said, "So like I was saying, ground isn't an option on this one. Any way to get to this camp from sea?"

"I looked at Jack and for a second we were both blank, then it came to both of us.

"*Blast charge.*

"There's a site up the eastern seaboard where a large aquatic evac took place maybe a month ago," Jack said. "That's where we were headed when we were captured and we passed the same point making our way here. It should be somewhere in the vicinity of Koto-Ri."

"You'll know the site because there's a giant scorched crater where we set off what looked to be one helluva blast charge," I said. "Nothing but soot and ash for a quarter mile square."

"I know the site you're talking about," a middle-aged man behind us said as the room turned to look at him. "I wasn't there, but I know Sergeant Muehler was. He'll be able to tell us right where it's at."

"And we can take you in from there," Jack said. "We could even guide you on ground, but from sea that's your best bet."

"Hix looked around the men in the room and said, "What do you gentlemen think? I know we're under pretty heavy fire, but we can't leave a camp of our own out there with no chance of recovery."

"A murmur of talk went up from around the room and I said, "Captain, what if I told you it could be done with a minimal detachment of men?"

"The murmuring died down and the Captain crossed his arms in front of him. "I'd be very interested to find out how."

"I turned and pointed to the trio of South Koreans I had drawn my weapon on that morning. "Every person at that camp is Korean. No Chinese anywhere. We could give you their exact patterns, how they run their pickups, how they guard the water detail."

"Jack's eyebrows raised beside me and everyone turned their attention back to Hix, who stood and rubbed his chin. "You know, that just might work. Set up a little ambush and get a group of our guys in there, could even arm the prisoners coming back with water. What would you say their total forces are there?"

"Twisting my face a bit I looked to Jack and said, "Maybe a hundred? At the very most?"

"Jack turned to Hix and said, "At any given point there are no more than twenty guarding the prisoners. The rest stay in bunkhouses which sit about a quarter mile away from the camp along with the officer's quarters and such."

"A half smile grew across the side of Hix' face and he said, "I'm liking this more and more by the minute." He spun his gaze around the room and said, "Gold, Molina, you two work on getting us a ship ready to depart at dawn, two days from now. Bergen, you get me forty men, twenty Korean and twenty American and let them know they'll be going on that ship."

"Activity burst out around the room as Jack and I requested permission to be dismissed. Hix granted it, told us to be back the next day at noon for planning purposes and released us.

"Jack and I left the room and I said, "I don't know who Spires is, but he must have some serious pull."

"Jack nodded. "You see the way they all got real interested when we brought him up?"

"I never had the chance to respond.

"Instead, a voice from the past called out, "Well if it ain't them damn Birch Grove boys!"

"It took a moment for the words to sink in as Jack and I looked at one another, then back in the direction of the voice.

"Marks. On either side of him were Buddy, Manus, Caldwell and Sims, all grinning wide.

"The same grins spread on our faces as we walked forward to meet them, starting with handshakes and ending with hugs.

"We thought we lost you boys way back on the ravine," Buddy said, still smiling.

"Ah, were not from Kentucky. They make us a little more resourceful up in Ohio," I said as the group laughed aloud.

"Where the hell you fellas been?" Marks asked. "Hiding out, waiting for us to win the war for you?"

"Jack bobbed his head and said, "Where *haven't* we been, thought for sure you'd have this thing finished by now. Imagine our surprise to find you aren't a day closer to anything than when we left."

"Sims held a hand to the sky and said, "Gentlemen, I propose in honor of the return of our friends from the dead, we take this some place a little more fitting a celebration."

"All I wanted to do was eat and sleep, and I could see Jack's face saying the same thing, but we decided to join them anyway. It was clear they wouldn't be denied and to be honest we were both glad to see familiar faces after all we'd been through.

"The boys took us to a hole in the wall joint so small I doubt it even had a name. There were but four tables in the whole place and we shoved them together and piled around.

"A waitress attempted to approach and take our order, but Marks told her not to bother. "We'll have two bottles of the house specialty and as much food as you could rustle up for our friends here."

"Within a minute the waitress returned with the alcohol and Buddy poured healthy drinks for everybody. Jack and I had never drunk a drop of anything in our life and weren't real thrilled to start, but the boys raised their glasses in salute of us and it would have been rude to refuse.

"Here's to the Birch Grove boys, best soldiers I ever had that I didn't have to teach every damn thing they know!" Marks said and the group downed their glasses.

"The alcohol was rancid and bitter and burned like hell going down. Tears welled in my eyes as it made its way to my stomach and I heard Jack cough beside me.

"The boys laughed even harder and poured another round, this time Buddy raising his glass and saying, "Here's to the Robert's brothers, the craziest, most heroic men to be brought back from the dead since Jesus Christ himself!"

"By the time the waitress arrived with the food my head was spinning. I tore through bowl after bowl of cheap brown rice and vegetables but it didn't much matter.

"By mid-afternoon we were all pretty darn drunk.

"We spent the entire day in there, the six of us laughing and talking and drinking. Every now and again other soldiers would wander by and we'd buy them a drink. Women would get as far as the door and have second thoughts but we didn't care. We played bad Korean music on the radio and danced with the waitress and sang old songs as loud as we could.

"At one point Dwayne happened by and poked his head in, the surprise on his face evident as he found Jack and me sitting around drinking with the boys. To his credit he stayed and had a drink with us and even pretended to be civil, which we all joked was quite the stretch for him after he was gone."

My uncle stopped there and locked his gaze on the setting sun, a closed smile on his old and weathered face.

"As I sit here this very minute, I can still remember everything about that day. I can taste the bitter vodka and the worse food. I can hear the boys singing and smell the flowers in the waitress's hair.

"The next page in the book is a label from the vodka we drank that day. It's written all in Korean and I still have no idea what it says.

"Truth is, I don't much want to know.

"We decided to include it in here for a couple of reasons. First, it marked the end of our journey. We were both a little worse for the wear but we had lived to tell our tale and that was what mattered.

"Second, that night before we all stumbled off to sleep we made a pact that from then on whenever we were to see each other we would commemorate that night by passing around the cheapest, nastiest vodka the place had on hand.

"Even now, the only alcohol Jack or I have ever had is cheap vodka with the other men in that group. The days we were married we shared a glass of Korean liquor and the days our children were born we shared some more.

"Each time we drink we raise our glasses and say "Here's to being alive" because against the odds, that's what we were.

"Alive."

# Chapter Forty-Three

The smile on my uncle's face grew a little larger as he said, "The next morning I felt like I'd been in a head on collision with Hell itself.

"I awoke atop a stack of flat woven grass mats in the back of a storehouse, Buddy sprawled out beside me and Jack sitting with his back against the wall opposite us. My mouth tasted like I'd spent the night eating sand and my head throbbed as every beat of my heart pushed new blood through it. I thought my leg was bursting through the dressing the medic had wrapped it in and my joints felt as if they'd been dipped in both acid and concrete.

"How you doing?" I muttered to Jack.

"Without lifting his head from the wall, he said, "I feel about like you look. My head hurts too much to sleep and cool concrete is about the closest thing we've got to medicine."

"I nodded my understanding and lay back on the mats. Using my thumb and forefinger I rubbed my eyes and asked, "What time is it?"

"It's late morning," Jack said. "Few more minutes and I was going to wake you. We should get washed up, find a change of clothes before we go over there."

"Buddy rolled over with a low moan. "And some coffee. Good Lord, you boys know how to come back in style."

"Where are we?" I asked, opening my eyes to let the low light filter in.

"Back of an old lady's shop, name of Oh. She makes mats and sells them, let's me stay here most of the time. There aren't any barracks in Pusan, so you kind of have to fend for yourself."

"It took the better part of an hour for us to wrestle ourselves up from the storehouse floor. Several times I took my feet only to feel the pain in my head and legs well up and be forced back to the ground. After the third attempt I managed to find my bearings enough to walk out into the day.

"Buddy led us through the side streets to an old public bath for us to wash up in. The water was quasi-fresh and icy cold and did wonders for our aching bodies. From there we found the makeshift Army supply in Pusan and drew fresh winter fatigues.

"Our last stop found us back in the same little bar we'd been in the day before.

"The waitress laughed when she saw us coming and laughed even harder when we ordered eggs and coffee. Three pots of straight black and a dozen greasy eggs later, we left Buddy and went off to find the Captain.

"Pusan wasn't a very big town and it only took a few minutes for us to get back to his quarters. It was even busier than the day before and we slid inside the door and stood in the corner, watching the flurry of activity around us.

"Maps were tacked to the walls and spread across the desk. In the center of the room was Hix, pointing left and right and talking to a group of men. We stayed where we were for several minutes until he noticed and motioned for us to come forward.

"As we approached one of the men made a face and said, "Damn, you boys smell like bad coffee and cheap booze."

"I half smiled and Jack nodded his head, but we said nothing.

"Hix looked from one to the other for a few seconds before tapping the map on the desk in front of him. "Show us what you know."

"Jack moved forward and asked, "Have you yet identified where that blast charge was detonated?"

"Hix glanced to his left and said, "We should within the hour, right Sergeant Reyes?"

A man with dark hair and a moustache nodded his head, but said nothing.

"So for now let's just assume we're starting from here. You said you went right by the site anyway, right?"

Jack looked down at the map again. He shook his head and said, "Do you have a topographical map? Everything we've got is based on landmarks."

The crowd to the left parted and Hix held a hand out for us. He grabbed a box of pushpins off his desk and inserted one at Pusan. Handing the box to Jack he said, "We are here. Where do we go next?"

Jack studied the map for a moment and put a finger on Chosin. From there he counted south three clicks and found the deep ravine that had served as our guide line for several months now.

"The blast charge is going to be somewhere around here," Jack said, pushing a red tack into the map near where the ravine and the ocean would intersect. "We've traveled this ravine three times now, I'm certain this is our landmark."

"From there you go east the better part of a day's march, probably fifteen or twenty miles," I said. "You can't see it here but there's a heavy trail that runs between this ridgeline and this pass."

As I spoke I motioned to the map and Jack inserted pins.

"It winds more or less due north until it reaches the river, where the trail hooks hard west for another five or ten miles."

"Jack pushed another pin in where the camp had been and we turned to face the room. Some of the men looked from the map on the wall to the map on their desk and an unknown officer asked, "How far we looking at all told?"

"I glanced at Jack with uncertainty as he said, "No way of knowing for sure."

"Took right at about three days moving," I said. "Best guess? Fifty miles or more."

"A low murmur went up from around the room and Hix raised his eyebrows. "You two covered fifty miles on foot?"

"Jack shook his head and said, "Nope. We covered fifty miles to the blast point. From there went due south for another day and a half's hard march. Probably close to a hundred all told."

"A short man with a head shaved bald and a thin blonde moustache stepped to the map on the wall and said, "What kind of terrain we looking at in *this* general region?" As he spoke he drew a circle around the pin Jack had inserted at the camp, covering several inches in all directions.

"I pursed my lips for a second and said, "Pretty standard with everything else we've seen. Some cliffs, a ravine or two, a few rivers and the woods sprinkled in."

"The man turned back to us and said, "What I mean is, anywhere in there you think we can land?"

"Confusion worked its way across my face and Jack asked, "Land, sir? The boats won't be able to get much past the shoreline. There's a river in there, but nothing large enough to get any major watercraft down."

"Not to mention we'd be asking for an ambush," I added. "Very tight turns, lots of trees, they'd pick us apart."

"The man stared from Jack and I and then to Hix, the confusion on his face matching our own.

"Gentlemen, this is Lieutenant Colonel Larry Fitzpatrick, United States Air Force. We don't have the time or manpower to send a unit in overland so we're looking at an aerial approach. Lieutenant Colonel Fitzpatrick is being kind enough to handle the logistics for us."

"Both of us nodded and Jack returned his gaze to the map. He bunched his brow for a moment and said, "What kind of aircraft will you be taking? How much room is needed?"

"Fitzpatrick shook his head and said, "This is to be done entirely by helicopter, no runway of any kind will be needed. We can sit down and liftoff from anyplace flat and clear that's a hundred feet in diameter or more."

"For a few moments we both sat and thought hard and Jack said, "There were a few small clearings downstream from where we put in. I'm sure if you were to swing in and come up from the south you could get a helicopter in there undetected.

"The road coming in due east has a lot of traffic and if you come down out of the north there's nowhere to land because of the ridgeline. You could go from the west, but you're going to have to be a ways further out to account for the Korean quarters."

"Fitzpatrick nodded his head and together he and Hix began pointing to the map again. I sat and stared at the wall for several minutes and said, "Captain, Colonel, I'm not trying to tell you guys how to run your operation but I'll tell you what you could do."

"They both turned and Hix said, "That's why we asked you here. Anything you got is helpful."

"I cast a glance to Jack and said, "To be honest, the best landing place you have is right in the middle of camp. If you can send in one team of South Koreans downstream and take out the guard detail, you could bring in the rest of your team there."

"Jack stood beside me and said, "We can show you within a quarter-mile where their barracks and headquarters are, you could run a couple of planes over them and wipe them out in a hurry."

"Hix nodded and said, "What do you think Larry?"

"Fitzpatrick made a non-committal turn of his head and said, "It needs a little tweaking, but it could work. Always easier to shoot an enemy from the air than face to face."

"Jack and I followed the conversation between them with our eyes and when Fitzpatrick finished Jack stuck another pin into the map just southwest of the camp. "That's where they stay."

"You're sure of this?" Fitzpatrick asked.

"Jack lifted his chin and pointed to the scar running beneath it. "Very sure. We've been there and seen it in person."

"Hix looked at each of us and said, "We have some more planning to be done here, but I assume you two want in on this?"

"Yes sir," we echoed in unison and turned to leave the room.

"You boys be ready at 0500 hours," Hix called as we left. "And try to lay off the booze tonight. Tomorrow you're going for a little trip."

## Chapter Forty-Four

"That evening was one of the best nights of sleep I ever got. Most times when I knew we were facing combat I'd toss and turn and wake up a hundred times, and that was if I was lucky enough to find sleep at all. That night though, I curled up on a stack of grass mats and fell into a deep slumber.

"I don't know if it was my body realizing how exhausted it was, the need for rest as a way to heal injuries, or maybe I was just growing used to the life of a soldier. Regardless, I slept as if I hadn't a care in the world.

"The next morning Jack and I rose while the world was still dark and left Buddy sleeping in the corner. We picked our way through the quiet streets across town and found several large helicopters being loaded on the beach by men running back and forth.

"A handful of South Korean soldiers in North uniforms stood bunched together waiting to board their helicopter as a group of American soldiers milled about next to another.

"Well, look here," I said as we approached to find Marks and Dwayne on the outer edge of the group sharing a cigarette. "These two decided they might want try this whole soldier thing for a change."

"Marks took a long drag off the cigarette and cast it aside. "Naw, we just wanted to get a good look at the bastards that were man enough to smack around the mighty Roberts brothers."

"Dwayne shook his head and said, "I didn't think such men existed. I'm half expecting to find Hercules or Xerxes or something." His voice still carried the same indifference towards us, but the fact that he was speaking at all meant progress had been made.

"Hix called us to formation and we assumed positions before him, two rows of ten men each.

"Gentlemen," Hix said, "you all know why you've been asked here today so I won't go into some dramatic speech." He paused for a moment to make sure he had attention and said, "This morning's raid will be conducted in four different waves.

"Alpha Team, the South Koreans, is departing now and will put in downstream from Ah-San. They will arrive in time to intercept the morning water run and will arm the prisoners they find. They will stand in as the water detail as well as conceal themselves in the barrels. They will enter the camp through the rear gate and secure the camp.

"We are Bravo Team and will be departing in twenty minutes. We will touch down right in the center of camp and help clean up with anything that needs to be done.

"Shortly after we take off two fighter planes will be departing en route to the barracks of the Koreans at Ah-San to provide heavy air fire. Because the terrain will not allow for them to land, it will be up to us to move in on foot and secure the area.

"The last departure will be additional helicopters to aid in prisoner evacuation. Once the camp is secure, you are to help in any way you can. Are these orders clear?"

"Yes sir!" sprang up from all twenty men in unison.

"Hix dismissed us and strode from the scene while men began to file onto their respective helicopters. As we boarded I looked over my shoulder to Jack and said, "What about the other camps?"

"Jack drew his mouth tight and shook his head. "There's probably no way Hix can arrange this kind of operation for non-military personnel."

"But Josephine and Mercer..." I began.

"We'll put in a word when we can," he said, "but right now is not the time."

"I knew better than to argue with someone who had the same opinion I did and was just looking at things in a more logical manner. I boarded the helicopter and within minutes we were whistling through the early morning sky.

Daylight was less than an hour old and mist rose from the forest beneath us and enveloped the world in silver.

"Sir, how long does it take to reach our destination?" a soldier behind me asked.

"ETA t-minus thirty seven minutes," Hix responded.

"Jack leaned against my shoulder and said, "Total ride of a little over an hour. How nice would that have been?"

"And miss a week of pure hell?"

"Jack smiled with one side of his mouth as the men around us sat in various stages of preparation.

"You can always tell the ones that have seen a great deal of action by the way they carry themselves before it hits.

"Those that are relaxed, calm, cracking a smile are those that have done it. I don't mean to say they've grown used to it but they've come to accept the fact that things happen in battle that just can't be helped. Sometimes heroes die and cowards live, good men perish and evil persist.

"The new ones have eyes that never stop moving. They don't talk to anyone, always have a hand shaking or a knee bobbing up and down. Their nerves are on fire and there's nothing they can do to stop it."

Uncle Cat paused again and looked down at his own hand and smiled.

"Hix gave us the heads up that we were arriving and each of us donned our helmets and checked our weapons. The helicopter banked right and began to descend as we prepared for whatever lay behind the closed door of the helicopter.

"The aircraft landed with a jolt and the doors swung open the second we touched down. Jack and I were one of the closest to the outside and we jumped to the ground and fanned forward with guns raised.

"Around us hundreds of prisoners stood with hands high above them, confusion written across their faces. A few scattered shots could be heard in the distance, but otherwise everything seemed quiet.

"Bravo Team, south gate. Move!" Hix barked and we drew up into formation and headed that direction. As we passed through camp men cheered for us, clapping and yelling.

"We burst through the south gate to find our crew of South Koreans poised to join us. They had shed the North Korean uniforms they were wearing when they left and piled them atop the stack of North Korean guards amassed outside the camp gates.

"Together Alpha and Bravo covered the route Jack and I had laid out for them towards the barracks, the sounds of planes and machine gun fire heavy over head.

"Fan out!" Hix called as we drew close and almost fifty men thinned to a single file line and closed in on our target. Some of the prisoners stripped weapons from the fallen North Korean guards and together we made a large wave moving forward.

"As we drew close we could see smoke rising from some of the buildings and Koreans lying on the ground around them. A few had weapons out and were trying to fire at the passing planes, but they were rewarded for their efforts by line after line of machine gun fire.

"By the time we arrived, much of the action had already taken place. Hix broke us into three groups and sent each of us into a building. There were no more than fifty men in the camp and most of those had been dispatched by air support.

"When each of the buildings was clear we reconvened and returned to camp. The sense of urgency was gone from the air and we used a light jog in returning.

"We arrived to find a small handful of helicopters on the ground, rows of weak prisoners being given food and helped aboard. Jack and I went straight for the medical tent to find Quincel and Rothchild, but were intercepted before we got there.

"They saw us before we saw them, Phelps calling out, "So I take it you boys made it back alright?"

"Jack and I each stopped and walked towards the three of them. It was the first time we had seen them up and about and to be honest, I was a bit surprised at how well they all seemed to move.

"I don't know about alright," I said, "but we made it. As promised."

"Took your sweet time getting back here too, didn't you?" Atwood sneered.

"In one of the few times I've ever seen Jack crack, he turned and snapped.

"We covered over a hundred miles without any real food or weapons," Jack said. "We slept a total of six hours in four days, killed Koreans with a homemade spear and Army crawled over five miles in the dark to get back here."

"Not mention got shot for our efforts," I added.

"Jack took a step closer to Atwood and said, "All to get back here and save your sorry ass."

"Atwood's face grew red and he said, "You forget yourself. I am a superior officer—"

"No," Jack said, "you're a higher ranking officer. There's nothing superior about you."

"Atwood face swelled with anger but Spires stepped between us and extended his hand. "You risked your lives to save ours and you managed to pull it off in less than a week. Thank you."

"Spires shook each of our hands in turn. "And Atwood? Stop acting like such a prick, either one of these two could kick your ass."

"Phelps yelped a laugh and shook our hands as the four of us moved towards the helicopters. Atwood's face grew an even deeper shade of crimson, but he said nothing as he followed behind.

"We got to the helicopters to find Hix directing people and introduced him to Phelps and Spires. The ranking officers began discussing plans for evacuation and Jack and I wandered off to find the doctors.

"Quincel and Rothchild were in their usual tent, tending to bedfast patients. As we entered they both gave the exhausted smile of men tired of holding on and hugged us each in turn. Together we began helping them move soldiers to the helicopters.

"The numbers at the camp had swelled in the week we were gone and the helicopters were forced to head to Pusan with a full load and return again. The South Koreans escorted the first load of prisoners back and while they were gone we readied the rest of camp to depart.

"Hix found Jack and I helping the doctors move the last of the dysentery patients and said, "You weren't exaggerating. Another week or two and we would have lost a good many of these men. As is, there's plenty here who may not make it."

"We nodded in unison and I said, "Things have gotten worse since we left. Looks like once we escaped the Koreans really started coming down on them because most of these men have been beaten."

"Hix shook his head. "You can't look at it that way. If you hadn't escaped, you'd still be here and not a single one of these men would be going home."

"Captain!" a voice called out, drawing our attention away from the discussion. "Over here! Come quick!"

"Hix ran towards the middle of the camp, Jack and I close behind him.

"Two soldiers were inside the tent holding a Korean on either side. The captive wore khaki pants and a white shirt with a scarf tied around his neck that had become unraveled and hung loose around him. Blood ran from his nose and mouth and dribbled down onto his shirt.

"Would you look at this?" I said aloud, recognizing the man upon arrival.

"This an old friend of yours?" Hix asked.

"Jack pointed to his chin and said, "You could say that, right Major Han?"

"Han's body was slack and weak and his head hung towards the ground. At the sound of his name he raised his head and shuddered when he saw us standing before him. His shoulders sagged, tears streaming down his face.

"Jack removed the Korean sidearm he had taken several days before and walked up to Han. He placed the barrel of the gun under Han's chin and used it to lift his head and stared down at him.

"Didn't think you'd be seeing me again did you son of a bitch? Didn't think you'd ever have to answer for all the times you've tortured and maimed people did you? Didn't think I would ever find your ass did you?"

"With each question Jack asked his voice grew angrier. Between each one he pistol whipped Han, thick slashes of flesh being removed with each swing.

"After the third question Jack drew Han's face up again. Every man in the tent was silent and watching as Jack cocked the hammer back and slowed his breathing."

My uncle paused and watched the full golden ball of the sun begin its final slip below the horizon. The world was suspended between day and night and for a moment everything had a glow about it.

"In war, you do what you have to do," Uncle Cat said. "Most of the time you move and react before you have time to consider what you're doing. It's the body's natural tendency to act in a manner of self-preservation and sometimes that means having to kill another man.

"Over the course of the war I had watched my brother kill men, but I had not watched my brother become a killer. We had both done what we had to do to survive.

"In that moment, watching him stand over a helpless and quivering Han, I had to step forth and put a hand on his shoulder. "Don't do this Jack. There's no going back from this."

"Jack pressed the barrel harder into Han's face and raised his face higher, staring down the bridge of his nose. He stayed that way for several seconds as Han quivered, then lowered his weapon.

"He took two steps back from Han and continued to stare at him as I slipped between them. "You won. It's over."

"In one fluid motion Jack raised the gun and fired half a dozen rounds into Han. I turned to see Han's chest explode with blood and bullets and I saw him fall back to the ground.

"It wasn't until he hit the ground that I noticed the small gun fall from his hand."

My uncle stood and walked back to the edge of the porch. His gaze was pinched tight to block the on-coming sun and I could see crow's feet folded around his eyes. He returned to the pole in front of us and rubbed his hand along it.

Without turning back to me he said, "The next page in the book is the last remnant we have from Korea. It's a patch of Hans' scarf, still has some of the bastard's blood on it.

"We each had our own reasons for deciding to include it. To me it was important because it marked the last time Jack saved my life, the last of many times.

"To Jack it signified that he wasn't just even with the man that scarred him for life, but he had won in the end.

"Together we decided to include the scarf because it marked something even more important to both of us. It was the last shot we ever fired at another human being as long as we both lived."

## Chapter Forty-Five

My uncle remained with his back to me for several long minutes, standing and rubbing his hand along the grain of the wood. He didn't look at it as he did so, just ran his hand the length of it and stared off into the distance.

The sun was now a half circle on the horizon, flaming orange as it seemed to sink into the lake before us. The sky glowed orange around it like dying embers in a fire and gentle streaks of purple extended from it.

"Five hundred and fifty six," Uncle Cat said. "That's how many men we pulled from Ah-San. I don't know how many ended up making it, but that's how many we gave a chance.

"Three days after the raid Hix called us back into his office. Spires was with him and there was a certain ominous feeling in the air.

"Please, sit," Hix said as we walked in. He was seated behind the old desk with Spires standing close by. Spires's arms were folded across his chest and both wore stony expressions.

"I shot a quick glance at Jack as we both took our seats, already not liking where this was going. We were both healing well, but still in no real condition for another assignment.

"Hix leaned forward over his desk and studied a piece of paper for several long seconds, glancing between it and us as he did so. "I'll be honest with you both. Right now I'm sitting here with very mixed feelings.

"As I commander I am sickened. There are men that have been in the Army for years and years that haven't amassed the kind of record you have in less than a year. You boys are rare stock and I'm none too pleased about what I've been ordered to do.

"As a man that saw what you did at Ah-San, I am overjoyed. You risked your lives for men that now get to go home to their families.

"And so will you."

"The last words hung for a second and my eyes bulged as Hix sat looking at us. He tossed the paper towards us and said, "It has been handed down by the United States War Department that we are to begin pulling out of Korea. As such, any and all men that are or have been wounded in the line of battle are to be discharged, effective immediately."

"The words fought hard to resonate with me and for a second it was difficult to breath. It was the very last thing

I had expected to hear. The notion of home seemed so far away that I had almost removed it from my mind.

"We were going home. Back to Mama and the river, to Birch Grove and bucking hay.

"Home.

"Jack picked up the paper and I looked down to see the words, "Notice of Discharge" and our names written across the top.

"Sir, I would hardly say we qualify as wounded," Jack said, looking up at him.

"Spires shook his head and said, "I told you this wouldn't be an easy sell Earl.

"Son, you've got a scar running from ear to ear and a cluster around your eye there that looks like shrapnel's still in it. Your brother has a hole in his leg. Neither one of you have anything but scar tissue on your forearms and wrists. I'd say that qualifies as wounded."

"Sir—" Jack began, but Hix raised his hand to cut him off.

"It's out of our hands, it's already been done. You depart this evening."

"This evening, sir?" I asked, shocked at the events unfolding before us. I took the paper from Jack's hand and read it to find it stated just what Hix had already told us.

"I've barely known you a week and already I can say you boys will be missed," Hix said, reaching out to shake our hands.

"I can second that," Spires said, extending his own hand. "What you boys did for us at Ah-San, I'll never forget. Maybe one of these days when we're all back home I can buy you a beer and you can tell me how the hell you managed to pull it off."

"The two of them dismissed us. Jack and I left the office and for the first time in days stepped out into sunshine. The air still had a brisk chill in it, but standing there with the sun on our faces felt incredible.

"We're going home," I said, the sound of the words sounding funny in the morning air. "You believe that?"

"Jack shook his head. "Home. Damnation."

"Together we went and found Buddy and Marks, Sims and Caldwell, Dwayne and the other remaining members of the $5^{th}$. The lot of us spent the afternoon exchanging stories and throwing back more bad Korean vodka, laughing and slapping back and raising toasts to whatever we could think of.

"Neither one of us had to pack because neither one of us owned a thing. Where we were going didn't have a call for knives or guns or rifles, and even if it did we'd find some when we got there. If we could have left the clothes on our back we would have.

"We both wanted to leave behind everything that had anything to do with Korea. We were both going home with our share of permanent souvenirs; there wasn't any need to carry along more, the few small items in this book excepted.

"Jack and I stayed in the bar until almost dusk and bid farewell to the boys. One by one they told us their hometowns and to give them a few months before looking them up. We told them if they were ever in Ohio they had a friend and a place to stay.

"I even shook hands with Dwayne and told him he could swing by too.

"Jack and I slipped from the bar and again made our way to the landing strip that only three days before had been taking us deep into the heart of Korea. This time it was taking us home."

My uncle turned towards me and rested his left shoulder against the post. The orange sun illuminated the left side of his face and deep shadows played across the right. He pointed to the album as it lay on the floor in front of us chair and said, "Go ahead and turn the page."

I slid my legs from the chair and in two quick steps went to a knee beside the album. There was just a precious few pages remaining to be turned as I peeled back one thin page and passed it from right to left.

On the page was a white rectangle of paper, a few inches wide and several more long. There was no writing on it, just dingy white paper.

I looked up to see my uncle staring down the length of the porch.

"For the longest time Jack and I wondered what to put in this slot. At first we both wanted to leave it empty, to symbolize that we were leaving everything behind us on the shores of Korea, but in the end decided it wasn't a strong enough symbol of that day.

"Instead we went to the War Department and got a copy of our discharge papers. We folded them in three equal parts and there they are before you now, the official documents ending our time in Korea.

"With just a couple of pieces of paper, we were going home."

## Chapter Forty-Six

Evenings in the fall aren't like the summer. They don't maintain their warmth once the sun goes down, but stay in direct correlation, temperatures rising and falling with it.

A small chill worked its way into the early evening air and began to blow off the water and over the meadow to us. I shivered a bit when it hit me, but said nothing as my uncle stood motionless against the post, impervious to the air around him.

"Over fifty men were amassed on the tarmac when we got there, all of them in some state of disrepair," he began. "Jack and I were two of the healthier men present and I almost felt guilty about leaving as I looked at them. Many had lost limbs or were on crutches, had their heads wrapped or were bound to wheelchairs.

"Don't," Jack whispered. "Don't do that to yourself. We have nothing left to prove. We're going home, just like these men."

"I already knew everything he was saying, but hearing it aloud helped emphasize the point.

"We aided as much as we could with loading the weaker soldiers and settled in for the longest journey of my life. The trip to Korea had seemed quite short because we were going to war. No man *wants* to face that and the more you dread something the faster it arrives.

"Going home was quite the opposite. The more time I had to sit and think of the coming summer evenings on the water, the golden waves of grain dancing in the breeze or the smell of Mama's cobbler on the window sill, the more I longed to be home.

"The flight from Korea to Hawaii took eighteen hours of air time. Twice we stopped on aircraft carriers in the Pacific, once on the *U.S.S Sherman* and once on the *U.S.S. Polk*. Each time we deplaned, used the restroom and got a quick bite of food while the plane was refueled, then we were back in the air again.

"The stops were so short that they didn't even bother to deplane those not strong enough to do it for themselves. Just wasn't enough time.

"We arrived in Hawaii on Thursday the 4th of April, the sun beating down on us at over eighty degrees. The first thing Jack and I did was lose the winter fatigues we were wearing and draw summer gear, as much to rid ourselves of them as to acclimate better to the Hawaiian heat.

"Two solid days we spent lying in the sun, eating anything we could find and enjoying the first women we'd seen in months."

My uncle chuckled and said, "It's a funny thing about women of the world. When we were in combat, we didn't have the time or the money to bother with them. Didn't matter though, to the women of Korea we were America and their ticket to it. Women in Pusan would have folded themselves into a duffel bag and let us carry them on to a plane if they thought it would get them here any sooner.

"Once we got to Hawaii though, we were just another couple of poor boys from the mainland, passing through to somewhere else. We had time and some money and plenty of desire, but couldn't so much as squeeze a sniff out of them."

My uncle kicked at the floor again, a tight smile on his face as he chuckled and swung his head from side to side.

"When we weren't enjoying our new life and freedom, we were completing a mountain of paperwork and reporting for mandatory check-ins at the base clinic. Most of the swelling in my leg was gone and the scabs were healing. The wounds on my arms and legs were faded to scars.

"Jack's face still bore the marks of shrapnel and the slash across his throat, but aside from the cosmetic wounds he was healing too. He was going to end with a little better collection of scars than I was, but neither of us were going to have any lingering functional problems and that's all we really cared about.

"On the morning of Saturday the 6th we boarded a plane to Los Angeles. Ten hours later we got on another one to Houston, Texas and stopped off there for the night. The base served as a go-between for the larger ones on the coasts and they had a small makeshift barracks for those of us passing through.

"The next morning, Sunday the 7th of April, we got on a plane to Rickenbacker Air Force base in Columbus, Ohio. Three of the most intense hours of my life as I tried and tried to imagine being home.

"How do you think we should greet Mama?" I asked Jack over and over. He must have been irritated as hell with me, but he never said anything. Just let me go on and on.

"We arrived into Columbus around midday and spent over two hours completing our discharge there. We had to sign and date everything they put in front of us and to this day they may still have claim over my first born child.

"I signed everything; I didn't care what it was.

"In return for our time spent in Korea, the last thing the Army did was grant us a Jeep ride home. We knew Mama wouldn't have a car and the notion of thumbing a ride south didn't appeal to either one of us. Lord knows we could have walked the thirty miles easy enough, but once you've gotten so close to your destination, you can't help but want to be there now.

"A young Private Airman named Seamus Bailey was appointed to drive us home. He was about the same age if not even a little older than us, but the past months had given us both something far beyond our years. Seamus still wore the bright eyed optimism and naivety of a man that hadn't seen war, still bore the hope that everything he had read in the papers was true.

"How'd you guys fare over there?" he asked, trying to make small talk to pass the time.

"Jack had given the front seat to me and sat across the back staring out into the open fields. His jaw was set and his eyes were locked and I could tell he didn't have any interest in the conversation at hand.

"It was what it was," I said. "It was war and nobody really wins at war."

"Bailey nodded as if he knew what I was talking about. "For you boys to be coming home like this, you must have been wounded. Mind if I ask what happened?"

"He looked in the rearview mirror to Jack hoping for an answer, but none came.

"You can't mind him," I said. "Old Jack's not a hateful sort, I just don't think he wants to talk about it is all.

"To answer your question, Jack took shrapnel from a mortar round and was tortured in a prison camp. I was shot making our escape."

"Bailey's eyes bulged a bit and he asked, "Escape? Aren't there exchange programs and stuff for that?"

"I snorted and said, "Minimal at best. The camp we were in nobody even knew existed. Our only options were to escape or die along with five hundred others just like us."

"Bailey furrowed his brow and said, "So you all managed to escape? Five hundred men?"

"I shook my head. "The two of us managed to escape and travel over a hundred miles on foot to allied forces. From there we engaged in an aerial assault that wiped the camp off the map."

"Even as I said the words, I couldn't really believe everything I was saying. It seemed like a plot from a book or something, the amount Jack and I had been through together.

"Bailey exhaled and shook his head, started to ask another question.

"You can leave us here," Jack said. "We'll take the last mile or two on foot. Thanks a lot for the ride."

"Bailey's cheeks flushed red as he eased the car to the side of the road. Jack hopped from the backseat to the ground and I eased myself from the front seat out onto the dusty road. I thanked Bailey for the ride and shook his hand and we both waited as he turned the Jeep around and drove away, leaving a cloud of dust in his wake.

"Aren't you a ray of sunshine?" I said as we started the final leg of a journey that had taken over a week to complete.

"Jack shrugged. "Just didn't much feel like talking about Korea anymore. He's never been anywhere near combat but he'll go to a bar tonight and tell some girl about how he was in an unmapped prison camp and had to escape on foot and saved the whole place."

"I chuckled and said, "You could have let him drop us off a little closer you know. I *do* have a hole in my leg."

"Jack made a face and said, "You have two little scabs that are almost gone. You can make it a mile on foot."

"Together we walked down the old dusty road, an eerie familiarity hanging about it. We'd been gone not quite a year but everything looked almost the same, just different enough to be noticeable.

"Looking back it wasn't that anything about it was different, just the people viewing it. We'd seen too much to ever see things the way we had before.

"So how we going to play this with Mama?" I asked as we drew close, exiting off the road and entering onto the dirt path that led us home.

"Jack paused and said, "If she's outside, we'll walk up and pretend we're asking for directions. If she's inside, we'll stay out in the yard and make enough noise that she hears us and comes out."

"I held the images of both playing out in my head for several minutes and as we got closer I could see Mama out back, hanging fresh wash on the line. It took everything I had not to run and throw my arms around her, pick her up in a hug and spin her around and around.

"I've got a better idea," I said. "Let's slip in through the front door and sit down at the kitchen table. We'll wait for her to come in and act like we've been there all along."

"Jack turned to me and smiled. "I like it."

"Together we dropped into a low crouch and jogged the last few hundred yards to the house as Mama continued hanging laundry on the back line. The front door was standing open to let a breeze pass through as we crept in and took seats at the kitchen table.

"I pointed out to Jack the framed pictures of us above the stove and the candle and cross between them. I looked him a question, but he knew no more about it than I did.

"It took almost fifteen minutes for Mama to enter the house, laundry basket in hand. With every bit of our strength we remained silent, smiles stretched across our faces.

"I'm not sure what reaction I was expecting Mama to have, but it definitely wasn't the one she gave us. She didn't smile and she didn't run for us.

"She collapsed into a ball, heaving and crying.

"Jack and I rushed forward and dropped to our knees, wrapping our arms around her as she sobbed and sobbed. Her thin arms reached out for us and pulled us in a grip so tight it almost took my breath away and for several long minutes she stayed that way.

"Mama, we're home," Jack whispered once she quieted, sending her into another burst of tears that lasted several minutes more.

"The two of us helped her from the floor and set her in a chair. "What's wrong?" I asked. "Aren't you happy to see us?"

"Mama bobbed her head as tears streamed down her face and she tried to speak. Sniffles choked her voice as she reached into the hem of her dress and pulled out a folded envelope.

"Jack took it from her and read:

*The United States War Department would like to extend its deepest sympathies on the passing of your sons, Jack and Richard Roberts, killed in action November 27, 1950. They were good soldiers that served honorably. On behalf of a grateful nation, please accept these small payments of gratitude for your son's service.*

"Jack sat the letter down and pulled two more pieces of paper from the envelope.

"What is it?" I asked.

"Jack licked his lips and said, "Checks. One for each us. $20,000 apiece."

"I received that letter three months ago, but I refused to believe it," Mama said. "I knew you boys would be coming home. I want you both to know that. Those are the original checks they sent me; I never went and cashed them. I knew my boys would be coming home."

"With the last sentence my mother's voice tailed off and she began to cry again.

"I stepped forward and put my arms around her and she buried her head against my chest. I looked at Jack and asked, "Why did they think we were dead?"

"Jack studied the letter, his face twisted up in thought. "November 27$^{th}$. You remember where we were then?"

"I continued running my hand over Mama's hair as it hit me.

"Chosin."

"Jack nodded. "My guess is they sent a letter to every person's family in the entire 5$^{th}$. They had no reason to believe anybody survived."

"We should find a way to send word to Marks and the other families."

"Jack nodded again. "Tomorrow. Tonight, we're here with Mama." He moved in and kissed the top of Mama's head as she slid her right arm from around me and grabbed him too.

"Much like the night we left, we spent that one wrapped up together at the kitchen table."

My uncle stopped short and I looked up to see him gazing down at the album. Moisture had worked its way from his eyes into the crevices of his face and he turned his head to hide it from the last glow of sunlight.

"The next page holds the very checks the government sent my mother, $20,000 for each of our lives. We both wanted to burn them, show the world we were very much alive, but Mama wouldn't hear of it.

"Said she wanted those checks around to remind her that no matter where her boys went, they were always coming home."

## Chapter Forty-Seven

The door swung open behind us again and my parents walked from the house. My mother had my father's suit coat around her shoulders and said, "Come on Austin, it's time to be heading home."

I looked down at the album and said, "Can we stay just a little longer? I want to hear the rest of the story."

My father shook his head and said, "Come on now son, listen to your mother."

Before I could protest further my uncle said, "If you folks wouldn't mind, we won't be but a few more minutes. We're almost done with our conversation out here."

My mother drew her mouth into a tight line and sighed. "Alright Uncle Cat, I guess we can stay a few more minutes."

Uncle Cat nodded and murmured a low thank you as my parents retreated back into the house.

My uncle followed their path back inside and I said, "Are we really almost done?"

The sun was sending its last fading rays from beneath the horizon and stars were starting to poke through the evening sky.

He nodded and said, "Yes, we are. There's only one page left, a page that's taken forty years in the making and still isn't done.

"Today it took another step towards completion."

"Today?" I asked.

"Go ahead and turn to it," Uncle Cat said. I did so and found a page lined with small newspaper cutouts. They had clearly been taken over time because each was a little bit different in color, the type on them a touch unique.

The articles were lined four across the page; each cut to the same side and lay side by side. At the top of each one was a small picture of a man, every one of them in military dress.

"That page," my uncle said, "is the last remnants of the 5th." He walked over from the post and took his seat. He patted his lap twice and I picked the book up from the floor and gave it to him.

He ran his finger along the first row and said, "These four weren't lucky enough to make it home with us. The entire first row. Francis, Petersen, Avery and Sparks all fell on the road to Koto-Ri.

"These clippings weren't easy to track down and only Sparks and Avery even had graves we could visit. I wish I knew more of their story, how they spent their lives before we left and the family they left behind, but I don't. Just like Europe or the South Pacific holds secrets for so many from the World Wars, the fields of Korea hold just as many for us."

My uncle paused for a moment, then ran his finger to the start of the second row.

"Sims was the first of us that made it home to go," Uncle Cat, tapping the far right picture in the group. "We hadn't been home very long when we got a letter from Marks telling us about it.

"Sims went home after the war and returned to working on his parents' farm in Kentucky. One day he was out riding when he came across a flint ridge. He tried to stay on his horse and cross it, but the footing was too bad. The horse slid fifteen feet into the ravine and took him down with it.

"Sims hit his head on a rock on the way down, bled to death before anybody found him."

My uncle slid his finger across and said, "Manus went next. Automobile accident. One night he was caught in a rainstorm and spun out on some loose gravel. Car slammed broadside into a tree. He was killed on impact."

Moving sideways again he said, "Dwayne passed away in '60. Nobody's really sure what happened, but as best we can guess he was in a bar in Louisville and got into an argument with a couple of gentlemen farmers there.

"Last anybody saw he was leaving for the night. Police found him the next morning beaten so bad his face was barely recognizable." My uncle shook his head and said, "Dwayne was a hothead and Lord knows we had our share of disagreements, but he was also a good man and a good soldier.

"Didn't deserve anything like that."

My uncle paused again and stared down at the floor, shaking his head. This time though, there was no smile across his face.

"For several years after Dwayne passed we were pretty lucky. We were all young and in decent health and for awhile it was nice to keep in touch without having a funeral to attend while doing it.

"That changed in the late sixties, beginning with Marks. Marks had gone back home, married his high school sweetheart, and together they had four children. One day while taking a family picnic to a lake near their home they decided to go for a swim.

"They spent the afternoon playing about and with a large family it's easy for one to go missing." My uncle paused for a second and stared at the album page in front of him. "Marks drowned trying to find that child. Turns out she had just gotten bored and wandered off. By the time she returned an hour later he was gone."

Sliding his finger down to the bottom row he said, "Buddy made it well into the seventies before meeting his end. He went home and married a little girl several years younger than him from his hometown. Went to work in a factory making glass light bulbs and together they raised a nice family.

"We saw Buddy a couple of times a year and spoke as often as we could. To this day his wife and I still exchange Christmas cards.

"Buddy had a condition that caused his blood to thicken, something nobody even knew he had until it was too late. One Sunday morning he was sitting in church with his family when a blood clot worked its way to his aorta.

"Died on the spot from a massive heart attack. There were a couple of doctors in the congregation that morning but there was nothing they could do for him."

Moving his finger over again my uncle said, "Winter before last Caldwell left us. We hadn't known him as well when we left Korea, but over the years we grew closer. He always showed when the group got together, always threw back some cheap vodka with us, and always bowed his head and prayed with us when another of us passed.

"When he'd gotten back from Korea he'd moved west to Missouri and opened a hardware store outside of

St. Louis. By all accounts it was a rather successful business and he too raised a nice family and led a good life.

"Every day he'd open the store at six in the morning and close it at four-thirty in the afternoon. Did it that way so the early risers could get what they needed first thing and so he had time at the end of each day to walk the deposit to the bank before they closed.

"One very cold afternoon he was walking to the bank with snow whipping around when two hoodlums shot him from an alley as he walked by. They stole his deposit and left him lying on the sidewalk. In the thick snow nobody noticed him there until the next morning, at which point he was frozen solid.

"Coroner said it was the bullets that got him and he went without suffering, but those are the kinds of things coroners are supposed to tell people. Whether that's true or not, we'll never know."

My uncle stared out at the tiny sliver of sun left sinking beneath the horizon and said, "Jack and I put this book together so our story could live on. It's not that we thought our story was better than any other soldier that put on the uniform; it was just the only one we knew.

"When we returned home we weren't showered with ticker tape parades and affection like the soldiers from the World Wars. We weren't reviled and called baby killers like the soldiers of Vietnam.

"We weren't *anything*.

"I've heard the war in Korea referred to as The Forgotten War. To any man that served there that's a slap in the face. Not so much because of the name but because it was true. It was a forgotten war. People here at home treated us with an apathy that was appalling.

"Nobody ever asked us our story or if they could write it down, so we did it ourselves. We did it for each other and for the many other men in the story that went to war with us. Today people use it as an analogy to describe their friends or their teammates, but I defy you to stand next to a man in combat and compare it to a football game or a job."

My uncle fell silent for several minutes. I watched as his face went from hard to soft to sad and a tear slid from his eye.

He reached into his pocket and pulled another newspaper clipping from it and laid it down next to Caldwell's.

Another tear fell down his face and his voice broke as he said, "In all my years, I had but one brother. Later when Mama remarried, I got some step-siblings, but there was only one man that I would trust my life and the lives of my wife and daughters to.

"In Korea, Jack saved my life more times than I can count. Without him I have no doubt I would be nothing more than an unmarked grave in the countryside.

"I spent my life trying to make it up to him, but in the end there was nothing I could do. Cancer crept into his body and depleted him in a way that only he ever knew about. Just like Jack to the very end, he never said a word about his pain or suffering.

"None of us even knew how bad he was until the last days, the days when his weakened form betrayed him, when he could no longer hide his shriveled state or inability to do some things for himself."

Tears streamed down my uncle's face, dripping off his cheeks and down onto the front of his jacket. Watching his heart break before me tears began leaking from the corners of my eyes and ran slow and fat down the sides of my face.

Several long minutes passed as my uncle cried for his fallen brother. I didn't make a sound and as if the world knew what was happening, it didn't either.

I hadn't noticed the house behind us grow quiet, but I looked back to see faces lining the screened windows along the porch. Tears ran from the eyes of my mother, my aunt, my grandmother, as my uncle sobbed for the passing of his brother Jack.

"You saw me place the flag on Jack's coffin didn't you?" my uncle asked, his voice no more than a whisper.

Tears continued to run down my face as I cast a glance to the front windows and nodded my head.

"The reason I did that was because that's how Jack and I decided a long time ago we wanted to be buried. The only way a soldier should be buried.

"Wrapped in scars and stars."

Those were the final words my uncle uttered, the tears falling even harder from both of us as the last shard of daylight burned from the night sky.

The porch screen door opened behind us and the sound of feet could be heard coming towards us.

My great grandmother walked straight to us and grabbed both of us in a hug. She pulled us tight and the three of us together sobbed into the autumn night.

We sobbed for the loss of an uncle, a son, a soldier.

A brother.

# Chapter Forty-Eight

There is only one tiny piece of the album that was not put there by my uncle. I put it there myself a little over eleven years after that afternoon on the porch.

The winter of 1995 was far and away the worst of the entire time I lived in Ohio. From November through April, not a single week went by without an excused absence for snow. Each week a new storm would swing down from Canada and blanket the region in fresh powder. Gusty winds would follow and whip it around for several days, pushing and piling it to perilous levels.

That kind of weather can wear on a person and I was no exception. I was two months into wrestling season my junior year. Each day I would rise in darkness, drive to school in treacherous conditions, go to practice all evening, and return home again in darkness. I went weeks at a time without seeing daylight and my body and psyche ached.

On Tuesday January 19th I stayed late after practice to get some extra lifting in. The league schedule was opening that weekend and I was looking to face several rivals in the area.

I arrived home to find my family milling about in the kitchen, worried looks on their faces. My brother paced in the dining hall and as I passed I asked, "What happened?"

He cast a glance around the room and said, "Uncle Cat passed away today."

My eyes bulged as I looked to my parents. "I didn't know he was sick."

My mother shook her head and said, "He wasn't. He had a stroke sometime early this morning and died shortly thereafter. Nobody even knew anything was wrong until he didn't show up for a dentist appointment."

"When he didn't show," my father added, seeing my confusion, "the office called his daughter to see if everything was alright. She went over to check on him, found him still in bed."

"That's awful," I murmured as numbness crept through my body and for a moment I stood in the middle of the room. My duffel bag remained in my hand and I still wore the gym clothes I had left practice in.

Looking around the room I asked, "So, why are we standing in the kitchen? Is someone here?"

My mother walked to the dining room table with a box in hand. She sat it down on the table and said, "This came for you."

It was large and square and atop it written in large block letters was *"TO BE OPENED BY AUSTIN ROBERTS ONLY."*

Surprise crept across my features as I stared down at the box. I twisted my face and tried several times to find the words, but none came to me.

"Austin, it's alright," my mother said. "You take it upstairs and open it whenever you like."

I looked at each of them in turn and let the gym bag slide from my fingers to the floor. It landed with a dull smack as I picked the box up and looked at it.

Only one place made sense for me to open it and I walked from the kitchen out onto the front porch and lowered myself into a rocking chair. The cold air bit at my face as I sat the box on my legs to open it.

The box was old and thin and the flaps fell away, allowing me to peer inside. In it were but two items.

A letter and the album.

I started with the letter, "Austin" written across the envelope in my uncle's cursive hand. It crinkled in my hands as I opened it and pulled several sheets of white paper from within. Licking my lips several times, I unfolded them and began reading.

*Dear Austin,*

*I've known for some time now my days were numbered. It wasn't anybody's fault and there wasn't anything I could do about it. Some things just are the way they are.*

*As the end grew nearer I began taking measures to ensure that the things and people I care about in this world were taken care of. I made sure my daughters weren't burdened with any funeral expenses and I left explicit directions to my attorney on how my things were to be doled out.*

*This one item though I didn't trust even to him.*

*You are the only person that has ever seen the album or heard the story of your Uncle Jack and me. That day, the day I laid my brother to rest, was the only time in my entire life I had the strength to tell that story and I was truly lucky that you were there to hear it.*

*You were a blessing because you were a child. You hadn't yet been tainted by the world or developed your own notions of war and brotherhood. Everything I told you I knew was touching you for the first time, like a golden sunrise on a clear morning.*

*What's more than that is you too were given the gift of a brother. Watching the two of you grow has been like watching Jack and I again, you each with your own roles. You have always been old, even for your years. You are quiet and brooding and live your life from one calculated venture to another. Your brother is more of a free spirit. He lives his life from one second to the next and never worries on what tomorrow will hold.*

*Rely on one another, there's a greater strength there than you will ever know.*

*You were the only person to ever hear the story and the only person I trusted to have this album. If I had given it to my daughters or anyone else they wouldn't know what any of it meant and they wouldn't be able to pass the story along the way you can.*

*I apologize for leaving you with such a burden, but this story is now yours. If Jack, myself, the other men in it are to live on it will be by your hand. I trust you'll do what's right when the time comes.*

*Sincerely Yours,*
*Richard 'Cat' Roberts*

> *P.S. I trust also that you'll see to it that I am laid to rest in a proper soldier's burial. I believe you know what that means.*

 

Three days later we laid my uncle to rest. The entire proceeding held an eerier similarity to the one so many years before and I couldn't help feeling like the same little boy standing in the warm autumn sun.

Despite my flashbacks, the two funerals couldn't have been more different. We lay Uncle Cat to rest on a Saturday morning, clear and cold, during the only break we had from the snow that entire winter. For one hour the winds died down and the snowfall ceased, allowing us to bury our friend.

I stood shoulder to shoulder with my brother as the honor guard fired their salute. I held my mother's hand as she cried.

The day before the funeral I went to the home of my uncle and removed the battered American flag he flew every day of the year. I folded it up tight and kept it in my coat and when every other person had marched by and paid their respects, I tacked it in place just the way I had seen him do it so many years before.

That night I made the last addition to the album.

I bought a fresh copy of the Birch Grove paper, cut out his obituary and placed it alongside the others. He and the eleven other men that went into the water that night at long last rejoined their platoon.

The final chapter in an incredible story over seventy years in the making was finally complete.

*December 11, 2013*

Eric,

*When your mother arrived home she stood with*
mouth agape for a moment, staring at a house that was barely touched. The look of shock and anger was soon replaced by understanding as I handed her the box you now have before you.

*She didn't need me to explain, didn't need me* to apologize or tell her how I had spent the week.

*She knew.*

*If you are reading this now I trust you have* made it through the story of your great-great uncles and the life they lived. I apologize again for not being able to share it with you in person but find solace in knowing the story has been passed on and rests in safe hands.

*So many years ago I was entrusted to watch* over the story, and now that task becomes yours. If the tale lives on it will be by your hand and if not it *will be something the four of us alone share for eternity.*

*With that son, I must bid you adieu. Your uncle and I are going fishing and Lord knows I can't be late for that. Afterwards, we'll cook whatever we catch over an open fire, made using steel and flint, the old fashioned way, just like Uncle Cat taught us.*

*Here's to being alive...*

*Your father,*
*Austin*

# About the Author

Dustin Stevens is the author of fourteen novels, including *The Zoo Crew* series, *Just a Game, 21 Hours, Liberation Day,* and *Catastrophic.* He is also the author of several short stories, appearing in various magazines and anthologies, and is an award-winning screenwriter.

He currently resides in Honolulu, Hawaii.

Made in the USA
Lexington, KY
10 December 2014